The Mirronstep

by

J. M. Nydam

Dedication

To Lee with thanks

Acknowledgments

I would like to thank the following people for their contributions:
Dr. Tony Valley
Glen Bledsoe
Lee Shaw
Peter Collins
Amanda Clarke
Gareth Nydam
Nick Nydam
Freddie Pymer
Kathy Pattison

Prologue

Four miles from Oaklade, there is a small town where people go about their daily business pretty much the same today, as they have done for hundreds of years.

The local Church stands by a main road that leads down the hill to Oaklade. The gravestones in the cemetery date back to as far as 1539, and church records date from 1290 AD onward.

There is a vault underneath the floor of the church, which was usual for the churches built during that era.

It is dark down there, and it has been many a long year since it was used for anything but storage. Some old furniture and a few boxes are scattered around. One or two stone effigies that had been carefully placed on the floor many years ago along with a few other objects, are now broken at the edges.

Wandering around down there is a monk, who carries his head under his arm, as he moves aimlessly among the bits and pieces.

Brother Ignatius was put to death for his beliefs by beheading, a long time ago. The unfortunate end to his life came at the hands of a Roundhead soldier, ordered by Cromwell to kill any of his kind at the time.

Before he lost his head, however, he was the guardian of an exceptional artifact.

So special was this object, that when Brother Ignatius lost his life, he could not move on to wherever good monks go. Although the artifact had been taken to another location upon his death, he was still bound to his task.

And so he waited through the centuries, hoping for the artifact to be returned, and whenever that was, he would be ready to protect it again.

Chapter One

Elizabeth Ghenestone was soaking up the sun and idly watching the river on the other side of the garden wall. She thought back to when she first met the elves, and the consequent discovery of the five Grymlons – the mystical orbs that control the air, water, earth, fire and wind. She hung her head a little, and closed her eyes for a moment, remembering the death of her mother, father and brother. Heaviness landed in her chest as she felt the aching sorrow of losing her precious family.

A smile ran across her face, as she remembered meeting Prince Gideon for the first time, and finding out that her Grandma Rose knew of the elves. She opened her eyes, remembering the battle to save the Grymlons from Verina, the Elviron Princess.

She leaned back on her chair a little, thinking of her upcoming wedding to Prince Gideon. Movement caught the corner of her eye. She turned toward the garden wall and saw an elf emerge from the willow tree on the other side of the river. She looked around to make sure no one else was watching. He, too, looked from left to right, as he reached the river's edge, before he strode over the bridge. He entered through the garden gate and when he reached her, he bowed slightly.

"My apologies for interrupting you, my lady, but I have a message from the king," he said, handing her a small blue envelope.

Elizabeth opened it, read the contents and nodded to the elf.

"You go on ahead. I will be along in just a minute."

The elf bowed again.

"Very well, my lady."

He headed back to the willow tree, and disappeared inside of it.

Elizabeth went into the cottage and scribbled a note for her Grandma Rose.

She headed for the back gate and went over the bridge, following the elf into the drooping branches of the same tree.

As Elizabeth neared the trunk, it split open. She shrank down as she entered and the tree closed behind her, leaving no trace of an opening.

Two guards stood aside and saluted as she passed then, turning left onto a street carved out of rock.

She looked up as she entered the cavern, and could only see darkness above her. She continued downward, passing elves and humans (who secretly worked for the elves), as she went. Lights shone through the windows of the shops, helping to illuminate the constant darkness of the streets. Glass domed candles sat on ornate stone pillars about three feet high, giving extra light along the way.

A few minutes later, Elizabeth came to a wall with a door large enough to ride a carriage through. To the right of it was a smaller door for foot traffic.

"I have been through this door so many times over the last few years," she thought, turning the handle and stepping through, "and still my heart jumps at the beauty of it all."

Ahead of her was a vast countryside of rolling hills, under a blue sky. Birds flew overhead. She shielded her eyes from the sun, as she looked across the countryside to the town of Kimadria, laid out around the high-spired castle.

"Magnificent as always," she thought.

A carriage with four horses awaited her. Elizabeth stepped in and sat on the plush green velvet seat. She was jolted back slightly as the horses took off at a gallop.

When she arrived at the castle, Elizabeth was escorted through the main hallway and directed to the main library.

There, she found King Morvand, seated at a round table next to his wizard Vandrayven. Across from them was King Kalidryd, the ruler of Distardrian and beside him, his wizard, Drewmannus.

Elizabeth took the only vacant seat between the two wizards.

"I'm quite sure these two don't like each other," she thought,- looking either side of her, "and now I am in the middle of them."

"Why have I been called here?" she asked.

King Morvand was the first to speak. "We have discovered that the Grymlons are dying and we don't know why."

"And why are these two here," she said nodding to the Elviron King and his Wizard.

"That sort of talk is unbecoming of a future queen, Elizabeth," said King Morvand. "King Kalidryd and Drewmannus are here to help."

Elizabeth fixed her gaze on King Kalidryd. "You mean the way they helped my mother, father and brother into an early grave?"

King Kalidryd looked up, openly returning her stare.

"In fact, I think we know that you caused the death of practically all of my family!"

Drewmannus turned to her with a glare, then turned to King Morvand.

"You did not tell her, did you!"

He stood, reaching for his staff, propped against the wall, making it clear he intended to leave.

"Sit down Drewmannus!" said King Morvand. "All will be explained in good time, but for now, we have more important matters to attend to."

Drewmannus re-took his seat, glancing balefully at Elizabeth as he did so.

She ignored the wizard, turning her attention to King Morvand.

"What is he talking about?"

"I will explain later," said King Morvand, "but for now we need to address the problem at hand. King Kalidryd is here today because he has a suggestion that may be helpful in seeking that solution. Please, Kalidryd, let us know your thoughts on the matter."

Elizabeth let out an exasperated sigh.

King Kalidryd stood.

"Your Highness, Morvand, thank you for allowing my wizard and I to visit you today. I…"

"While we are all here," Elizabeth interrupted. "I have a question that so far, I simply cannot get an answer to."

King Kalidryd's shoulders slumped. His head tilted to one side slightly.

"What is it, Elizabeth?" said King Morvand.

"I have asked questions about my parents and brother for the past five years. Am I ever going to get a straight answer from anyone?"

"Elizabeth. Now is not the time," said King Morvand. "Please, let King Kalidryd speak."

King Kalidryd bowed to Elizabeth. "Perhaps at some later time, we can discuss your concerns."

She stared at him. "I will agree to that, but are you sure you want to?"

King Kalidryd turned away from Elizabeth. He wiped his brow with the back of his sleeve, turned to all present and began his story.

"As we all know, five hundred years ago, we were a race of elves much like the elves in this Realm.

We had our own set of Grymlons, identical to the ones at Kimadrian. That is, until one day, an elviron by the name of Renmar decided to sell our set. He had access to them because he was in our employ as a royal guard. One of his duties was to oversee the safety of the Grymlons sanctuary."

"Another trustworthy elviron, I assume," Elizabeth remarked.

King Kalidryd turned to King Morvand for help.

"May I make a suggestion?" said Drewmannus, quickly.

"But of course," said King Morvand.

"Yes, please do," King Kalidryd muttered.

"I cannot take Elizabeth back in time, but I can show her the events that we know took place: at least most of them."

"How do you intend to do that?" asked Elizabeth.

"All of the wizard's in Distardrian have studied the history of the Grymlons. So if you will hold onto my hand, I can cast a spell to let you into the part of my mind that holds the information regarding the events that led to the way we are today. That is, if you are not too afraid."

"I am not too sure that it would be fitting for you to subject Elizabeth to that," said King Morvand.

"No, no. It's perfectly all right, your majesty," Elizabeth said.

"It will not harm her, will it?" asked King Morvand.

"Are you suggesting that I would intentionally hurt the future Queen of Kimadrian?" asked Drewmannus.

"No, of course not," King Morvand quickly replied.

"Then we should proceed," said Drewmannus. "Time grows short, does it not?"

The Mirronstep

"What do you want me to do?" Elizabeth asked.

"Just sit still," said Drewmannus. "Take my hand and I will do the rest."

Elizabeth sat back in her chair. Drewmannus pulled his chair to the side of her and held out his hand. Elizabeth looked down at his bony fingers, as she took it.

"Please close your eyes and allow me to introduce you to Renmar, the elviron who began our existence as we know it today," he said, closing his eyes.

Chapter Two

Elizabeth opened her eyes and found herself standing in a dimly lit passageway. She glanced around her, as she stepped forward and put her hand on the door directly in front of her.

"I'm underground. This door is the same design as the one in Kimadrian," she thought, touching the locking mechanism."

She turned peering into the passageway, feeling the heat from the flaming torches hanging from the walls with iron clasps.

"What a gloomy place. It feels like a sauna down here."

An Elviron came around the corner.

"This must be Renmar," she thought, "and he looks nothing like the Elviron I know today!"

As he approached her, he looked back to see if he was being followed.

Elizabeth stepped out of the way when Renmar reached the door. He turned the rounded symbols on it, until the door clicked open. He pushed against it and entered the room. She followed him.

"The Grymlons in Kimadrian are housed in the castle's highest tower," she thought, looking around her. "These Grymlons look the same, but it's dark and un-inviting down here.

The Grymlons began to glow in the dimness, seeming to sense Renmar's presence.

He stepped around the room, popping the orbs into the pouch he had pulled from his pocket, until he had all five. He turned and looked straight at Elizabeth.

She felt panic begin to rise in her, but he passed right through her and out of the door.

Elizabeth looked down as her body reassembled itself. "That felt too creepy for words." she thought, following him out of the room.

The Mirronstep

Renmar closed the door, spinning the circles of the lock, until they were out of sync, then he headed back the way he came. Elizabeth followed close behind.

They climbed to the upper part of the castle, where it was bright and cheery.

Elizabeth looked up at the paintings of the elviron posing in regal positions. They were surrounded by brightly coloured banners hanging from the walls.

"I don't know how long ago this was, but it certainly doesn't look like this now," she thought, noticing how clean and tidy everything was.

She followed him out of the castle, and into a small wooded area. They continued on, and a minute or two later, approached a large tree. He pushed on the base of its trunk. As it opened up, he entered into the darkness. Before the door closed, Renmar plucked a torch from the wall, produced a flint box and flamed it into life.

A few feet along the passage, they came to some steps leading upwards to a trap door. Renmar ran up the steps, pushed on the door, and climbed out into the Human Realm. She followed him and watched as he grew to human size.

Renmar slung the Grymlons over his shoulder by the strap, and began walking until he reached the road. He continued on, until the road became lined with trees on both sides.

Suddenly he stopped, squinting into the trees. "Is anyone there?" he called.

Elizabeth glanced over his shoulder, and thought she saw something move, but Renmar began to walk again.

He had not gone but a few more paces, when a figure came out of the trees. When Renmar turned, the figure stopped.

"Who are you?" he asked.

"A friend in the night, looking out for your safety," the stranger replied.

"You don't look very friendly to me," thought Elizabeth.

"Then why do you hide?" asked Renmar.

"You may have been a robber or worse, a murderer."

"And so might you," said Renmar.

"You offend me," said the stranger.

"I apologize," Renmar found himself saying, not wanting to make the stranger angry.

"May I come a little closer?" asked the stranger.

"You may," said Renmar, ignoring the uneasy feeling in the pit of his stomach.

The stranger caught up, falling into step beside him.

Elizabeth followed them, listening to their conversation.

"Where are you going?" the stranger asked.

"Into the town," said Renmar.

"I have never seen anyone like you," said the stranger. "Where are you from?

"I am not from around here, if that is what you are asking," said Renmar.

"You have no relatives or friends around this area?" asked the stranger.

"No," said Renmar.

"And what are you doing out on this road for no apparent reason?" Elizabeth thought, as she followed behind them.

She turned, looking back, and hadn't noticed that the stranger abruptly stopped walking. She halted right in front of him. It was then she noticed how grotesque he looked.

He had long thick hair. His eyes had somewhat of a red tinge to them, and seemingly glowed slightly in the moonlight. He also had unusually long incisors that jutted out just enough to peek below the top lip of his closed mouth.

"I wonder if you've noticed how strange your walking companion is," Elizabeth thought.

Renmar, also stopped walking, and turned to the stranger.

"I'm curious…," he began. A scream escaped from Renmar, as the stranger pounced on him before he could finish his sentence. The stranger pulled viciously at Renmar's collar, ripping the material away from his body, exposing his neck.

Elizabeth staggered back a few paces, as she watched Renmar fight courageously, but his attacker was strong.

The stranger had now transformed into a hideous creature, with straggling matted hair. His unusually long incisors were luminescent in the moonlight. Renmar screamed as the creature buried his head in Renmar's neck.

The Mirronstep

Elizabeth watched in horror. She put her hand over her mouth to stifle a scream. Her stomach did a flip flop, when she heard the sound of gurgling, sucking noises, as the creature began to draw Renmar's blood from his body.

Renmar dropped the pouch containing the Grymlons and grabbed his dagger. He pushed the creature away, and slashed at its face. The creature heard the sound of his own scream as the dagger's blade dragged across his cheek. He put his hand to his face and dropped to the ground.

Renmar struggled to his feet, holding his dagger with one hand and his neck with the other. The creature also scrambled to his feet and backed away from Renmar. Elizabeth watched the creature as he turned towards her, and began to run.

"Back away witch!" he hissed at Elizabeth, as he passed her by. Elizabeth jumped back.

"He saw me!" Fear suddenly gripped her, as the creature disappeared into the trees.

Renmar lost his balance and fell to the ground. He pulled himself onto his knees, then struggled to his feet, picked up the bag with the Grymlons and began walking, Elizabeth following behind.

When they reached the village, he led her to an Inn, but didn't enter. Instead, he staggered down the alley way next door.

"He looks like death warmed up," Elizabeth thought, as she watched him lean against the wall of the Inn.

Hearing footsteps, she turned to see a tall, thin man dressed in white robes approach.

"Oh, Alomer, I thought you would never get here!" Renmar gasped. "I have the objects we discussed."

Alomer looked closely at him. "You do not look well, my friend."

"I was bitten by something on my way here," said Renmar, holding his neck. "A creature attacked me! I managed to fight it off, but I think he sucked my blood. I feel so weak, I can hardly move."

Alomer stepped back. "I… I've changed my mind, Renmar. The deal's off."

Elizabeth saw fear in Alomer's face as he retreated a few more paces.

"But we had an agreement," said Renmar, moving towards him. "I cannot return to Distardrian. If I go back now, I will be punished as a traitor!"

Alomer put up his hands. "Don't come any closer, Renmar. You have been bitten by a vampire. Do you know what that means?"

"No. What is a vampire? We have no such thing in the Realm."

"It's a creature of the night. Anyone who is bitten by a vampire: becomes one. Go home Renmar. If you can get back before anyone knows you're gone. You may be able to return the Grymlons before anyone knows they are missing."

"But!" said Renmar, taking another step towards him.

Alomer headed towards the street. "I'm sorry, Renmar!"

"Wait!" said Renmar, trying to catch up to him, but Alomer was already on his way down the road.

Renmar fell against the wall. "What will I do now?"

Elizabeth followed him back to where he had come out of the ground.

Then everything went dark.

As the darkness began to fade, Elizabeth noticed she was now standing on the pavement of a street. Renmar was just ahead of her and was letting himself into one of the terraced houses.

"He doesn't have the Grymlons anymore. I wonder what he did with them?" she thought, following him into the house.

Renmar pulled a chair from the table in the kitchen and sat down.

"I feel exhausted," he uttered.

He put his head on his hands and promptly fell asleep. Elizabeth sat in the chair opposite… waiting.

When he woke an hour and a half later, Renmar went to the pantry; he cut a slice of bread and a wedge of cheese and placed it on a metal plate. He sat back down at the kitchen table. He placed the piece of cheese on the bread, took a small bite and began to chew. Suddenly, he spat the food onto the plate and promptly vomited on it.

Elizabeth put her hand up to her mouth and turned away, as the warm, acid stench of his vomit hit her nostrils.

The Mirrorstep

He jumped up, "By the Grymlons!" He shouted, shocked at his own involuntary reaction.

Renmar quickly cleaned up the mess. He pulled a metal cup from another cupboard at the other side of the sink and put it under the pump, pulling the handle to fill the cup with water. He took a drink from the cup and vomited it back up into the sink.

"Whatever is wrong with me?"

He ran his fingers through his hair and made his way to his bedroom.

"Perhaps if I try to rest, I may feel better," he said to himself, lying on his bed. He was asleep again within seconds.

Elizabeth sat in an easy chair in the corner of the room and watched him as he slept.

Renmar slumbered on for two more hours before waking. He sat up and put his legs over the side of the bed, and ran his fingers through his hair again. He looked at them in horror as hair slipped through his fingers and onto his lap. He hurried to the mirror on the wall at the end of his bed, and recoiled when he saw his reflection. In disbelief, he slowly turned back to the mirror.

"My skin!" he said, touching his face, which was now the colour of cold grey stone, "and my eyes! They weren't that shape when I went to sleep!"

Renmar pulled at some of the hair left on his head. More strands attached themselves to his now sweaty fingers.

"What is happening to me?" he asked the much changed reflection in the mirror.

Elizabeth followed Renmar into the kitchen. She stood quietly, watching him pace the floor, becoming more and more agitated. His face became contorted with rage. He calmed down, only to become enraged again. He picked up the chair he had been sitting in earlier, and threw it across the room. Elizabeth flinched as it hit the wall, breaking off two of the legs. He went to the cupboard by the sink and pulled out cups and plates, hurling them at the wall. Finally, he could no longer contain his rage. He opened the front door and ran out into the street, but when the sunlight touched his skin, he screamed in pain, running back into his house and closing the door.

Renmar strode back and forth across the room, instinctively waiting impatiently for night to come.

"He is going to wear a path in the floor if he doesn't stop soon," Elizabeth thought.

Eventually, Renmar went to the window and looked out into the darkness.

Elizabeth followed him as he left the house.

Renmar turned down a dimly lit street. He stepped back into the shadow of a now closed shop, and waited.

An unsuspecting passer by turned the corner. Elizabeth stood beside Renmar as the stranger approached.

When he entered into the shadows, Renmar grabbed him. He pushed him up against a wall, and sank his teeth into his neck. Elizabeth could hear the familiar sucking, gurgling sound, as Renmar drank from the stranger. The stranger pushed Renmar away and ran, but not before Renmar had gorged himself on a good amount of his blood.

Renmar stood for a moment, dazed. A few seconds later he turned back the way he had come. Elizabeth followed him back to his house. She followed him to his bathroom and stood by the door, listening to him retch violently into the toilet.

"He looks as though he might die!" Elizabeth thought, as he left the bathroom and staggered to his bedroom.

"Why am I craving blood, but can't keep it down?" he mumbled, as he fell onto his bed and passed out.

"I know why," thought Elizabeth. "You're changing into something else. Not quite the vampire from the human realm, but a different kind of creature, Gideon told me about."

Elizabeth wandered the house, waiting for him to wake. The living area had a settee with green throw pillows and a dark green blanket placed neatly over the back. There was a high back armchair by a large stone fireplace. A table sat beside the chair, upon it, half a dozen books, a table lamp filled with oil and a pipe in a tray. She noticed the not unpleasant sweet smell of tobacco smoke lingered in the room.

"He has good taste in furniture," she thought.

She looked around the rest of the house, noticing that Renmar lived rather well.

Elizabeth turned, feeling dizzy and disorientated. Then she realized that she was no longer in Renmar's home.

The Mirronstep

She now joined Renmar in a room with a high window. It was night time, and fire torches lit the bare stone walls. Renmar's hands were tied to a heavy metal ring hanging from the ceiling, and his back was bare and bloody. An elviron guard was standing behind him with a whip. The sickly smell of blood now wafted up her nostrils.

In the corner, hot coals glowed from an iron basket. A long, slim poker was buried in the middle of them.

"I've been here before. We're in the dungeons of the elviron castle," she thought.

An elviron dressed in the heavy colourful robes of a Wizard, stood to one side.

"Where are the Grymlons, Renmar? If you tell me, I can have you killed quickly, without suffering," said the Wizard.

"I keep telling you. I left them at the entrance to the Elviron Realm. In my haste to get home, I left them up there."

"They are nowhere to be found. We have searched the entire area," said the Wizard.

"I swear I am telling the truth," said Renmar.

"Why did you steal them?" asked the Wizard.

"I have already told you. I was going to sell them."

"And you say you took them to the Human Realm. Is that correct?"

"Yes, but the buyer changed his mind," said Renmar, moving his hands, in an attempt to find a more comfortable position.

The elviron guard raised his whip, lashing it down on Renmar's back.

"Ow! What was that for?" Renmar half shouted, half screamed.

Blood spurted from the new wound, spraying the guard, who wiped the blood from his face with the back of his hand.

"Answer when you are spoken to."

Renmar eyed the elviron guard. "I would try and drink his blood," he thought, "but I might throw it up."

"I think you did sell them, Renmar. That is why you no longer have them," said the Wizard.

Renmar turned his attention back to the wizard. "I was going to sell them to a druid, but for some reason, he decided not to buy them from me. He told me something at one of our meetings that may save me, though."

"I am not sure anything can save you now," said the Wizard, "What was the druid's name?"

"He never gave me his name," Renmar lied, "but I do know it has to do with magic."

The Wizard laughed. "Magic, you say?"

"I have information that the druid told me," said Renmar.

"What sort of magic did he tell you about?" asked the Wizard.

"I will only tell you if you give me your word you will spare my life," said Renmar.

"I will promise you nothing, until you have told me what the druid said," replied the Wizard.

"The druid gave me some information during one of our conversations that may be of interest to us both."

"The king's orders are to have you executed. I find it difficult to believe that you have any information that would stop me from carrying out those orders." said the Wizard.

"The druid told me of a device called a Mirronstep."

"What does this device do?" asked the Wizard.

"It can send one backwards or forwards in time."

The Wizard, being a Wizard, became curious at this point.

"Let him down," he told the guard.

"But the king, my lord," the guard protested.

"I said let him down. It will only be for a minute."

The guard stepped forward and untied Renmar's hands, letting him drop to the floor.

"Give him some water and a stool to sit on," said the Wizard.

"Oh, now I am a manservant?" said the guard.

"No, but you could become a rat or perhaps a beetle, if you don't do as I ask," the wizard replied, in a menacing voice.

The guard grabbed a stool by the wall and plopped Renmar ungraciously on it. He went to his own water flask and poured Renmar a drink.

"I don't know why you are trying to make him so comfortable," said the guard, looking Renmar up and down. "He will be dead by the day's end. He looked half dead when he got here. Are you sure he doesn't have anything that's catching?"

The wizard ignored the guard, staring only at Renmar.

"Tell me more of this device."

Renmar gingerly sipped the water, hoping he wouldn't throw up again. He heard gentle rumblings in his gut, but nothing came up.

"The druid told me that he knew of a device called a Mirronstep," he continued, handing the cup back to the guard. "It was some sort of mirror that could take an elf backwards or forwards in time."

"Of what significance would this device be to you?" asked the Wizard.

"Well, if it did exist, then perhaps I could persuade the druid to let me use it. I could go back in time to retrieve the Grymlons, thus redeeming myself."

The wizard thought for a moment.

"I will talk with the king," he said, leaving Renmar with his torturer.

Time passed by, as the guard and Renmar waited....

"He's been gone for ages," Elizabeth thought, beginning to get bored.

Eventually the Wizard returned. "The king says that you have made this story up so that you might escape."

Elizabeth watched as panic ran across Renmar's face. "But I tell you, the druid knows where the device is! He talked about it all the time, even said that he had used it."

"I am sorry Renmar," said the Wizard, motioning for the guard to approach. "He is to be beheaded at dawn."

The guard nodded as he grabbed Renmar's hands and tied them to the ring again.

***

While Elizabeth and Renmar were at the dungeons in the castle. Renmar's first victim, Denly, had just roused himself from a deep sleep.

"I feel absolutely awful," he told his wife, as he exited the bedroom. Denly's wife, who had been working in the kitchen, turned to him and screamed.

"Who are you?" she shouted.

"What are you talking about? It's me, your husband, you silly woman!"

"You are not my husband, you grotesque looking monster! Now get out of my house, or I will call the sheriff!"

Denly approached his wife, meaning to reassure her of who he was, but as he neared her, he noticed the vein in her neck standing out.

"I can hear the blood pulsing through her like a clock on a plate," he thought, feeling his mouth begin to water.

The thought of raw meat came into his head. "I don't eat meat!" he thought with disgust, "but it sounds really appetizing for some reason."

Denly's wife backed away. "What is wrong with you? I told you to leave this house. DENLY, WHERE ARE YOU? THERE IS A STRANGER HERE AND I THINK HE IS GOING TO ATTACK ME. HELP!"

"I am here, dearest," Denly said, as he grabbed his wife by the throat. He pushed her to the ground, and sunk his newly grown incisors into the vein in her neck.

Denly drank. He drank as though he would never be able to quench his thirst… then threw up. Twelve hours later, Denly and his wife waited for darkness. They waited, so they could pass on their bodily upgrades to the next and nearest unfortunate victim.

Chapter Three

As the sun came up the next morning, Elizabeth watched in horror as the guard decapitated Renmar with one swift slice of a sword.

"Just as well they cut it off," she thought, looking down at Renmar's head. "Not sure if he would have stayed dead, if he hadn't. I'm glad they covered him with a blanket too. I think he may begin burning before they set fire to him."

His remains were covered and then taken outside of the city to be burned.

Elizabeth wandered around for a few days, watching as total mayhem spread across the land.

Elviron running from elviron, until there were none to be found during the daylight hours. Then one morning there was no daylight, only a dull greyness during the day. The elviron wizard, now a vampire himself, had cast a spell to keep the sun at bay.

One by one, the elviron began to venture outside. With the sunlight hidden, they could go about their daily business. Elizabeth noticed that they were much changed.

"Now they all look like Renmar. I want to be gone from here," she said, but in the blink of an eye, she found herself at the edge of the Kimadrian border.

When darkness fell, she watched as hundreds of elves tried to stop the elviron from passing over the border to their realm, with the hope of stemming the infection.

"I'm in the middle of a war!" she thought.

She jumped out of the way of an elviron broadsword, as it came down upon the elf behind her. The sword landed in the middle of the elf's chest. Blood sprayed from the wound, and the elf screamed as he hit the ground. Some of it spattered against Elizabeth, passing through her to the ground behind. The elviron who had dealt the fatal blow, turned quickly, looking for his next victim.

Elizabeth watched elves and elviron slaughter one another.

When the fighting finally stopped, she moved among the dead and dying. She knelt down when she heard a very young elf moaning in pain.

"I wish I could help you," she said, trying to comfort him.

As she made her way across the battle ground, she saw heads separated from bodies. Limbs were strewn about, with nothing attached to them. The smell of faecal matter, blood and vomit was everywhere.

She dropped to her knees, unable to endure anymore.

"The smell, I can't stand the smell!" she thought, holding her stomach.

Then she opened her eyes....

Drewmannus stared at her as she pulled her hand away, not wanting to go back to the scene.

"How long have I been sitting here?" she asked.

"About five minutes," said King Morvand.

"But I was there for days!"

"You do not look well, Elizabeth. Would you like to stop this meeting?" said King Morvand.

"No, Your Majesty. It's just that I had no idea. There was so much suffering. So many died!" she said, with tears in her eyes: the stench of death still lingering in her nostrils.

King Morvand closed his eyes for a second, as though remembering the time.

"There is nothing romantic about war," he said, with a sigh.

"I hope you now have a better understanding of what transpired," said King Kalidryd.

Elizabeth nodded. "It has helped me understand what happened between the elves and the elviron, but I didn't see what happened to the Grymlons."

"No, and that is unfortunate. There is no written record of what he did with them," said King Kalidryd.

"I never saw Renmar take anyone's essence," she said.

Drewmannus explained. "Not long after all of our realm had been infected. We discovered that because we were elves and not humans, blood just made us sick. All we had to do was eat raw meat.

The Mirronstep

'We also discovered that we could put our hands inside the chest of our victims and take their essence. As you have witnessed in the past, if we swallow the essence while the light still shines within, it gives us great strength and power. The essence also gives us the ability to be semi invisible and pass through solid objects. Sadly, our appearance became abhorrent even to us. Over the years, we have eliminated all means of reflection."

"So that's why the paintings in the elviron castle are all slashed," Elizabeth said, remembering when she had sneaked into the castle with Gideon. "You can't stand to look at who you once were, but what does all of this have to do with me?"

"You asked why you were called here today?" said King Kalidryd. "You are very powerful in the ways of magic. If the Mirronstep does exist, you are the one most likely to be able to locate it and travel back in time: thus, preventing this from ever happening and restoring us to our former selves."

"We think our set of Grymlons is dying because the two sets are connected in some way," said King Morvand.

"But it has been several hundred years since the elviron set has been gone," said Elizabeth. "The Grymlons here have been regenerated many times since then. How come they didn't die sooner?"

"We are not sure," said King Morvand.

"What if I go back and save the elviron Grymlons and the elven ones still die?" she asked.

"The truth is," said King Morvand, "we do not really know what will happen if you save the elviron set of Grymlons. Ours may still die, but this is our only option at the moment."

"Have I missed anything? Do you think Elizabeth has all the information she needs?" King Kalidryd said, looking to King Morvand.

King Morvand thought for a moment. "I think Elizabeth has been enlightened enough. Now that she has seen your version of past events, it is up to her, whether or not she chooses to help."

"Do any of you have any ideas on how I might begin my search for the Mirronstep?" Elizabeth asked.

"Perhaps you could contact Thalios. He is after all, an Arch Druid, and you worked together to regenerate the Grymlons five years ago," King Morvand suggested. "He won't want to help you at first, but you must persuade him to do so. He will have access to information that might give you at least some clues."

"How much time do I have?"

"We think that the Grymlons will probably expire in about a month, if nothing is done to change anything. I also think this meeting is over," King Morvand said, standing.

"King Kalidryd, let me escort you and your wizard to your carriage."

King Kalidryd and Drewmannus stood to leave.

Elizabeth turned to King Morvand. "I'm going to find Gideon. If I try to find the Mirronstep, we'll have to put a hold on our wedding plans for a while."

"I am so sorry, Elizabeth. I wish the timing were better," King Morvand said.

As Elizabeth walked towards the door, King Kalidryd called to her.

"For what it's worth, I am sorry about your mother and father. I know you think we were to blame for their deaths, and to a point you are correct. But that deed was my daughter, Verina's and I did not know about it until it was too late. I thought King Morvand had explained this to you. He obviously had not."

Elizabeth looked into the elviron king's weary eyes.

"My brother was killed too, you know."

King Kalidryd glanced at King Morvand before dropping his gaze to the floor.

Elizabeth left the room. She moved quickly down the hallway, trying not to cry.

"I've shed too many tears for what couldn't be changed. It's time to move on."

Elizabeth ran up the stairs towards the royal residence and made her way along the hallways of the castle. When she reached Gideon's quarters, she knocked on the door. An elf servant, dressed in a black tunic, opened it. When he saw Elizabeth, he stepped aside.

"The master is expecting you milady," he said with a bow.

Elizabeth went through a small entry way, then turned left and came to another door. She knocked again.

The Mirronstep

"Liz, is that you?" a voice inquired from the other side.

"Yes."

"Well come in. I'm sure you have much to tell me."

Gideon was sitting at his desk. He looked up and smiled when he saw her.

"Five years ago my heart leapt at the sight of you," she thought, looking into his face. "Nothing has changed."

She glanced at the paperwork on his desk. "What are you doing?"

"I need help, Liz! My father had these really old documents brought to me from one of our libraries. It is supposed to contain some information on something called a Mirronstep, whatever that is?"

"That was quick! I've only just left the meeting with your father and the elviron king."

"My father and King Kalidryd had already discussed some of the situation before you arrived. He sent these papers and books up here. So that I might do some research and try to help."

Elizabeth looked down at the papers. Age had turned some of them brown around the edges. A musty smell wafted up her nose.

"It's nice to see you too, Gideon," she said, taking a seat by the fire place.

He got up from his desk and pulled her up out of the chair. She laughed as he put his arms around her waist and embraced her.

"How strikingly beautiful you have become," he said, as he looked into her crystal blue eyes.

"Flatterer," she said, feeling the colour rise on her cheeks.

He kissed her gently on the lips. "I have missed you. Are you going to stay for a while? The servants have your rooms ready."

"I was planning to stay for a couple of days, but your father has suggested that I try to find Thalios. I'm curious as to how much he knows about the Mirronstep."

Gideon held on to one of Elizabeth's hands, as he guided her to the couch and they sat down.

"What is the Mirronstep, Liz?"

Elizabeth explained the visions Drewmannus had given her.

"Do you believe what you saw?" said Gideon.

"I believe he believes the visions he let me see. I also believe that he might do anything to get his hands on the Grymlons."

"If the Grymlons die we don't know what will happen, but I do know that us elves and you humans will suffer greatly," said Gideon. "What about Renmar? If what you saw is what really happened. Do you think he was telling the truth?"

"Renmar's life was at stake. From what I saw, I think he believed that there was a Mirronstep. I also believe that if he would have had the chance to find it, it may have saved his life."

Gideon frowned. "All this is very disturbing."

"You know that we will have to postpone the wedding don't you," Elizabeth said.

"My father can arrange for us to be married tomorrow, if it's what you want," Gideon said, gently brushing her cheek with the back of his fingers.

"I won't let this situation ruin our chance to have a lovely wedding. I want to walk down the aisle to you, and I want to wear a white dress. I want my gran to see us married. I want the wedding we deserve."

"Then you shall, my brave and patient, Elizabeth."

"I have to go," she said. "Will you look after Merlyn for me for a while? I don't want to leave him up in the human realm, if I am to be gone for a few days. He likes to escape and hide from Gran, and she's getting a bit too old to be chasing him around."

"Of course. Any excuse to look after that little dragon. He is so much fun!"

"You be nice to Merlyn," Elizabeth said, wagging her finger at him. "I don't want you making him angry, and him turning you into a lump of charcoal!"

"Don't worry, Liz," he said, with a laugh. "I will take care of your precious dragon."

They kissed briefly.

"Let me know if you get any information from that clutter on your desk, Mr. Organization," she said, heading for the door.

"I will do my very best, my lady," he replied, with an exaggerated bow. Elizabeth laughed as she left his rooms. She made her way down the stairs and out of the castle.

A carriage was waiting for her at the entrance.

She stepped up into it, sat on the plush velvet seat, and looked out of the window.

"It's time to find out just how much Gran and Thalios know about this Mirronstep," she thought, as the carriage pulled away.

Elizabeth came out of the willow tree by the river and made her way along the pathway to Willow View Cottage.

As she approached the back door, she heard voices. When she entered the kitchen, Grandma Rose was drinking a cup of tea, and Charlie the cat was sitting on one of the chairs at the kitchen table.

Elizabeth touched the back of Charlie's head and she stood, arching her back and purring loudly, at her touch.

"What are you doing here, Charlie?"

"Just came to do a little mousing. You're back early. How is the ever handsome Gideon?" Charlie asked between purrs.

Elizabeth sat in the chair next to her. "He's well. I have just had a very interesting meeting with King Morvand and King Kalidryd."

At the mention of King Kalidryd, Grandma Rose raised an eyebrow. "What was the elviron king doing at Kimadrian?"

"If you make me a cup of tea, I'll tell all," said Elizabeth.

Grandma stood. "One cup of tea coming up."

Charlie jumped off the kitchen chair and brushed against Elizabeth's legs, Elizabeth reached down, stroking the top of her head.

"I think I am going down to the Elven Realm to see Vandrayven," she purred. "I will come back and visit tomorrow if it is all right with you, Grandma Rose. I would like to come and play with Merlyn."

"Where is Merlyn?" said Elizabeth.

"I called him when Charlie arrived, but he didn't appear," said Grandma.

"I'm going to take Merlyn down to Kimadrian tomorrow. He's going to stay with Gideon for a few days, because I have to go on a trip. Charlie, you can help Gideon look after him if you want."

"Yes, I would like that," said Charlie. "Will you tell Merlyn I will see him tomorrow?"

"He'll be excited to see you," said Elizabeth.

Grandma Rose put Elizabeth's tea in front of her and opened the back door. The cat scampered along the pathway and disappeared around the corner.

While they drank their tea, Elizabeth told her grandma what occurred at the meeting with the two kings.

"I've heard of the Mirronstep, but you could be searching for years and never find it," said Grandma. "Thalios might not tell you anything, even if he does have some idea of where it is. The druids are scared to death of even the thought of the Mirronstep. They are afraid of what might happen if something like that ended up in the wrong hands."

"How do you know about the Mirronstep, Gran? You've never mentioned it before, and I've never seen anything about it in the books I've read."

"The Mirronstep has been mentioned from time to time, over the years," Grandma said. "There are brief references to it in one or two of the books in our little library. The only books you have read so far; are the ones you needed to read for the guardianship of the Grymlons. There are many more that tell the history of the Elven Realm. There are also books that give information on the druids. I don't think there's enough information to speculate where the Mirronstep might be."

"I have to try and find it," said Elizabeth. "The Elven Realm has never been without the Grymlons. The books of prophecy and learning say that the Elves are the Grymlons."

"How will you find Thalios? Grandma asked.

"I'm not sure. I've never had to go looking for him. Don't you know how to find him?"

"I've never had to contact him either. He always seemed to know when to appear," said Grandma. "Only the chosen one that has to renew the Grymlons has dealings with an Arch Druid. I have no idea where he would be."

"Well, I think if I go to Stonehenge, I may be able to contact him if I stand by the Heel Stone, and just ask the stone to find him."

"It's worth a try," said Grandma, "As you well know. The public aren't allowed near the stones without paying to see them. So if you want to get near the Heel Stone, it will have to be when there's no one around. If we get caught we might get arrested. I'll go with you and keep a look out."

"I think I may be able to avoid that," said Elizabeth, finishing her tea. "The advantage of magic helps, but you're right, it would be better not to draw attention. I'm going to go and look through the books in your room. If there's a reference to the Mirronstep anywhere, I need to find it. Do you remember which book you found the information in?"

"No I don't," said Grandma. "I'm the retired guardian. Your mother would have known, and I haven't looked in most of those books for years."

Elizabeth entered Grandma Rose's bedroom and moved the bed to one side. She touched the base of the wall and a door slid open. She reached her hand in to the left side of the interior and flipped a switch. A light came on, giving a somewhat murky illumination inside the windowless room.

She looked around, letting her eyes get used to the dimness. The room was filled with books stacked high around the walls. Elizabeth went to the back of the room. She picked up a step ladder that was laying on the floor and pulled it open.

"I may as well start at the back and work my way forward," she thought, climbing up to the top step.

She brushed the dust off the books and pulled three of them from the stack.

As Elizabeth stepped down, she heard a rustling in the corner of the room and immediately turned in the direction of the noise.

"The room is dark and dusty. Light my way and reveal," she said, raising one hand.

A small ball of light appeared. It hung above her head, as though waiting for instructions. Elizabeth moved her hand outward, pointing to the corner. The light moved to where her hand indicated. She peered into the corner and let out a sigh of relief. Sitting on top of half a dozen books was Merlyn. He had a piece of scrap paper stuck in one of his talons and was trying to pull it off.

"A little help would be nice, please?" he pushed into her mind.

"What are you doing in here?" Elizabeth asked him, as she pulled the paper from between his claws. "I thought I told you to stay out of Gran's library."

"I try to find mice for Charlie. She likes it when I tell her where they are, and there are lots of mice in here."

Elizabeth pointed to the door. Merlyn hung his head and trudged slowly out of the room. Elizabeth raised her hand and snapped her fingers. The hanging ball of light poofed into nothing, as she picked up the books and followed him out.

Once outside, she knelt down on the floor with Merlyn at her side, and thumbed through the books, one by one.

A couple of hours and dozens of books later, Elizabeth found a brief reference to the Mirronstep, in a book containing information about ancient druid rituals.

"This must be the reference Gran told me about," she said to an uninterested Merlyn. "It says here that members of the druid council used the Mirronstep, hundreds of years ago, to move around in the future and the past.

"Hmm… 'primarily used to attend rituals'. I wonder what sort of rituals?"

Elizabeth put the books back where she had found them and switched off the light. She touched a panel in the inside of the room and the wall slid back into place, leaving no trace of a door. She put the bed back into its original position, taking care to put the legs of the bed back into the indents in the carpet.

"Well, that was a waste of time," she said, patting Merlyn on the head.

She heard Grandma Rose calling her.

"Come on, Merlyn, supper's ready."

Elizabeth and Merlyn left Grandma Rose's bedroom and headed towards the dining room.

"Did you find anything?" Grandma asked.

"Only a small section about how the druids used the Mirronstep. I think it's the same piece that you found."

Grandma and Elizabeth ate in silence, while Merlyn sat under the dining table, snoozing.

"We should leave at about 4:30 a.m." Grandma told Elizabeth, after supper. "That will give us time to get to Stonehenge and away again before it gets light."

Elizabeth stood and kissed Grandma Rose on the forehead. "I'm going to bed, Gran. I'll see you in a few hours."

Chapter Four

Elizabeth was in a church, or was it a cathedral? She couldn't tell. She was standing in the aisle, halfway between the door to the side of her and an alter in front of her. As she looked to her right there was an oblong hole in the floor, with steps going downward into darkness. A hooded figure stood about three or four steps down, beckoning her.

Elizabeth tried to see the hooded figure's face, but the cowl was down in front just enough to hide it.

"Why do I feel I know this person?" she thought.

"Follow me," the figure said, walking down the steps.

The figure turned, facing Elizabeth again.

"Grandma is coming," he said.

The picture in front of her grew dim.

"Elizabeth? Elizabeth? Wake up," said Grandma, gently shaking her.

Elizabeth opened her eyes.

"Were you having a nice dream?" asked Grandma.

Elizabeth shook her head, trying to gather her thoughts.

"I was in a church and there was someone there with me."

Grandma smiled. "Well, you were supposed to be getting married soon. You may have had that on your mind."

"No, it was something else," Elizabeth said, glancing at her alarm clock.

It was 4:00 a.m.

"We need to get to Stonehenge," said Grandma. "I'm going to take a quick bath. Will you make us some breakfast?"

"Want some coffee?" asked Elizabeth.

"That would be wonderful. I'll join you in the kitchen as soon as I've bathed."

Elizabeth dressed, went to the kitchen and filled the coffee percolator with water. She put ground coffee in the top and put it on the stove. She dropped four pieces of bread into the toaster and took the butter out of the fridge.

"Who will live in the cottage when Gran dies?" she wondered. "Once I am wed, I am destined to become queen of Kimadrian. Gideon will be king, and he can't rule from the "Human Realm" as he calls it, and I can't be in both places at once.

Willow View can never be sold. The druids would never let that happen."

"I can't worry about that now," she said aloud, as she poured coffee and put plates out for toast.

After breakfast, Elizabeth drove her grandma to Stonehenge. The darkness was just beginning to fade, as they reached what was left of the stone ring.

They parked by the gift shop.

"I'll wait here," said Grandma. "If anyone comes along, I'll try to keep them talking until you get back."

"I'll be quick, Gran."

Elizabeth jogged across the car park, and out onto the road. She waved her hand in front of the chain link fence, and a hole appeared. She stepped through it and crossed the grass to the stones. She hopped over the rope that cordoned off the pathway to the stone ring, made her way through the centre of it, and out of the other side, until she reached the Heel Stone at the outside edge of the circle.

She touched the stone, putting her face up close.

"If anyone can hear me, this is Elizabeth Ghenestone. I need to talk to Thalios."

After a few seconds, she thought she could hear something. She leaned inward and put her left ear against the stone.

"Go home and wait," she heard a faint voice say.

"All right," Elizabeth said, more to herself than the voice she had just heard.

"It's so quiet around here, it's almost creepy. I feel as though the stones are part of me when I'm near them," she thought, feeling the hair on her arms stand up.

The Mirronstep

The shadow of the stones began to engulf her, as the sun peeped over the horizon.

Elizabeth hurried to Grandma Rose, who had gotten out of the car and was standing by the passenger door.

"We have to go home."

"How do you know?" Grandma asked.

"Because the stone said so."

"I'm glad you came back when you did," said Grandma.

"Why?" Elizabeth asked.

"I think I'm seeing things. I could have sworn I saw someone by one of the stones, watching you."

"But no one knew we were coming here," said Elizabeth.

"That's why I think my eyes were playing tricks on me. I turned away for a second and when I looked back, the figure was gone."

"A trick of the light, perhaps?" Elizabeth suggested.

"I think so," said Grandma.

They got back into the car and drove homeward to Oaklade.

Elizabeth dropped Grandma Rose at the front of the cottage, parked the car and entered the house through the back entrance.

"Would you like a cuppa?" Grandma asked, as Elizabeth came in through the door.

"Yes please," she said, taking a seat at the kitchen table.

"I suppose all we can do now, is wait," said Grandma.

"We can't do much else for now. I'm going back to bed for an hour, Gran, I feel a bit sleepy."

"Here, take your tea with you, dear," Grandma said, handing Elizabeth her cup. "I'm going to drink mine and perhaps do the same."

Elizabeth drank her tea, and stretched out on her bed. She pulled up the crocheted blanket that her mother had made before she died, and snuggled down underneath it.

She woke an hour and a half later, and decided to take a bath before doing some more research for the Mirronstep.

Elizabeth had just finished dressing, when Grandma Rose called to her. When she reached the kitchen, there was an elf guard standing by the back door.

"Lord Thalios is at the castle waiting for you," the guard informed her. "The king requests your presence as soon as possible."

"Please go on ahead and tell the king I'll be there in a few minutes."

"Yes, My Lady."

"I'll go down now, Gran. So I don't keep him waiting. Merlyn, are you here?"

Merlyn shimmered into solid form in front of her.

"Why is it, he will come when you call him, but he won't appear for me?" said Grandma.

Elizabeth looked from Merlyn to her grandma. "Well? Why won't you come when Grandma calls?"

"Grandma makes me clean up my mess," Merlyn pushed into her head.

"When Grandma calls you, you are to appear to her. Do you understand?" she pushed back.

Merlyn took a sideways glance at Grandma Rose. "Yes, I suppose so."

"We are going to the Elven Realm," Elizabeth told him.

"We are? How long for?" Merlyn said, jumping around the kitchen with excitement.

"Until I return from a trip I have to go on. Make yourself invisible until we get inside of the Willow tree."

Merlyn's shape shimmered for a moment and disappeared.

"We will see you in a bit, Gran."

"You go ahead, dear. I'll wait to hear from you."

Grandma Rose walked to the edge of the path and watched Elizabeth until she disappeared into the branches of the Willow tree.

"I hope she stays safe," thought Grandma, "All these years with no worries, and now this."

Grandma Rose returned to the kitchen. She made herself another cup of tea, took it into the living room and took a seat in her favourite chair.

"I think I'll take a little nap."

Gideon was waiting for Elizabeth at the entrance of the castle.

"Merlyn, why don't you go and find Charlie?" Elizabeth suggested.

"I'll go to Vandrayven," Merlyn pushed into her head. "Charlie is usually with him."

"Good. I'll find you later," said Elizabeth.

As Elizabeth approached Gideon, he took her hand, and they started through the entrance to the steps that led to the king's private rooms.

"You look worried," she said.

"Thalios won't talk about the Mirronstep," Gideon replied. "He says that it is a sacred artifact, and even if he did know where it was, he wouldn't tell us. He says the Mirronstep is too dangerous to use, even for good."

"We'll see about that. How did he get here so fast?"

"I don't know," said Gideon.

The two of them walked the rest of the way in silence. The guard at the entrance to the king's chambers stood back when he saw them approach. He saluted, as he opened the door to let them pass.

Thalios was sat by the fireplace with Keslyn, Merlyn's mother, and his constant companion. He stood when they entered.

Elizabeth went to him and they embraced, as would a father and daughter.

Keslyn put her head under Elizabeth's hand.

"How is Merlyn?" she pushed into Elizabeth's mind.

"Happy and very energetic!" Elizabeth replied. "He's here with Charlie. Why don't you go and find them?"

Keslyn scampered away.

Thalios looked from Elizabeth to Gideon, then back to Elizabeth.

"I think I will let you two talk. I am going to find my father. He and I have business to attend to. If you need me, please send a guard," Gideon said, excusing himself.

Elizabeth and Thalios sat by the fireplace.

He turned to her, putting his hand on her arm. "Gideon has told me about the Grymlons. I hear that you are looking for the Mirronstep. Do you know what you are getting yourself into?"

"I think so," she said. "I know how dangerous this is going to be, Thalios, but I don't have any choice. The Grymlons are dying, and I don't know what else to do. So if you know where the Mirronstep is, will you please tell me, so I can try to stop this disaster?"

Thalios stood. He went to the window that looked down into the private court yard of the king and queen. He watched as Charlie, Keslyn and little Merlyn played on the grass below.

He seemed deep in thought for a minute or two, then he turned to Elizabeth. "I do not recall ever hearing, or reading about the Grymlons dying for any reason. If they are dying, then the Realm truly does have a disaster on their hands," he said, "still, the Mirronstep? Could it make a difference? I would be risking my life to try and find it. I'm not too sure that if I do, it would be of any use. Besides, Elizabeth, I don't know where the Mirronstep is, and I am not happy about looking for it. The Mirronstep is more dangerous than you realize. I also know that you will look for it, and probably find it eventually."

"So I think I may be able to contact someone who may know something of where it may have been."

"I would appreciate your help, Thalios."

He stood. "Give me a few days, and I will see what information I can come up with. If I find out anything, I will contact you."

Thalios turned and left without saying goodbye.

"I've upset him, and that's unfortunate, but it means the Mirronstep exists!" Elizabeth said, looking out of the window.

She stayed until she saw Thalios walk across the garden to Keslyn. He looked up at her just as he reached the little Dragon, and waved. Elizabeth waved back.

Thalios and Keslyn left through the gate at the side of the garden.

Elizabeth sat on the couch by the fireplace and shivered.

"I'm beginning to feel a bit overwhelmed by some of this," she said, wrapping her cardigan around her.

A few minutes later, Gideon knocked on the door, and let himself in.

"You are as pale as a ghost. Are you all right?" he said, taking a seat beside her.

Elizabeth put her head on his shoulder. "I'm just disappointed about postponing the wedding."

"I am too, but we have the rest of our lives together, and it's not for long," he reassured her.

"You are ever the optimist. That's what I love about you, Gideon. Come on, let's go and see Grandma Rose. I could murder a good cup of tea," she said, as she stood, holding out her hand.

Gideon grasped her outstretched hand and she pulled him off the couch.

"Just how do you murder a cup of tea, Liz?" he asked, following her to the door.

Elizabeth laughed at her handsome elf.

"Oh, shut up, Gideon. You know what I mean."

He chuckled as they made their way out of the castle and up to the Human Realm.

Chapter Five

Bindyl had worked late at the castle in Kimadrian.

"I feel exhausted," he thought, as he rode towards home, "but I like to be tired. When I sleep, I don't think of the death of my Zoe. She's been gone for five years now, but it may as well have been yesterday, I miss her so much."

"Sleep brings with it dreams, and in my dreams I still see her and hold her. In my dreams, Zoe is still alive to me. I do enjoy the property King Morvand gave me in gratitude for saving Gideon when he was attacked by the Perichron, but I wish I could be here living with Zoe as my wife. She would have loved the cottage I live in. The stables would have been perfect for her favourite horse."

Bindyl rode through the gate and across the courtyard.

"Can I take your horse, sir?" his servant asked, as he approached the stables.

Bindyl stepped down from the saddle. "Yes, thank you."

He entered the back of the cottage and went to the kitchen sink. "Everyone tells me that life goes on," he thought, as he washed his hands. "Yes, life goes on, but I still miss her."

He entered the dining room and took a seat. The cook brought his supper.

"You can leave for the night," Bindyl told her, "and tell the rest of the staff I'll see them tomorrow."

The cook nodded. "Very well, sir."

Bindyl was about to put a fork full of food into his mouth, when there was a knock at the front door.

"Who can that be at this time of night?" he thought.

He got up from the table and opened the door. Standing in the darkness was Tevyn, Zoe's brother.

"It's late, Tevyn. Why are you here?" he asked, already knowing the answer.

The Mirrorstep

"Mother and father are arguing again. I couldn't stand it any longer. Can I stay here tonight?"

Tevyn was only ten years old, but his time as a slave to the elviron princess Verina, had affected him. He appeared much older.

"He looks so tired," Bindyl thought, glancing at the boy. "You're lucky that I live so close," he told Tevyn, "come in and I'll get you some supper."

"I'll get my supper, Bindyl. You sit down and finish yours."

"I'll send Seth to let your parents know where you are," said Bindyl.

While Tevyn was in the kitchen, Bindyl went to the stables.

The horses let out a low nickering sound, as he called Seth's name into the darkness.

"Yes, sir," answered Seth, emerging from his groom's quarters in the attic.

"I'm sorry. I know I told you that your duties were finished for the night. Would you ride over to the Mindar Estate. It will only take a few minutes, and let Tevyn's parents know he is with me. You may retire for the night when you return."

"Yes, sir," said Seth.

After supper, Tevyn sat with Bindyl for a few minutes, reading.

"I'm tired. Do you mind if I go to bed, Bindyl?"

"Not at all, I'll take you to school in the morning."

"Thanks. Good night."

Bindyl sat by the fire for a while, then he decided to retire for the night.

***

Bindyl was standing in front of a young man dressed in the brown robes of a monk.

"He reminds me of Elizabeth," he thought, looking into the man's face.

Bindyl glanced around him. "I'm in the Human Realm, in one of their graveyards by the look of it."

The young man turned to Bindyl, and pointed to a pathway between the gravestones, that led to a church.

Bindyl passed by him, pointing to the church ahead of him, glancing back at the young man. The young man nodded. Bindyl nodded back, and began to walk faster.

At the entrance to the church was an alcove. Inside was a bench seat on either side.

Bindyl could not quite see inside until he got closer. Then he noticed a small figure dressed in white, sitting on one of the benches. Bindyl was about to enter the alcove, when the young boy stood, blocking his way. Bindyl noticed the boy's complexion was completely white, as was his curly hair.

"I think I am supposed to go in there," Bindyl said, peering around the ghostly boy.

"I think not," said the boy, shaking his head. "You cannot enter here. You can make the journey, but you may not pass into this place."

"What journey?" Bindyl asked.

Fear grabbed Bindyl's heart. He turned back towards the gravestones and the urge to run overtook him. He tried to move, but his legs felt heavier and heavier. The harder he tried, the less he could move. He turned, looking back at the alcove, convinced that the ghost of the boy was right behind him.

The figure of the boy did not follow, but merely re-took his seat on the bench, as though waiting for the next visitor.

Bindyl woke, and shot upright in bed; his nightshirt drenched in sweat.

"No more bread and cheese for me before sleep!"

He got out of bed and made his way down the hallway. When he reached Tevyn's room, he peeped in, to make sure the boy was asleep. He closed the door and went to the kitchen. He poured himself a drink of water, and stood for a moment sipping it.

"What an odd dream," he said, trying to shake the images from his head.

Bindyl looked down at his now cold feet. He put the empty glass by the sink and returned to his room, changed his nightshirt and climbed back into bed.

The image of the young man with red hair, stayed in his mind's eye, even as sleep overcame him.

The Mirronstep

***

The next morning, Bindyl drove his carriage into Kimadria. He dropped Tevyn off at the school, and continued on to the castle. A groom took his carriage, and he headed to the guardroom.

"BINDYL!"

Bindyl turned, following the voice, and saw Gideon waving to him.

He stood to attention, saluting.

Gideon gave a quick salute in return, motioning Bindyl to follow him up to his quarters.

"I'm going to be late," Bindyl said, running up the steps behind him.

"I work here too, and I'm your commanding officer. So I give you permission to be late."

"What's wrong?" Bindyl asked, as Gideon closed the door.

"We have a problem, old friend. I think that you and I are about to experience another of Elizabeth's adventures."

Bindyl, who had just sat down in a chair by the window, immediately stood, shaking his head.

"No, no more adventures for me. I had my fair share of excitement the last time Elizabeth went on her little quest. No offense Gideon, but elves seem to die around her, and I for one, intend to live for a very long time."

Gideon held up his hand, "None taken Bindyl, but you have not heard me out. It could mean the end of both Kimadrian and Distardrian as we know it. Goodness knows what will happen in the Human Realm."

"All right," Bindyl said, sitting back down. "I will at least listen to what you have to say, but I don't think you are going to change my mind. I love Elizabeth. She is one of the nicest humans I know, but she has those powers and she can be more than a bit scary."

"She can be a little spirited at times, I will admit, but she would never harm anyone, Bindyl, you know that!"

"Tell me what is going on," said Bindyl.

Gideon took a seat and explained what was happening with the Grymlons, and what the plan was.

"We need you, Bindyl, because you can be trusted to stay quiet about this situation. If the elven population found out about this, it may cause panic. We must try to keep it from the elviron too."

"How can I help?" asked Bindyl.

"I'm not sure yet. I'll let you know as soon as I get more information."

"I have to get down to the guard room," said Bindyl. "You won't be working today. Someone has to do some work around here!"

They both laughed.

"Keep me posted my friend. I will do what I can to help you," Bindyl said, as he headed towards the door.

"I'm glad you changed your mind," said Gideon.

"I hope I don't regret it," Bindyl replied.

"I will come and see you as soon as I know more," said Gideon. "I'm going to go up to the Human Realm to talk with Elizabeth. I will let the king know you are in charge until I return."

When Gideon entered his father's rooms, his mother and father were there. They both glanced at him at the same time, as they stopped talking.

"What's the secret?" Gideon asked.

"We were discussing how handsome you have become," said Queen Paulina.

"Mother, shame on you! You were not talking about me, but never mind. If you don't want to tell me, then it's obviously none of my business. I just came to let you know that I am going up to the Human Realm to visit Liz. Bindyl is in command of the royal guard, until I return."

"Tell Elizabeth that we are thinking of her and looking forward to seeing her soon," the Queen said.

"I will pass on the message," said Gideon, kissing his mother on the cheek.

He bowed to his father and left.

The queen turned to the king, as Gideon closed the door behind him.

"Should we tell him?" Queen Paulina said, with a frown. "If the boy does not wake, and he may not after all this time, Gideon will eventually have to look after him."

The Mirronstep

The king had been pacing nervously while Gideon had been in the room. He sat down beside the queen. "If we tell Gideon, he will want to tell Elizabeth."

"I think she should know," said the Queen. "Now the elviron know that Jesse is alive, there is no more need for secrecy. She may be able to help him, Morvand. She saved Gideon when he was sick, and Zoe too."

"Elizabeth was devastated at the death of her mother and father," said the King, turning pale at the thought. "She missed her brother even more. They were very close before the accident. Elizabeth has become very powerful over the past few years, under the watchful eye of Vandrayven. She may not be too happy that she has been deceived."

"Jesse has been in a coma for almost seven years now. Over the past few weeks, he has almost regained consciousness several times. What if he wakes?" said the King. "It is true that Elizabeth may be able to help him, but what if she gets angry? What then?"

Queen Paulina took the king's hand. "If we tell Gideon, perhaps he can soften the blow for her. It may be safer if he tells her. I have grown tired of the deception anyway."

King Morvand thought for a moment. He smiled at his Queen. "I agree, but it's such a nice day. Let's not worry about it now. I am going for a walk in the garden. Would you like to join me?"

He smiled at her as she took his hand, and they walked out to the back patio and down the steps.

A guardsman took Gideon's horse at the gates of Humadria, and he made his way up through the town in the rock. He turned at the fountain, and headed towards the hollow tree trunk.

The two guards at the opening saluted him and stepped aside when the tree opened. Gideon looked out through the willow tree's branches, growing to human size as he did so. When he was sure there was no one around, he stepped out into the open. He crossed the bridge and passed through the gate to the back garden of the cottage.

He smiled, enjoying the sunshine, and the scent from the many flowers that lined the garden path.

"This would be a good place to live if I didn't have to be king, in a year or two," he thought. "I like the food up here and the tea. I wish I knew more humans."

Elizabeth was at the kitchen table, surrounded by books. She turned and smiled at Gideon when he entered through the back door.

As he looked into her eyes, his heart leapt in his chest, and his palms became sweaty. He could feel the colour rising on his cheeks.

Elizabeth got out of her chair. She had just kissed him on the lips when Grandma Rose came into the kitchen.

"I feel so blessed," Gideon thought, looking down at her. "I think I have loved her since the first time I saw her. This is as close to heaven as any elf can get!"

"Would you like a cup of tea, Gideon?" Grandma asked.

"Yes please, Lady Rose. I came to see how the research was going," he said, taking a seat at the kitchen table. "I couldn't find any more information in my father's library."

Elizabeth closed the book she had been skimming through. "I need a break," she said, with a sigh. "You have given me the excuse I needed, to stop looking through these dusty volumes."

Grandma Rose put a cup of tea in front of her.

She took a big swig. "Ah, thanks Gran."

"I haven't had any luck yet either," said Gideon, "but I'll keep looking, at least until Thalios returns. Don't give up, Liz. You might find something."

Elizabeth pushed the books away from her and finished her tea. When Grandma poured Gideon another cup, he put spoonful after spoonful of sugar into the hot liquid. He stirred it and drank it down, almost in one gulp. Elizabeth laughed at him. He put the cup down and smiled back at her.

"He so loves his cup of sweet, sweet tea," she thought, smiling back.

***

Two days later, Gideon arrived at the cottage.

"Thalios is at the castle and he wants to see you as soon as possible."

"What are you doing delivering messages? I thought you had servants for that," said Elizabeth.

"Thalios wouldn't let anyone but me give you the message. He said it was too dangerous," Gideon said, handing her a note.

She opened the folded paper.

"My dearest Elizabeth,

I have some information of the object you seek. Please come to the castle and we will discuss the matter.

Your friend,

Thalios."

Elizabeth turned to her grandma. "I have to go to the castle."

"Well don't keep Thalios waiting." Grandma replied, "I have some things to take care of around the cottage, so don't worry about me."

"I will send a guard to let you know, if Liz is going to be gone for a while. He can check up on you," said Gideon.

"I appreciate the concern, but there is really no need," said Grandma.

"May I remind you that you were kidnapped a few years ago, from right under my nose?" Elizabeth commented.

"Oh, all right. I would be delighted to have the company of an elf from time to time, and yes. I would like to know if you are going to be gone for a few days."

"It's settled then," said Gideon. "Come on Liz, Thalios is waiting."

Grandma Rose followed them out of the cottage. They turned and waved to her when they reached the gate at the end of the garden.

"I'm glad I didn't tell Elizabeth, I haven't been feeling too well lately," thought Grandma, returning their wave. "The doctor said that the pain in my chest was not indigestion this time. It was caused by angina, a condition that causes blood constriction around my heart. He said the nitro-glycerine pills he has given me will help when the pain gets too bad. I hope I have a few years yet, but I'm in my seventies now and I'm beginning to feel a bit tired."

A slight breeze brushed by Grandma Rose's face, interrupting her thoughts. She went back into the house, and made herself a cup of tea, before sitting in her favourite chair and dozing off.

Thalios was waiting in Gideon's rooms when Elizabeth reached the castle. He had been pacing back and forth across the living room, going to the window occasionally and looking down at Keslyn, who was playing with Charlie and Merlyn.

He turned away from the window when Elizabeth and Gideon arrived.

"Where have you been?" he asked. "I have been waiting too long in Kimadrian. It must not be known that I was here. It could be dangerous for us all."

"We got here as fast as we could," said Elizabeth.

Thalios stood for a moment. He looked from Gideon to Elizabeth. He shook his head and went to the window again. Gideon touched Elizabeth's arm and glanced towards Thalios. She nodded.

"Thanks," Elizabeth whispered, kissing him on the cheek. "I'll fill you in later."

As soon as Gideon left, Thalios turned to Elizabeth and motioned for her to take a seat.

"Elizabeth, I have done a most terrible thing. I am afraid that if I am discovered I may pay with my life!"

"What have you done?" she asked, as she sat on the couch.

He sat beside her. "I will explain, but first I have some things for you."

He reached into a black bag he had with him, and handed Elizabeth a book and a small mirror, with an intricate pattern around its entire edge.

"What are these for? The mirror is beautiful," she said, holding it up and looking at her reflection.

"You must be careful with that," said Thalios. "It is very powerful."

She placed the mirror on her lap. "Thalios, what's going on?"

He stood and began pacing the room again.

"I requested an audience with the Judicial Druids," he began to explain. "When I was presented to them, I asked for information about the Mirronstep...

..."I am here today my lords as I learned that the Grymlons in Kimadrian are dying."

"That is dire news, Thalios. What can we do to assist you?" said Peter, the druid seated in the middle chair of the five council members.

"Elizabeth Ghenestone requested an audience with me and asked me if I knew of a device called a Mirronstep."

"The Mirronstep is a legend, Thalios, nothing more than a fairy tale." said Peter.

"Elizabeth told me a story about a druid long ago, who testified to the existence of the Mirronstep. I myself have heard rumours. The druid in question stated that he had used it."

"And who might this druid be?" asked Peter.

"I believe his name was Alomer."

"Alomer, yes, he was a druid who oversaw the regeneration of the Grymlons long, long ago," said Peter. "How would Elizabeth know of him?"

"I was not privy to that information, my lord. Only that Elizabeth was aware of his existence and that he was a less than honest druid. I have known Elizabeth for a few years, and have no reason to believe that she is not telling the truth."

"Alomer was indeed dishonest. According to our records, he disappeared and was never heard from again," said Peter.

"Could it be that he went through the Mirronstep to save himself from punishment for his misdeeds?" Thalios asked.

"I believe that there was such a device back in Alomer's time," said Greyson, the druid next to Peter.

Peter turned to Greyson. "He does not need to know that!" He whispered.

"He already knows about the Mirronstep," said Greyson, "and he is no fool."

"Greyson is correct, Thalios. The Mirronstep did exist a long time ago, but I believe it was destroyed," said Peter, glaring at Greyson.

"Yes, yes, my apologies" said Greyson, quickly. "I remember. It was destroyed."

"Now, is there anything we can do to help you with the Grymlon issue? I mean other than the Mirronstep?" said Peter.

"No, my lords, but I thank you for your time…"

"I left the council chambers feeling great despair," Thalios continued. "I was deep in thought as I walked along the corridors. I feared that our world and that of the elves was about to be changed forever. Then I heard a voice call my name and turned around."

"Who is there? I called into the darkness of the halls.

A hand came out from the dimness of one of the passageways, beckoning for me to follow.

I pulled a flaming torch from the wall and followed the robed figure. After a minute or so, the figure stopped at one of the many doors that lined the very long, dimly lit passage.

The figure pulled a key from under his robe and unlocked the door. He entered, bidding me to follow. Once inside, the figure pulled his cowl from his head. I was very surprised at who had summoned me. ...

"Greyson! Why have you brought me here?"

"I have, over the years, tried to be impartial in my decisions regarding matters of our Order. I am however, very concerned about the plight of your young friend. I am also fearful of the consequences we may pay if she does not get help from the Mirronstep," Greyson explained.

"But there is no Mirronstep. You and the council have just told me that it was destroyed."

"That was a lie, Thalios."

"Then where is it?"

Greyson looked down at his feet. "I don't know."

"Then how do you know it exists?"

"Because it was hidden long ago. I don't know where, but I can give you some things that may help you to find it. You must keep them safe. I caution you, Thalios. If the council finds out that you have the tools to find the Mirronstep, I will deny all knowledge of you and this meeting. The punishment for taking anything out of this room without permission from the council is death."

"The objects in this room are rarely checked on, so I don't think anyone will miss them. There is however, only one way in and out of this room. If you are caught wandering these passageways, you will be punished. No one is allowed in this part of the council chambers without permission from one of the judicial members."

Greyson unlocked a cabinet resting against one of the walls. He reached in and pulled out a bag.

"Take this, Thalios. If you step out of this room and extinguish your torch, you will see on the ground, a thin green line that glows in the dimness of these passages. Follow it until you get to the large round room at the entrance. Don't veer away from the green line, or you may get lost. These corridors go on for miles."

"Is the Mirronstep in here?"

"Goodness me, no," said Greyson. "The Mirronstep resembles a full length mirror. Or so I've heard. No, the objects in the bag will lead to the Mirronstep, if they are placed in the right hands. I believe those hands may belong to your young Elizabeth."…

"So here I am," said Thalios. "I don't know what you are supposed to do with the things I have just given you, and I don't want to know."

"Thank you, Thalios," Elizabeth said. "I think you've done enough for now. If I succeed in finding the Mirronstep, I'll contact you and we will decide what to do from there."

"Please be careful, Elizabeth. A great deal depends on you," said Thalios.

He left the room quickly, eager to be as far away from the objects that he had given Elizabeth as possible.

A few minutes later Gideon popped his head around the door. "Has he gone?"

"Yes," she said.

"What has gotten into him?" said Gideon, as he entered the room, closing the door behind him. "He looked scared to death."

"Thalios left me this bag," she said, holding it up.

"What's in it?" Gideon asked.

"A mirror and a book. I'll look at them closer, but you and I need to go and see your father."

She put the bag in the cupboard by her bed.

Gideon took her arm and they made their way to the king's apartments.

They found only the queen when they reached the royal apartments.

"We need to talk to father," Gideon told his mother.

"The king is in a meeting with Vandrayven. When he returns I will let him know you wish to see him."

"Thank you, mother," said Gideon, taking Elizabeth's arm to leave.

"Gideon?" said the Queen, "I would like to speak with you alone, if I may, on a personal matter."

"Anything you have to say to me, you can say to Elizabeth. We will be married soon, mother."

"Yes, yes, but this is a personal matter between Gideon and I. Elizabeth, I hope you understand."

"Of course I do, your majesty," said Elizabeth. "It's quite all right, Gideon. I'll meet you back at your rooms."

Gideon showed Elizabeth out.

When the Queen was quite sure the door was closed, she took a seat and motioned for Gideon to sit beside her.

"I have something to tell you, my son. Elizabeth's brother Jesse, is still alive."

Gideon looked at his mother for a moment, then stood and went to the fireplace. On the mantle, were several small portraits of himself with both the king and queen.

"I cannot even think of how I would feel if I lost you both," he said, staring at the pictures. "Where is he?"

"He is here… in the castle," said the Queen.

"How long has he been here?"

"Since the accident," the Queen replied.

"Why didn't you tell me before, mother?"

"At first, we were hoping that Jesse would get better," said the Queen. "He has been in a coma for years, but he has recently regained some consciousness. It is only for a few minutes at a time, though, and it may not mean anything."

"Grandma Rose knows he is still alive. She comes down every now and then to visit him. She was going to tell Elizabeth, but then when she temporarily lost the use of her legs after the car accident, Rose decided not to.

It was the plan to tell Elizabeth when Jesse was more stable, but then she revealed herself as the chosen one."

"We knew how distraught she was about losing her family. If we had told her that Jesse was still alive, we would have had to tell her how he came to be here."

"Who caused the accident?" Gideon asked.

The queen avoided her son's gaze.

"King Kalidryd said it was princess Verina who ordered Elizabeth's family to be killed. She knew that the protector of the

Grymlons, on this occasion would have had the training that was required over the years. Verina knew that if Elizabeth's mother was dead, then Elizabeth would have to replace her when she became of age to be the guardian. She also knew that Elizabeth's chances of succeeding in the task of regenerating the Grymlons would not be good. Verina was a little older than Elizabeth, and had been studying the regeneration of the Grymlons for years."

"She didn't bargain for the fact that Elizabeth would become so powerful, and so quickly."

"But why is he here?" asked Gideon.

"Jesse was brought here to protect him. The elviron thought that Elizabeth's mother, father and brother were all dead. When Rose found out Jesse was still alive, the king arranged for him to stay here. If Verina had found out he was not dead, she would have tried to finish the job."

"Why are you telling me this now, mother?"

"Because your father and I want you to tell Elizabeth."

She watched, as Gideon turned pale.

"You want me to what?"

"We want you to break the news to her. She may take it more calmly from you," said the Queen.

"I can't mother," Gideon said, as he sat back down beside her. "I don't think she is going to be very happy. I don't think she is going to be very happy at all! You have kept this secret all these years. Now you want me, the one person who has pledged to love and protect her: to reveal to her a huge deception. Well, I won't do it."

Gideon stood to leave.

"Why?" asked the Queen, shocked by his refusal.

She was about to protest, but Gideon stopped her.

"You created this deception. You tell her! Or better yet, let Grandma Rose tell her. I think it is Grandma Rose's responsibility to reveal your deceit."

"Gideon, I am sorry it has come to this," said the Queen, "but if we tell Elizabeth about Jesse, she may be able to heal him. Grandma Rose is getting a bit too old to have to deal with the stress of this situation, and besides, she is unwell."

"Grandma Rose is unwell? What is wrong with her?"

"It is her heart," said the Queen.

"But I thought the doctor said that it was some sort of stomach acid problem."

"Gideon, that was years ago," said the Queen. "Grandma Rose is in her seventies now. She grows tired quickly these days. She has had some tests done by her human doctor, and he suspects that her heart has grown weak. Elizabeth does not know yet. Grandma Rose wants to get the results of the tests first."

Gideon headed towards the door.

The Queen stood. "Where are you going?"

Gideon turned to his mother, as he opened the door. "I need to think about this, I am going to see Liz, then I'm going for a walk. I need to get this straight in my head."

As Gideon headed towards Elizabeth's rooms, he felt slightly panicked.

"I'll go and see Liz: make some excuse to be alone. Then I'll go to Bindyl's until I can work this out," he thought.

***

Elizabeth had just bathed and was getting ready to look at the mirror and book, when Gideon arrived.

"He has an odd expression on his face," she thought as he entered the room.

"Is everything all right?" she asked.

"No," Gideon said, sitting by the window.

"Would you like to talk to me about it?"

"No," Gideon replied, in a sullen voice.

"Have I done something to upset you, Gideon?"

"No."

"If you don't want to talk about what is troubling you, why are you here?" she asked, becoming more annoyed with each 'No'.

"My mother has just told me something that is very disturbing."

"Does it have something to do with me, or us?" Elizabeth asked.

"Yes," said Gideon, staring out of the window.

"Look at me," said Elizabeth.

Gideon turned and faced her.

"You are beginning to annoy me," she said.

"And you are asking too many questions," said Gideon, "and that is also a little annoying."

"So you have come here with a look on your face that would drop a horse, but you don't want to talk about something your mother said about us both?"

"Correct," said Gideon.

"Then please leave."

"What?" said Gideon.

"Don't come in here with that look on your face, and then sit by the window and not tell me what's wrong. If you want to be sullen and angry, and not tell me why, then get out of here and leave me to my studies."

Gideon stood. "I think you are right, it's best if I leave and think about what my mother said. I think I should be alone for a while."

As he made his way to the door, Gideon hesitated for a second. He looked at Elizabeth as though he was about to say something more, then stormed out of the room.

Elizabeth sat for a minute or two, trying to make sense of the conversation they had just had.

"I was a little short with him," she said. "I should go to him and try to find out what is wrong, instead of being angry."

Elizabeth left her rooms and headed to Gideon's.

Chapter Six

Bindyl looked up at the darkening sky, and patted his horse on the neck.

"A nice hot supper, a glass of good Elderberry wine, and an early night for me," he thought.

A few minutes later, when his cottage came into view, he noticed a carriage parked in the courtyard. He hurried his horse along to see who it was. As he grew closer, Bindyl saw Gideon step out and say something to the driver. The driver turned the carriage around, nodding as he passed Bindyl, and headed back towards Kimadrian.

Gideon stood by the back door of the cottage. He pulled his topcoat around him, shielding himself from the oncoming rain-storm.

"Something is wrong," thought Bindyl, stepping down from his horse. "He looks miserable."

Seth took Bindyl's reins from him and led the horse to the stables.

Bindyl crossed the courtyard to greet his friend.

Gideon smiled, but Bindyl could see he was struggling to be cheerful.

"What brings you to my little hideaway?" he asked.

"Can I stay here tonight?" Gideon said, looking into Bindyl's face.

Bindyl let out a laugh. "I'm sorry Gideon. I was not laughing at you. It's just that everyone wants to stay here lately. Tevyn's parents were arguing, so he stayed last night. What's your reason for using me as an escape?"

"I… I have some things I need to work out in my head, and I need some peace and quiet. Liz doesn't understand and I can't tell her what the problem is. If I do, I am afraid of the consequences."

"Let's get out of this rain," Bindyl said, stepping through his front door. "Would you like some supper?"

"That would be nice," Gideon answered, not feeling very hungry, as he followed Bindyl into the living room.

"MOLLY," Bindyl shouted down the hallway.

A slightly built female elf, wearing an apron entered the room, curtsying as she did so.

"Please put out an extra place at the table for his highness, and make up the bed in the spare room."

"Yes, sir," said the maid, exiting with another curtsy.

"Sit down and tell me what's amiss, while I get us a glass of wine," Bindyl said, opening a small glass cabinet.

He grabbed a bottle and began to uncork it.

Gideon sat in one of the easy chairs. "My mother has informed me that Elizabeth's brother is still alive, and at the castle. She wants me to tell Elizabeth."

Bindyl hesitated for a moment. Something hung at the edge of his mind, as though trying to make itself known.

"They have kept this secret for seven years," Gideon continued, "and now, after all this time. They want me to tell Liz, because they don't have the courage to do it.

"I told my mother that I needed some time to think about it. So I went to Elizabeth and told her I needed to be alone for a while. She could see that I was a little upset about something, but when I wouldn't tell her why, she got a bit angry with me. We ended up having an argument and I left.

"I feel so horrible, Bindyl. We argued about something that will upset her even more if she finds out. She just doesn't know it yet."

Bindyl handed Gideon a glass of elderberry wine, and took a seat opposite his friend.

"When did all this happen?" he asked.

"It happened today. I left Elizabeth's rooms and came straight here."

"You know," said Bindyl. "I thought I knew every inch of the castle. I am head of the king's guard, and it's my job to know every nook and cranny. Yet I have never come across any trace of Elizabeth's brother. Do you know where he is?"

Gideon shook his head. "What am I to do, Bindyl? How am I supposed to tell Elizabeth that my family has been keeping this secret from her all these years?"

Bindyl stood. He took Gideon's wine glass and refilled it.

"Tell her," he said.

Gideon almost choked on the sip he had just taken. "What?"

"Tell her, and get it over with: be braver than the others. Tell her the truth."

"I have a question for you, Gideon," he said, as he sat back down in his chair. "Do you know what Elizabeth's brother looks like?"

"Yes," replied Gideon. "Well, I mean, I have seen pictures of him. Why do you ask?"

"I had the strangest dream last night. In my dream, I was standing in front of a church. There was a figure there in a robe, like a monks robe. He reminded me of Elizabeth. He looked a lot like her.

"In my dream, he pointed to the church and gestured for me to go to the door. When I reached the entrance, the ghost of a little boy blocked my way. He told me that I could make the journey, but could not enter the church. I had no idea what he was talking about, but for some reason I became afraid and began to run. As I tried to run away, my legs felt too heavy to move. It was then that I woke up. It unsettled me for a while, but then I forgot about it until now."

"How strange," said Gideon, "Elizabeth has a picture of him in her room. I'll borrow it and show it to you."

Just then, the servant came in and announced that the evening meal was ready.

"Come on Gideon, let's have supper. In the morning, you should go and talk to Elizabeth."

Gideon got up from his chair and followed Bindyl.

"Thanks, I think I can talk to her now."

They went to the dining room and sat down to eat.

Chapter Seven

Elizabeth sat in the living room of Gideon's apartment, looking down on the gardens below.

"I wonder where he is?" she thought, trying not to cry. "I didn't mean to get so angry. He obviously had a very disturbing conversation with the queen. Why wouldn't he tell me what she said to him? And why was he so upset? I wish he hadn't just left."

There was a knock at the door. Elizabeth turned, as King Morvand entered the room.

"I must be careful of what I say to her," he thought, noticing her expression. "I think Paulina may have said something to Gideon about Jesse."

Elizabeth stood and curtsied. "I'm sorry your majesty, I was not expecting you."

"Why my dear, what is wrong? You are so pale."

"Gideon and I have had an argument," Elizabeth replied.

"Do you mind if I ask what the argument was about?"

"I'm not quite sure," said Elizabeth. "When he came back from your apartments, he was upset. He had been talking with his mother on a private matter. When I asked him what was wrong, he became angry with me. I felt as though I had done something, but he wouldn't tell me what it was. Have I done something, your Majesty?"

"Elizabeth, you have done absolutely nothing," King Morvand reassured her. "I will find out what is going on, and I promise you that I will get to the bottom of it."

The king left without saying goodbye. "I must find the queen!" he thought, hurrying along the corridor.

Elizabeth let out a sigh, as he closed the door.

"Has everyone gone mad?" she thought. "I'll go back to my

rooms and look a bit closer at the mirror and book, see if it gives me any clues about the Mirronstep. If Gideon wants to run off, that's his business. I have more important things to look into."

Chapter Eight

The king made his way to the queen's private apartments, but she wasn't there.

"Where is her majesty," he asked, her maid.

"In the gardens, sir," the maid answered.

The king looked out of the window. He saw Paulina sitting on one of the long stone benches, and hurried down the back steps and out into the gardens.

When Queen Paulina saw him, she stood. "Morvand, what have we done?"

The king put his arm around his wife and pulled her to him.

"We did what we thought was best," he said. "I still believe that we did the right thing. If Verina had found Jesse, she would have killed him. At least this way he is still alive."

***

When Elizabeth reached her apartments, she called for her maid.

"Would you please bring me some tea," she said.

The maid curtsied and left.

Elizabeth took the objects Thalios had given her and sat at her desk, placing them in front of her.

The maid arrived with the tea, knocking on the door, before she entered.

Elizabeth waved her hand. The objects on the desk disappeared.

"Come in," she called out.

The maid entered the room with a tray and went to place it on the desk in front of her.

"No!" Elizabeth shouted.

The maid jumped back, almost dropping the tray.

"I'm sorry," Elizabeth said, quickly. "I didn't mean to raise my voice. Please put the tray on the table in front of the settee."

The maid did as she was told. "Would you like me to pour you a cup?" she asked.

"No thank you. I'll do so in a minute. You may go."

"As you wish, my lady," said the maid, leaving the room.

Elizabeth waved her hand again and the objects reappeared.

She poured herself a cup of tea, and took a few sips before returning to her desk.

She picked up the mirror, turning it over in her hands, fascinated by its unusual design. As she was handling it, she accidentally touched the middle.

Her finger disappeared into the glass.

"Ugh!" She said, drawing her hand back. "It feels like jelly."

She opened the little book. On the first three pages, there were sketches of churches, a soldier in uniform, a sketch of the mirror and beside it; a much larger sketch of the mirror. There was also a picture of a boy dressed in white.

One of the sketches was of an old church. There was a pathway with gravestones either side of it. The pathway led to the entrance covered by an alcove, with a door just inside.

"Where have I seen that entrance before?" Elizabeth said.

She skimmed through the rest of the book, but the pages were blank.

"I'll go down to the main library and have a look around," she thought.

She put the book and the mirror back in the cupboard by her bed, waved her hand at the objects and said, "In sight only to me. When I ask I will see," then looked into the cupboard, which was now empty.

Elizabeth left her rooms and headed down the stairs to the library.

A guard stopped her as she was about to go down the stairs.

"I have a message from Prince Gideon, my lady," he said, handing her a note.

Elizabeth broke the seal on the paper and read the message.

"My dearest Liz,

I am at Bindyl's. I am very sorry to have upset you. It was not my intention. Please don't worry about me. I just need some time to think.

I will see you tomorrow.

All my love,

Gideon."

"Thank you," Elizabeth told the guard.

"Will there be a reply, my lady?" the guard asked.

"No, that will be all."

"I'm glad he is with his best friend," thought Elizabeth, as she continued to the library.

"Perhaps Bindyl can help Gideon with his problem."

She had been researching in the library for an hour, when one of the king's servants entered the room.

"I have been sent to invite you to supper with the king and queen, my lady," he said, with a bow.

"Please tell the king and queen thank you, but I'm tired. I will eat supper in my rooms tonight and retire early."

"Very well, my lady," the servant replied, leaving the room.

Elizabeth closed the book she was reading.

"I think I'm better off with my own company tonight," she said, as she gathered the rest of the books piled up on the desk. She put them all back where she had found them, before making her way up to her rooms.

After she had eaten, Elizabeth went to bed. She was just about to fall asleep, when she heard a noise at the window.

"I am two floors up," she thought, getting out of bed. "I only know one being that would knock on a window this high up."

She picked up a candlestick, just in case, and pulled back the curtain. Charlie stood on the window ledge staring back at her.

She opened the window, and Charlie jumped through and onto the carpet.

"Has it ever occurred to you to use the door, sometimes?"

Charlie let out something between a chuckle and a purr.

"Now where would be the fun in that?"

"It's late Charlie, I'm tired, and you almost got wacked with this candlestick," Elizabeth said, putting it back on the dresser.

"I didn't mean to frighten you," said Charlie.

"I am two floors up, Charlie? It's not every night someone taps on your window, when you're two floors up!"

"Oh come on. You didn't consider that only a cat could tap on your window from that high up?" Charlie said, with a purr.

"No, Charlie I didn't. Now what is it you want?"

"Can I sleep with you tonight?" Charlie asked, sitting at her feet. "I miss you, and Merlyn keeps disappearing. It gets a bit un-nerving after a while."

"Come on, get on the bed," Elizabeth said, patting the bed cover, "but you stay down the end. I don't want cat hair all over my pillows."

Charlie jumped up and stretched out at the end of the bed. Elizabeth crawled back between the sheets and put her sleepy head on the pillow. She turned over on her side to get comfortable, and as she did so, she opened her eyes.

Lying on the pillow beside her was the faint image of a little Dragon. It was so faint that you could practically see right through it.

"Merlyn," Elizabeth said, quietly. "If you are going to sleep in this room, please have the good manners to show yourself."

She heard a heavy sigh.

Slowly, the image on the pillow became more and more visible, until Merlyn was in solid form.

"Thank you," she said.

"Good night Lizzy," a little voice pushed into her head.

Elizabeth mumbled a tired good night, as she closed her eyes.

Elizabeth woke at 6:00 a.m. to someone knocking on her door. She got out of bed, put on a robe and went to answer.

"Can I come in," said Gideon, as she pulled the door open.

Elizabeth stood back to let him pass. He brushed by her, and stood for a moment, uncertain of what to do or say next.

Elizabeth closed the door and went into her bedroom. Gideon followed her. He sat down in one of the easy chairs and noticed Charlie sleeping at the end of the bed, and Merlyn asleep on one of the pillows.

"I see you had company last night," he said, with a grin, hoping that the backlash from his behaviour the day before would not be too bad.

Elizabeth leaned against the foot of the four poster bed with her arms crossed, staring at him.

"Is there something I can do for you, Gideon? You know you're not supposed to be in my bedroom."

"I know, I know," he said, sheepishly, "but I wanted to apologize for the way I behaved yesterday, and I couldn't wait until you woke up. I felt so bad about our argument. I just wanted to get it over with."

Elizabeth pointed to the door.

"Out, NOW!" she said, "and wait for me in the breakfast room. I need to get ready for the day. If you want to apologize, you can do it in the proper manner. Not here, where you know that you are not supposed to be."

Gideon got up out of the chair and bowed in a very exaggerated, but gentlemanly way. Just before he reached the door, he turned and was about to say something. Elizabeth glared at him. He hung his head and continued out of the room.

After Gideon had closed the door, Charlie began to laugh. Her laughter became louder and louder, until she was rolling around on the bed, paws flapping in the air.

"What do you find so amusing?" Elizabeth asked.

Charlie sat up. "Gideon. I have never, ever seen that look on his face before. He must really love you, Elizabeth. I have seen him hurt elves for much less than that."

"You two need to leave," Elizabeth said, trying to hide a grin. "I have to bathe and get dressed."

Merlyn woke and simply poofed away into nothing.

"See!" said Charlie, pointing a paw at Merlyn, as she headed to the window. "See what I mean? Not so much as a good morning or anything."

"Oh no you don't," said Elizabeth. "You go out of the door."

Charlie purred. She changed direction, walking to the door. She meowed like an ordinary cat, looking up at her. Elizabeth opened the door to let her out.

Chapter Nine

Gideon was in the breakfast room, pacing back and forth. His father was sat at a table eating breakfast.

"Gideon, stop pacing. I would like to eat my breakfast in peace!" said the King.

"How dare you and mother do this to me," Gideon said, continuing to pace. "Elizabeth is mad at me because I cannot tell her what mother told me. Now she thinks she has done something wrong and I…"

He was about to say something about Jesse, when he saw Elizabeth out of the corner of his eye.

"Good morning Liz, Can I get you some breakfast?"

Elizabeth passed by him with a frosty glare.

"You are not my servant and I'm perfectly capable of getting my own breakfast, but thank you for the offer," she said, turning to the buffet table.

The king sighed.

Elizabeth poured herself a cup of tea and spread some marmalade on a piece of toast.

She took her breakfast to the window and sat down to eat. Gideon picked up a plate of bread and honey and some elven tea, and joined her.

They ate in silence. When Elizabeth was finished, she motioned for the servant to come and get her cup and plate.

She did not move for a few minutes, but sat staring out of the window.

"It's so beautiful here," she thought.

The Mirronstep

Gideon looked out of the window, then at Elizabeth. He looked over at his father, who was finishing his breakfast.

"Liz, would you like to go for a walk in the gardens?"

Elizabeth looked into his eyes. Gideon squirmed slightly under her gaze, and the colour rose on his cheeks.

"Yes, I'd like that."

They stood. Gideon bowed to his father, who in turn nodded back. The two of them left the room and made their way down to the gardens below.

"Oh thank goodness," said the King. "Now perhaps I can have a little peace!"

Elizabeth and Gideon strolled along one of the many pathways that squared around the garden. As they were walking, Gideon gently took her hand. She didn't try to pull it away.

He guided her over to one of the garden seats and motioned for her to sit down.

"Liz, I have something to tell you and before you get upset, I should say that I think it is good news. You however, may not initially see it that way."

He looked at her, trying to predict the outcome of the conversation.

Elizabeth returned his gaze with a blank expression on her face.

Gideon decided to press on.

"I had a conversation with my mother yesterday, as you well know. You also know that what she told me, well, it upset me somewhat."

Elizabeth nodded.

"Well," said Gideon, nervously. "What Mother told me was something that was so completely unbelievable; I needed some time to sort it all out in my head."

Elizabeth continued to nod, as though agreeing with him.

"I don't know how to say this, so I am going to just … well … Elizabeth, Jesse is still alive."

Gideon stood. He looked down at her. Wondering what was coming next.

Elizabeth got up from her seat, facing him.

"Liz, are you all right?" he asked, noticing that her face had turned white.

He caught her, as she slumped to the ground in a dead faint. Fortunately for Gideon, the king had been watching them from the window. He quickly summoned four guards, who ran down to the garden to help. They took Elizabeth to her rooms and the king's physician was sent for.

The king's physician examined Elizabeth, then, found Gideon and the king.

"She is suffering from extreme shock," he informed them. "She is to be kept warm. When she wakes, give her some hot, sweet tea."

"Thank you Frederick," said the King.

The physician bowed to the king and left.

Chapter Ten

When Elizabeth woke, she was lying on her bed. It took a minute or two for her head to clear.

Gideon was sat beside her.

"What's he doing here?" she thought.

Gideon was reading a book and had not noticed that she was awake. Then she remembered.

"Jesse!" she said, sitting bolt upright.

Gideon, unaware that she was awake, jumped out of his chair.

"Heavens, Liz. You scared me half to death!"

"How can he be alive? I was at his funeral. Mum, dad and he were all buried at the same time. There were three coffins. I saw them put into the ground."

The vision of that day came into her head with sickening clarity, as though it were yesterday.

"Has Jesse somehow returned from the dead?" she said.

"No, Liz. He never died," Gideon said, sitting on the side of the bed.

"Where is he? I want to see him now!"

"I will take you to him," said Gideon, "but first we have to go and see the king."

"Why? Why can't you take me to Jesse, Gideon?"

Gideon stepped back as Elizabeth got off the bed.

"Liz, I don't know where he is," Gideon replied. "Mother only told me that he was alive yesterday. I was so angry at her for deceiving you for all these years. I left without finding out where he is in the castle. I thought I knew every inch of this place. It seems I was wrong."

Elizabeth had gone into the bathroom while Gideon was explaining things. She came out with her hair brushed and in a ponytail.

"Does my grandma know that Jesse is alive?" she asked, quietly.

He turned away from her.

"Gideon, I asked you a question."

Gideon continued to avoid eye contact, nodding.

Elizabeth sat down. She closed her eyes and began to cry.

Gideon rushed to comfort her, but as he reached her, she stood. She looked at him and he saw incredible sadness in her face.

"I want to see my brother. Let's go and find the king."

Gideon took her hand and they made their way to the royal apartments.

The queen stood when they entered. Elizabeth approached the king. She didn't curtsy. Instead, she looked him straight in the eye.

"Please take me to my brother."

The king said nothing. He left the room with Gideon, with Elizabeth following behind.

The three of them went down into the depths of the castle, until they reached Vandrayven's rooms. The king first knocked on the large Oak door, then entered without waiting to be invited.

Vandrayven was busy working with his bottles and jars when they arrived. He turned, saw the king and bowed. The king nodded. When Vandrayven saw Elizabeth, he headed towards the back wall of his rooms, held up his staff, said something in elvish, and a door appeared.

"Well I'll be…," said Gideon.

Vandrayven opened it. Elizabeth pushed him aside and entered.

The room had everything one would need to live in comfort, except the occupant of this room had few needs.

In a bed in the middle of the room was a man. He had long red hair and a beard. He seemed to be sleeping.

Elizabeth approached him.

"Oh, heavens! It is Jesse," she said, quietly. She suddenly felt a weight in her chest, and her eyes fill with tears. You look so much older now."

The Mirrorstep

Gideon looked from the man in the bed to Elizabeth. He noticed a striking resemblance between the two.

She stared down at the man in the bed in disbelief. "I'm going to wake up in a minute and all of this will be a dream," she thought, touching his hand.

He flinched, she jumped.

"It's all right Elizabeth," said Vandrayven. "He regains consciousness a little now and then. He may know that you are here. Talk to him, he might respond."

Elizabeth directed an icy stare at the wizard, and turned back to her brother. She bent down close to his ear.

"Jesse, it's Liz. I'm going to try to help you. Can you hear me?"

At the sound of her voice, the fingers of Jesse's left hand moved slightly.

"I'm going to go and see Grandma, but I'll be back. I promise."

Jesse's left hand twitched again.

Elizabeth turned and left the room, with the rest of the group following closely behind.

"Is there anything I can do to help you, Elizabeth?" the King asked.

Elizabeth turned on her heel.

"Yes," she said. "When I get back from seeing my gran, you can give me an explanation!"

She turned and continued to walk at a brisk pace.

"I will explain everything, Elizabeth, but we must move fast. Time grows short," the King called after her.

Elizabeth stopped and turned around again.

"You can take your Grymlons and...," she said, angrily, but stopped herself. He was, after all, the king. She continued along the hallway. This time, no one followed her.

Elizabeth exited the willow tree, making sure as always, that there was no one around to see her. She was crossing the bridge when she saw her grandma in the garden.

Grandma Rose was knelt down on a small mat, pulling weeds from among the flowers.

"Autumn is coming. She's doing some last minute pruning and clipping. She so loves her garden," Elizabeth thought, stepping through the gate.

Grandma Rose looked up. When she saw Elizabeth, she stood and waved. Elizabeth waved back.

Grandma shaded her eyes with her hand, watching Elizabeth approach.

The two of them stood face to face for a moment, looking at each other.

"Why didn't you tell me that Jesse was still alive?" Elizabeth asked.

Grandma Rose's shoulders slumped, and she turned her gaze away.

"She looks old and tired," thought Elizabeth, suddenly regretting her outburst.

"Can we talk about this over a cup of tea, Elizabeth? I have been in the garden all morning and I could do with a break."

Elizabeth nodded, stepping onto the garden path.

Grandma Rose followed her through the back door of the cottage and into the kitchen.

"Sit down, gran, I'll make us some tea, then we can talk."

Grandma sat down at the kitchen table. Elizabeth made the tea and put a cup in front of her. Grandma Rose drank a few sips.

"When the crash happened," Grandma began to explain, as she put her cup down, "all three of them were pronounced dead at the scene. You didn't know much of this. When the news caused you to go into shock, and you went into the hospital. I was advised by the doctor not to discuss any of this with you in case it increased your distress. But I grew suspicious when the police couldn't find the driver of the car that hit them. The car was registered to a person who had reported it stolen a few years before, and had since died.

As you know, your dad was an only child and both of his parents were dead, so it was up to me to go to the morgue and identify all of them."

Grandma Rose paused for a few moments, closing her eyes, as the memory of three white faces lying on cold metal slabs came flooding back.

She took a deep breath and continued.

"I identified your mother and father, and then the mortician took me to a different room to identify Jesse. Just as he pulled back the sheet to reveal Jesse's face, the phone rang in the other room. I told him it was all right to leave me alone with my grandson, that I needed to say goodbye to him anyway. So he left to answer the phone.

I looked down at Jesse. I touched his face and told him I loved him. I was just about to pull the sheet back up over him, when I saw a small tear appear at the corner of his right eye."

"Well, even I know that dead people don't cry. So I touched his face again. He felt cool to the touch, but his eyes twitched. I was about to go and get the mortician, when a thought occurred to me. If Jesse was still alive and it was the intention to kill my family, perhaps I should let it stay as it seemed."

"When the mortician came back into the room, I told him that I didn't want Jesse embalmed. At first he protested, but when I insisted, he gave in to my request. He asked me about your mother and father and I told him that they had both requested embalming before their burial, which was true. The mortician informed me that because of health issues, if he couldn't embalm Jesse, he would have to enclose him in a coffin as soon as possible. I hurriedly picked out one of the coffins for sale at the morgue. I knew that if I was to keep Jesse alive, I would have no choice but to have him placed in one, for the time being.

I left the morgue, contacted King Morvand and told him the situation. He got in touch with a couple of humans who lived in the Elven Realm."

"That evening, we broke into the morgue and took Jesse out of his coffin. We filled it with enough bags of flour sealed in plastic to make it about his weight, and we brought him down to Kimadrian. He has been there ever since.

"We thought he may stay that way for the rest of his life, then a couple of weeks ago he regained consciousness for a moment, but then lapsed back into a coma."

"Three days ago, King Morvand sent word for me to see him, he said it was urgent. Fearing the worst, I hurried down to the Realm. When I got there the king told me that Jesse had been mumbling something: trying to talk. When I reached Vandrayven's rooms, Jesse was rambling about going on a journey. He said he had to contact someone and help with a task. I listened to him, thinking that he was making no sense whatsoever, when he said Bindyl's name."

"At first, Vandrayven and I were a bit shocked. Jesse had never met the elves, and Bindyl had no knowledge of him. Vandrayven said that one or more of us may have mentioned Bindyl's name and he somehow heard it and remembered it. A few minutes later he lapsed back into a coma again.

"I wish you had told me before, Gran. I've missed so much time with him."

"I'm so sorry, Elizabeth, but the time passed so quickly. Before I knew it, not months, but years had passed. Do you think you could help him? If he woke up once, he may be able to do so again."

Elizabeth sat for a second or two, trying to take the whole thing in.

"I'll try to help in any way I can, Gran. I want you to come back down to Kimadrian with me. We'll do it together."

Grandma Rose began to cry. Elizabeth put her arms around her. "Don't cry, Gran. I promise I'll try my best."

Grandma blew her nose loudly. "It's just that I have had to keep this secret from you for so many years. Now it's out in the open and I feel such a sense of relief!"

Elizabeth smiled. "Come on Gran, let's go. I have work to do."

"Wait a minute," said Grandma.

She went to her room and put a few clothes in a small case. She picked up the bottle of pills, the doctor had prescribed for her. "I'll have to tell Elizabeth about my heart eventually," she thought, "in case I need these and can't get to them for some reason. I'll wait a while, though, let her try to heal Jesse first."

Grandma pushed the pill bottle down into the bag and headed to the kitchen.

"Are you ready?" asked Elizabeth. "We need to be on our way. I want to get Jesse sorted out, so I can try to solve this Grymlon problem."

"Yes, yes. Let's go," said Grandma, leading the way out of the cottage.

The Mirronstep

***

Gideon was waiting for them when they arrived.

He glanced at Elizabeth, not sure how to act. As she approached him, she smiled, then reached up and kissed him on the cheek.

"We're going to see Jesse. I have to look into this Mirronstep situation, but I need to take care of my brother now," she said, looking into his eyes.

Gideon looked down at her. "I'm sorry Liz. My father feels awful."

"First things, first," she said, "let's see if I can help Jesse, then we'll deal with your dad later."

When they reached Vandrayven's rooms, Elizabeth sat on the side of Jesse's bed and took his hand.

At her touch, his eyes twitched, and he began to moan and move around. Suddenly, he opened his eyes and looked directly at her.

"Where is Bindyl?" he asked, then closed his eyes again.

"What?" Elizabeth said, shocked at his question.

Gideon was talking to Vandrayven. When he heard Jesse say Bindyl's name, he turned. "Did he just say Bindyl?"

Elizabeth turned to Gideon. "Do you know what's going on here?"

"I think I might. When I was at Bindyl's house. He told me he had dreamt about a young man who looked like you. The young man directed him to a church. Can I go and find him?"

"Yes," said Elizabeth, "and hurry back."

Before the words were half out of her mouth, Gideon was sprinting towards the door.

"I'm going to try and use magic to coax Jesse out of his coma," said Elizabeth, taking his hand.

She chanted words in elvish, in the form of a spell.

Jesse didn't move.

Elizabeth tried again, nothing happened. She stood and began pacing the room.

"I know there's something," she thought. "I just can't get my mind around it. Why is the spell eluding me?"

After a few minutes, Gideon reappeared with Bindyl. When they entered the room, Jesse became agitated again.

"This is the man in my dream," Bindyl said, "The one who pointed to the church and gestured for me to walk the pathway to the entrance."

When Bindyl spoke, Jesse opened his eyes.

"No! You must make the journey, but you can't go in!" he said, before closing his eyes again.

"What is he talking about?" Bindyl asked. "The boy in my dream said the same thing."

"Gideon, can I speak with you outside please?" Elizabeth said.

They went out into the hallway and Elizabeth closed the door. "I can't get Jesse to respond, and I don't know what else to do."

"Why don't you leave it for a while," Gideon suggested. "Perhaps if you wait a few days, it may work better?"

"I don't have a few days, Gideon. I have to find the Mirronstep."

"Then go, Liz. Jesse has been this way for years. A few more days probably won't hurt him."

"But to talk to Jesse again, to laugh with him!" Elizabeth said, "Even to argue with him! But you're right. He has been this way for a long time. If he is meant to come out of it, I may not be the one who is supposed to make it happen."

"I promise we will look after him," said Gideon.

Elizabeth returned to Jesse's room.

"What is happening?" asked Bindyl. "How does he know me? We have never met."

"I don't know," Elizabeth said, staring at Jesse.

"I have to get back to the castle guard. Will you find me when you get some answers?" said Bindyl.

"As soon as I know, you will, too," said Elizabeth.

Grandma and Elizabeth waited for about an hour, but Jesse didn't wake again.

"Don't worry, Elizabeth, you go. I'll come back later," said Grandma, "check on him and make sure he is all right."

Elizabeth joined Gideon, Grandma, and the King and Queen later, for the evening meal.

There was an awkward silence between them all, while they ate.

The Mirrorstep

Having finished her meal, Elizabeth was about to leave, when the queen stopped her.

"I'm sorry," she said.

"You should have told me sooner," Elizabeth said.

"We should learn to trust you more. We will learn by our mistakes, Elizabeth. I give you my word, no more secrets."

"I want to be a good wife to Gideon and a good daughter-in-law to you," said Elizabeth.

The queen stepped forward and embraced her.

"You already are," she whispered, into Elizabeth's ear.

After dinner, Elizabeth went to her rooms. When she entered her bedroom, Charlie was asleep at the foot of her bed, and Merlyn was asleep on one of the pillows.

Elizabeth rolled her eyes.

"I'm being a big softy, but they look so comfortable," she said quietly. "I'm tired, and it's been a trying day. I suppose it wouldn't hurt to share a bed with them, again."

***

Elizabeth was standing in front of Jesse. He was dressed in a brown robe with the hood up, but she could still see his face. She looked around her at the gravestones peeping up from the grass.

"I've been here before," she thought, seeing the church behind her brother.

Jesse pointed to the entrance. She looked where he was pointing, stepped onto the pathway and approached the stone alcove. She entered and put her hand on the metal ring that was the handle to the large oak door. She tried to turn it, but it wouldn't move.

Elizabeth turned and saw her brother watching her, a little way off. She kept her eyes on him as he got farther and farther away, until he was a tiny figure. Then he was gone.

She woke.

"More dreams, but I feel rested," she thought.

"You two need to go and play," she told Merlyn and Charlie.

"Watch this!" said Charlie. "Merlyn has discovered he can take passengers."

Charlie stood beside Merlyn and touched him on the shoulder. Merlyn became transparent, and Charlie faded with him.

"Partners in crime," she said, shaking her head and laughing, as she headed to her bathroom.

She bathed and dressed, then joined Gideon and his parents for breakfast. Grandma Rose sent her apologies for not joining them, but spent some time with Jesse instead.

After breakfast, Bindyl found Elizabeth. "May I speak with you in private?"

"Of course. Is everything all right?"

"Yes. I just need to discuss something with you," he said.

They went into the portrait room and Elizabeth asked a servant to bring some tea for them both. She sat down in one of the plush chairs.

Bindyl stood by the stone fireplace. "I had another dream last night."

"What about?" she asked.

"Your brother. He spoke to me."

Elizabeth sat up in her chair. Bindyl was about to tell her about his dream, when a servant came in with the tea tray.

She poured some tea for them both.

"Jesse spoke to him! I must try to stay calm. Bindyl has a tendency to panic and I don't want to frighten him," she thought.

"Well, come on Bindyl," she said, cheerily. "Sit down and have some tea with me, and tell me what he said."

Bindyl sat next to her. Elizabeth handed him a cup of tea and he sat back sipping the hot liquid.

"Elizabeth, what is a Mirronstep?"

"Why do you ask, Bindyl?" Elizabeth said, almost dropping her cup.

"Because your brother told me that you are going to try to find this Mirronstep, and I am to help you. He says he is going to help you, too."

"How is he supposed to help?" she asked.

"Jesse says that he died the night of the crash. He says he walked towards a bright light, but was pulled back by someone. When he turned around to see who was holding him back, he saw his mother. She told him that he would get well, but first he would sleep. She told him not to worry and that the sleep would be long, but seem much shorter. Then she told him that in his sleep, he would help you perform a great task, sometime in the future. His mother told him that he must stay asleep for his own safety.

"When Jesse questioned your mother about why he had to be asleep to help you. All she would say was that his spirit would be able to travel through time, and that if he helped you in spirit, his body would remain safe."

"He said all that?" What did he say about the Mirronstep?"

Bindyl took another sip of tea. "He said that you would be looking for it."

"Did he say where the Mirronstep was?" she asked.

Bindyl chuckled. "Jesse said you would ask that. He doesn't know where it is."

"Well," she thought with a smile. "It was worth a try."

Elizabeth explained about the Mirronstep.

"So that's why Gideon asked me to help. I don't think I want that much excitement in my life!" Bindyl said.

"Don't worry, Bindyl. "I'm the one who will be stepping into the mirror, if we find it. I'm not sure, but I think I may be the only one who can."

"Well, in that case," said Bindyl. "I will do anything I can to help."

"I'm going to do a bit more research. I'll find you when I know more," said Elizabeth.

"I have to go back to my duties with the castle guard. I'll probably see you later, Elizabeth."

They parted company at the bottom of the main stairs.

Elizabeth was heading up to her rooms, when a voice echoed gently in her ears.

"Sit down and sleep," it said, faintly.

"What?" asked Elizabeth, looking around.

"Sit down and sleep," the voice said.

Elizabeth looked around again, but she was alone in the corridor.

She entered her rooms, then made herself comfortable in a chair, closed her eyes and relaxed.

"Hello sis, long time, no see."

Elizabeth opened her eyes. "So it was you talking to me."

"Yes," Jesse said.

Elizabeth stood. She went to him and put her hand out. It came to rest just above his elbow. "I can touch you! But how?"

"It's magic, Liz. Did you think you were the only one who was special?"

Elizabeth laughed as the two of them embraced. She laughed and cried, then laughed again. When she had settled down a bit, Jesse took a seat.

"I can only be with you like this, as long as you can stay asleep. If you wake up, I will disappear. If you have any questions, ask them now. It's not good for you to stay this way for too long. It drains your strength."

"Well, I know you can't tell me where the Mirronstep is. So why are you supposed to help me?"

"Mother has given me the task of protecting you while you are on your quest, but I can only be with you when you are in the places that you are supposed to be," Jesse replied.

"How will I know where those places are?"

"I don't know that answer, but I do know how smart you are. So I know that you will figure it out," Jesse said, beginning to fade.

He looked down at himself, then at Elizabeth. "You are waking up. Don't worry Liz. We'll meet again," he said, as he faded away into nothing.

Elizabeth opened her eyes.

"I feel as though I haven't slept in days," she said, climbing onto the bed. She fell into a deep sleep as soon as her head hit the pillow.

Chapter Eleven

Elizabeth returned to her rooms after breakfast, and took the mirror out of the cupboard. She sat down at her desk, studying it. As she stared at her reflection, it became hazy and a picture came into view.

"It's a church!"

Fascinated, she continued to look into the mirror. A cemetery came into view. Behind the old cemetery there was a sign above a Cotswold stone wall that read, 'St. Michaels Church.'

"I know this church. We travelled there on field trips to do brass rubbings on the gravestones. I remember going down into the vault to where they stored the old stone effigies. I'll go and find Gran, see if she wants to come with me to visit the church."

Elizabeth found Grandma Rose with Jesse.

She looked down at her brother, and put her hand on her grandma's shoulder. Grandma Rose looked up at her and smiled.

"I'm going on a little trip. Would you like to come with me, Gran?"

As she spoke, Jesse's head began to move from side to side, and his hands grasped at the bedcovers.

"Jesse, it's all right," said Grandma.

He settled down a bit, at the sound of her voice. Grandma Rose kissed him on the forehead and the two of them left Vandrayven's chambers.

"Where are we going?" she asked Elizabeth.

"To Highwell, to the church by the main road."

"Why?" Grandma asked.

"I think I'm supposed to go there," Elizabeth replied, and explained how Jesse had visited her in her rooms, and what he had told her.

"When I woke, I looked into the little mirror Thalios gave me, and it showed me the church. I'll tell Gideon where we're going and meet you at the main entrance."

"I'll order a carriage to take us to Humadria," said Grandma.

"Thanks, Gran. I'll be quick," Elizabeth said, hurrying down the hall.

She found Gideon sitting at his desk.

"I think I may have a lead on where the Mirronstep is," she told him.

"That's wonderful news! Where are you going?" he said.

"We are going to Highwell. It's a small town about four miles away from Oaklade," Elizabeth replied. "There's a church there. When I looked into the little mirror, it showed me the graveyard with the church signpost, by the road."

"Do you think the Mirronstep could be there?" asked Gideon.

"Wouldn't it be nice, if it were that easy," Elizabeth said.

She kissed him lightly on the cheek. He looked down at her and smiled. "Be careful."

"As always," she replied.

Gideon watched her hurry down the hallway. Only after she had turned the corner, did he go back to his rooms.

"I have a feeling that this Mirronstep thing is going to be a bit more of a challenge than she thinks," he thought, closing his door.

***

Elizabeth ran down the castle steps to meet her grandma, who was already seated in the carriage. As she neared the entrance, she noticed Bindyl standing by the carriage door, talking to her. He turned and smiled at Elizabeth, when she approached them.

"Where are we going?" he asked.

"Why?" she said.

"I have to go with you, Jesse said so," said Bindyl. "I have to go with you wherever you go. If Jesse says that I play a part in this latest adventure of yours, then I go where you go. Believe me, Elizabeth,

I would rather be at the castle doing the work I know and actually enjoy, but it seems I have no choice."

"Well, get in," she said. "I don't have time to argue. But when we get up to the cottage, you must stay out of sight."

Bindyl got into the carriage, and took a seat next to Grandma Rose.

"Where are we going?" he asked, again.

"We're going to the church in Highwell," Elizabeth answered.

"Why?" asked Bindyl.

"Because I saw the church in the. … Well, never mind. Just believe me when I say, I may find the Mirronstep there."

"Just like that," Grandma commented, with an ironic grin.

Elizabeth looked out of the window, ignoring her grandma's remark.

When they reached the willow tree, Elizabeth stepped through its branches, followed by Grandma and Bindyl. They made their way over the bridge, through the gate and across the lawn. Grandma unlocked the back door to the cottage and entered the kitchen. Bindyl took a seat at the table.

"Would you like a cup of tea before we go, Gran?" Elizabeth asked.

"No thanks. If we're going to Highwell, we need to get going," said Grandma, fumbling in her handbag. "You two go and wait by the car. I'll be there in a minute. I can't find the car keys."

Elizabeth and Bindyl made their way around the side of the cottage and through the gate to the car.

"When we get to Highwell, Bindyl," Elizabeth said, "I want you to shrink to your elf size and make yourself invisible."

"All right," he agreed, "but can I stay human size on the way there, so I can see out of the window? I have never ridden in a car before."

Grandma Rose came around the corner and unlocked the car.

"Sorry to keep you," she apologized. "I seem to be forgetting things more and more, lately."

"I can drive if you like, Gran," said Elizabeth.

"No thank you," said Grandma. "I'm not quite that old yet."

The drive to Highwell took about ten minutes. The church was on their left, on the main road. Grandma drove past the church and turned left at the traffic signal. She drove along the main street to the centre of the town. She turned left again and parked in the town market square.

Grandma Rose and Elizabeth got out of the car. Bindyl shrank down, and jumped out when Elizabeth opened the back door to get her brass rubbing supplies. They walked along the street, past the shops that sat in front of the church and turned right under a stone arch.

Directly in front of them was the side entrance to the church. Grandma pushed open the wrought iron gate and they headed through the pathway that led to the side door.

Grandma Rose and Elizabeth entered the archway, but when Bindyl tried to follow them, he was pushed back by an unseen force. Try as he might, he could not enter the archway.

He finally gave up.

"You two go on without me. I will sit on the grass and wait."

"Are you sure you'll be all right here by yourself?" asked Elizabeth.

"No one can see me, and I don't seem to have much of a choice, do I."

"We won't be long," said Grandma.

A blast of cold air hit Elizabeth's face as she opened the church door and stepped into its stony interior.

"It's cold in here," said Grandma, pulling her jacket around her.

"It's always cold in here, Gran. The walls are inches of thick stone. It's been years since I was here last. They have redone the stonework. It looks much brighter in here than it used to."

Grandma put a couple of one pound notes in the collection box by the door. Elizabeth walked along a short pathway that led to the aisle. She turned right and saw the vicar tidying the altar.

He turned when he heard Elizabeth and her grandma approach.

"How may I help you?" he asked.

"Good day to you, Vicar," Elizabeth said. "My name is Elizabeth and this is my grandmother, Rose,"

"Good day to you both," the Vicar replied.

"I was telling my gran about this church when we were having tea this morning," Elizabeth explained.

"I don't recognize your face," said the vicar.

"We are from Oaklade," said Elizabeth. "My school used to come here on field trips. We used to do brass rubbings on the head stones in the front of the church."

"Ah yes," said the Vicar. "You must have attended Our Lady of St Luke's. Haven't had a visit from them in a while."

"I left school five years ago," said Elizabeth.

"Well, what can I do for you today, miss?" asked the vicar.

"When I told Gran about the beautiful rubbings we did here, she suggested that we come back today and do some more."

The Vicar's eyes lit up. "I think that is a splendid idea. We don't get many people asking to do rubbings on the stones these days," he said, with a grin. "Where would you like to begin?"

"Would it be possible to go down into the vault?" asked Elizabeth.

"I don't know about that. I don't remember when we last allowed the public down there."

"I brought these with me," said Elizabeth, producing some rubbings she had done the last time she was at the church.

Among them was a rubbing of an effigy that was no longer in the graveyard.

The Vicar rolled out the waxed paper on the floor. "This is an excellent specimen, and it is now stored down in the vault."

"I would like to give this one another try, if you would allow me, Elizabeth said.

Yes, I think I will make an exception this time. Be careful down there, though. It's very dusty and the light isn't very good."

The vicar moved to the right side of the altar. Just in front of Warnefield chapel, there was a wooden door in the floor, with a brass ring embedded in it. He twisted the ring anticlockwise and pulled on it, until the door rested on the floor beside the opening. Grandma noticed a damp smell wafting up from below.

"Be careful of the steps," he said, "they're a bit worn in spots."

The Vicar went down a couple of steps and flipped a light switch. The black hole turned into a gloomy, semi darkness.

Elizabeth turned to her gran. "Want to come with me?"

"You go on. I will wait here for you," said Grandma, taking a seat in one of the pews.

Elizabeth made her way down the first few steps. She stopped for a moment, waiting for her eyes to get used to the gloom. A couple of seconds later, she continued down. The vault travelled the width and length of the church. There were old broken gravestones scattered around, along with a few effigies, an old dresser and some broken chairs.

She stopped. "What to do now? Well, I said I was here to do a rubbing, so I'll do one," she thought, pulling charcoal sticks out of her pocket.

Elizabeth unrolled a line of waxed paper and placed it on top of one of the stone effigies. She began rubbing the charcoal against the paper, picking up the outline of the face beneath.

"You were always very good at those rubbings."

Elizabeth jumped up and turned around.

"Jesse! You scared me half to death."

Jesse chuckled. "Well, you're in the right place for that."

"What are you doing here?" she asked.

"I told you that if you were where you are supposed to be, I would be there to protect you."

"Is the Mirronstep here?" Elizabeth asked, feeling a rush of excitement.

"Not exactly, Liz… I… a… would like you to meet Brother Ignatius."

Jesse stepped aside. Behind him was a monk with no head. It took Elizabeth a second or two, before she realized that the monk's head was nestled under his left arm. As she focused her eyes on the head, it smiled at her.

"How do you do?" the head of Brother Ignatius enquired.

"Quite well, thank you," Elizabeth replied, trying not to panic and run for the steps.

"I understand that you are looking for something?" said Brother Ignatius.

"I'm looking for the Mirronstep," Elizabeth said.

"Alas," said Brother Ignatius. "I used to be the protector of the Mirronstep. That is, until my unfortunate demise. I stay here, in the hope that it will one day return, so that I may once again protect it from those who would abuse and destroy it."

"Do you know where it is?" asked Elizabeth.

The monk's head shook from side to side, casting its eyes sadly downward.

Then he looked up. "I do not know where it was taken, but I was told to say a riddle to anyone who asked."

"Yes?" asked Elizabeth. "What is the riddle?"

"Let me see now," said the head. "Ah… yes, I remember. At least I think I remember. You have to understand, the riddle was given to me many, many years ago. Yes, yes! I remember now, it goes like this.

> *Climb atop the Silbury Hill.*
> *When all is quiet and the air is still.*
> *Seek out rocks high and low.*
> *Through the fields of grass you'll go.*
> *To find the bones of Glorranbow.*
> *Meet the knight from Arthur's time.*
> *He will give you a cluing rhyme.*

"That's it?" said Elizabeth.

"Yes, that is definitely the riddle," said Brother Ignatius. "Though what it means, I have not the slightest idea.

"If you find the Mirronstep, will you please bring it back here, so that I may protect it again?"

"I'll do my best," Elizabeth replied. "Although, I have no idea what the riddle means either.

"It's time to go, Liz," said Jesse, turning and looking up into the church. The Vicar's shoes could be seen on the top steps of the vault.

"Is everything all right down there? I thought I heard voices," he called into the dimness.

Elizabeth looked up. When she turned around, both Jesse and the headless monk were nowhere to be seen.

"Yes," Elizabeth called. "I was just commenting to myself how intricate the workmanship is on some of the effigies down here. I'll be just a few more minutes."

She quickly finished her rubbing and gathered up her charcoal and waxed paper.

She was about to make her way up the steps, when a hideous looking animal with wings, snaked out a claw at her. She deftly jumped out of the way.

Jesse re-appeared behind her, waving his hands as if shushing it away. The creature backed into the darkness.

"What was that?" she said.

"Oh just a gargoyle that fell off the roof some time ago," said Jesse. "He was only protecting his territory. No harm done."

Elizabeth squinted into the gloom to where the creature had disappeared. A stone statue of a gargoyle stood against the back wall.

When Elizabeth looked back at Jesse, he had disappeared again.

She stepped up into the church, to find Grandma Rose engaged in polite small talk with the Vicar. They both turned when Elizabeth came up the steps. She held out the brass rubbing she had just finished for both of them to see.

"May I keep the one you showed me earlier?" he asked. "You seem to have a talent for this sort of thing."

"Of course," Elizabeth said, handing him the rubbing. "I must thank you, Vicar, for allowing me to come back and do another rubbing."

"Don't mention it," the Vicar said, tucking the rolled up wax paper under his arm.

"I may want to come back and do some more, if that would be all right with you?" said Elizabeth.

"Anytime, anytime," replied the Vicar.

They all shook hands. The Vicar returned to tidying his church. Elizabeth took her grandma's arm and led her to the exit.

Bindyl was still sitting on the grass among the gravestones when they emerged from the side door.

"You have been gone for a long time!" he said, impatiently.

"Sorry," said Grandma Rose, "but we had to get permission from the Vicar, before Elizabeth could go down into the vault. Come on, let's go home. Elizabeth can tell us what she learned and I'll make us all a cup of tea."

The three of them made their way to the car.

On the way out of Highwell, Bindyl changed back into human size so he could look out of the window.

"Why couldn't I go into that church?" he asked Elizabeth.

"I don't know," she replied.

"Am I evil?" asked Bindyl, obviously upset by the ordeal.

"NO!" Elizabeth and Grandma Rose said, at the same time.

"We'll get to the bottom of this," said Grandma, trying to console him.

"What happened in there?" Bindyl asked.

"Gran, Jesse was down there, and he was with a monk.... who's head was, well, under his arm."

"Why was Jesse there? And why was he with a monk?" asked Grandma.

"Jesse was there because I was in the right place for him to help me. The monk wanted to know where the Mirronstep was," said Elizabeth. "Apparently, he used to be its guardian."

"And now?" asked Grandma.

"Now, all he has is a riddle, which he told me," said Elizabeth.

"A riddle? What's a riddle?" asked Bindyl.

"I'll write it down when we get home," said Elizabeth.

The rest of the journey was made in silence, with Bindyl, looking out of the window, in deep thought.

"I'll be getting back down to the Elven Realm now," he said, when they reached the cottage, "got things to do."

"All right," said Elizabeth. "I'll see you in a bit."

She watched him disappear into the willow tree, then she went into the kitchen where Grandma Rose was busy making a pot of tea.

Elizabeth wrote down the riddle and Grandma read it. "Well, it's obvious that you have to go to Silbury Hill, but I've never heard of a place called Glorranbow," said Grandma.

"I'll know more when I get there," said Elizabeth.

"I could drive you?" offered Grandma.

"I will have to go at night," said Elizabeth. "I don't want you out in the middle of nowhere."

"But I want to help," said Grandma.

"I have to take Bindyl with me. He could probably be a good elf to have around if a girl needed help."

"I had forgotten about Bindyl," said Grandma. "You're right. He wouldn't let anything happen to you. Now I feel better about not going."

After Elizabeth and Grandma Rose drank their tea, they followed Bindyl down to the elven realm.

When Bindyl reached the castle, he had the groomsman saddle his horse and made for home.

"What, by the Grymlons, happened back there!" he thought, as he rode across the countryside.

Once home, he poured himself a glass of elderberry wine and sat in his favourite chair. Bindyl drank his wine and dozed off. He was awakened by a knock at the front door.

He waited for one of the servants to answer, but the knocking continued.

"I wonder where all the servants are?" he said, getting up to answer it.

Bindyl opened his front door, and looked up at the visitor staring for a moment in disbelief.

Standing in front of him, was his Uncle Brondly.

"Hello Bindyl," Brondly said. "May I come in?"

Without thinking, Bindyl stepped back and let his uncle in.

"You have done well for yourself, Bindyl. I am proud of you," Brondly said, looking around.

"You are dead. How can you be standing in my house," was all Bindyl could muster.

"Yes, I am indeed dead. That is why I am here."

Bindyl brushed by his uncle, surprised that he could actually feel him as he did so. He motioned for Brondly to go into the living room, and called for his servant.

"Don't bother trying to call your staff," said Brondly. "They can't hear you. Everything has stopped for you at the moment, so that you and I can talk. May I please sit down?"

Bindyl waved his hand, gesturing for his uncle to take a seat.

Brondly sat in the chair by the fireplace. Bindyl took a seat across from him.

"I have been allowed to come here," said Brondly, "because I have the chance to pass on to a better place than I am now, but I need your help to do this. I have disgraced our family. I'm sure you have suspected for some time that it was me who stole the Grymlon back when they were to be regenerated. Unfortunately, you have been cursed because of my crime."

"So I have to pay for your sins?" said Bindyl, looking down his nose at his uncle.

"In a way yes," said Brondly.

"I'm curious, uncle. Do you know who killed you that night? The sheriff investigated your murder, but never found out who did it."

"It was Verina," Brondly answered. "I thought I had done a deal with an old elf. He paid me well for stealing the Grymlon, but after I was paid, he followed me home. I let him in the house and he turned into Verina before my very eyes. Well, as you can imagine, I was shocked beyond all reason. She overpowered me, stabbed me then watched me die! It was terrifying! Before she left, she took the knife out of my back, put something on the hilt and stabbed me again! I was stuck in my lifeless body for the longest time. When the door opened, I was sure it was you, but it was Gavin Gross-tick."

"Do you mean the elf that lends elves money, and then takes everything they have to pay it back? Were you out of your mind, uncle?!"

"I, well, I sort of got a loan from him when I couldn't find a job. Yes, yes. I know it was a big mistake because he wanted his money back plus a hundred and fifty percent. He threatened to cut off my fingers if I didn't pay him back! He must have been watching the house and saw Verina leave. When he came in through the front door and saw I was dead, he looked around, and found the pouch with the payment for stealing the Grymlon. He left with it! I knew no more after that, until I awoke in… well, where I am now. I suppose your human friends would call it limbo."

"It was me. I found you," said Bindyl. "There was a note on your back that said 'Traitor.'

"Well now you know why I am here. You have been given a task to do for the human witch. If you are successful, both of us will be redeemed."

"Elizabeth is not a witch," said Bindyl. "She is the chosen one, and I would help her no matter what the circumstance."

"I know what you are thinking. You are thinking that you should not be accountable for my sins. And you should not, but I lied to the powers who decide where we go when we pass on."

"I knew you would save me. So I told them that you were involved in the stealing of the Grymlons. They sent me here to let you know that only if you succeed in helping the wi… ah… chosen one with her task, you will be permitted to pass on to the good place and so will I."

"You are despicable!" said Bindyl. "And yes. I have always suspected that it was you. That's why I helped Elizabeth back then, and I will help her now, but not because of you. I will do it because she is good and kind. She is trying to save all of us. Now get out of my house and don't come back!"

Brondly stood and headed towards the door. As he put his hand on the door handle, he turned.

"I knew you would do the right thing," he said, with a smirk.

Brondly left the house, not bothering to close the door behind him.

Bindyl watched as Brondly slowly became transparent. He had faded into almost nothing by the time he reached the gate.

"Well, now I know why I could not go into the church," Bindyl said to himself. "And now I know why I'm having the dreams. I am in disgrace with the powers that be. Now it's up to me to try to right a wrong that was not of my doing. I'll go to Elizabeth. She will know what to do."

Bindyl saddled his horse and left immediately.

When he arrived at the castle, he put his horse in the stables. He began to enter the main courtyard, thinking about what he would tell Elizabeth, when he suddenly stopped.

"What if I tell Elizabeth about Brondly's deception," he thought, "and she thinks I might have actually had some part in the theft, when my uncle stole the Grymlon from the castle in Kimadrian.

It was, after all, I who followed Zoe and took the Grymlons from her.

The Mirronstep

It was, after all, I who took them back to the castle. Yes, Zoe had admitted to digging up the bag that the Grymlons were in, after Gideon and Elizabeth had buried them. But for all anyone knows, Zoe may have lied to save me from being blamed. If a human or an elf were to put all the past events together, it might look exactly as though I had been involved with my uncle's treachery!"

Bindyl turned off the pathway that lead to the royal family's living quarters. He went instead, to the guard room and wrote out the duty orders for the next day.

After he had seen to his duties, Bindyl decided to stay in his own room at the castle barracks, and stretched out on his bunk.

"I don't want to meet with my uncle again," he thought, as he lay thinking of the nights events. "This is the last place he will bother me, dead or not."

Chapter Twelve

Grandma stepped out of the carriage at the castle entrance and went to see Jesse, while Elizabeth made her way to her rooms.

A few minutes later, there was a knock at Elizabeth's door.

When she answered it, Grandma Rose was there.

"Gran, what are you doing here? I only just left you," she said, stepping back to let her in.

"I was on my way down to see Jesse, when I thought it would be nice if you and I go into Kimadria and have supper. Would you like to?"

"I would love to," said Elizabeth.

The two of them left the castle and walked into Kimadria. They found the little café they had eaten in, the last time they were there.

"I'm sorry you and Gideon have to postpone your wedding, said Grandma as they ate.

"It was hard to deal with at first," Elizabeth admitted. "Gideon suggested that we just ask the king to marry us, but I didn't want that."

"I'm glad you decided to wait," said Grandma.

"I'm really enjoying this," said Elizabeth. "The last time we were here, I couldn't read the menu."

"I remember," said Grandma.

"And you became ill from the food that you had eaten," said Elizabeth.

"Yes," said Grandma. "I remember that too."

"Do you still suffer from the acid reflux, gran?"

The Mirronstep

"Sometimes," said Grandma.

***

Grandma Rose and Elizabeth had just returned, as Gideon was heading towards Elizabeth's rooms.

"Where have you two been?" he asked.

"We went to Kimadria and had supper," said Elizabeth. "Is everything all right?"

"You didn't tell the royal staff you were gone," he said. "I was getting a bit worried."

"We just went for a walk and a meal," said Elizabeth.

"You are soon to be the future queen of Kimadrian," Gideon said. "It is not fitting for you to be roaming around the countryside without an escort."

"I think I'm going to go to bed now," said Grandma.

"Good night, Gran," said Elizabeth.

"Good night, Lady Rose," said Gideon,

"Don't stay up too late, you two," said Grandma, leaving the couple.

"Let's go to the library and have some tea, shall we?" Elizabeth suggested.

"I don't want you to go into Kimadria again without an escort," said Gideon, following Elizabeth.

"You know, Gideon. I could turn anyone who came near me or my gran to stone with the blink of an eye. So an escort would be a bit much, don't you think?"

"I'm Sorry, Liz. I sometimes forget who you are, but please do this for me, will you?"

"Of course, if it would make you feel better," Elizabeth replied.

"Did your journey go well?" he asked.

"I think so," she answered, as she sat on a couch by the stone fireplace. "Bindyl couldn't go into the church, something stopped him. I could tell it upset him. He came straight back down here after we arrived back at the cottage. I haven't seen him since."

"Did you find out where the Mirronstep is?" Gideon asked, taking a seat beside her.

Elizabeth laughed. "Did you really think it would be that easy?"

"I was so hoping it would," he said.

"I did find out I have to go to Silbury Hill."

"Isn't that close to Avebury?" asked Gideon.

"Yes, Bindyl is supposed to come with me, which could make it a little difficult."

"Have you been down to see Jesse yet?" Gideon asked.

"No," said Elizabeth. "He came to me in a sort of a dream. He told me that he will stay asleep until all of this is over. So there isn't much point in trying to wake him."

"I hope you are right and he comes out of this," said Gideon.

"I told Gran what he said, but she is still going to go down and spend time with him. It was hard for her to keep the secret for so long. I think it has taken its toll on her health. She doesn't seem to be able to move around as well as she used to."

"My mother found it difficult too," said Gideon. "It didn't help when I got angry at her for keeping the secret from you."

"Your mother and father did what they thought was right," said Elizabeth.

"I know, but I wish they had trusted us sooner," said Gideon.

"What's done is done," she said.

Chapter Thirteen

Bindyl had fallen asleep in his bunk at the guard house. He woke with a start.

"Is anyone there?" he called into the semi lit room.

Jesse stepped out from a shadow in the corner.

"I'm dreaming aren't I," said Bindyl.

"In a manner of speaking," Jesse said.

"Why are you here, Jesse?"

"Elizabeth will be leaving tomorrow to go to Silbury Hill," said Jesse. "She will try to sneak away without you."

"But didn't you tell her that I have to go with her?" asked Bindyl.

"I did," said Jesse.

"Then why would she try to sneak away?" asked Bindyl.

"She thinks she can do it better without you," said Jesse. "So be ready. Elizabeth will try to leave in the early evening, when she thinks you've gone for the day."

Jesse began backing away into the corner, when Bindyl stopped him. "Jesse, do you know anything about my uncle Brondly?"

Jesse said nothing as he faded from Bindyl's dream.

"Wait!" was all Bindyl could manage before Jesse disappeared completely.

He woke, sweating again before returning to a restless sleep.

At 6:00 a.m. he rose. He made sure the guards knew what their duties were for the day, before he headed up to Gideon's rooms.

Gideon's servant appeared and let Bindyl in.

Gideon was eating breakfast at his desk.

"Good morning, Bindyl. Would you like something to eat?"

"Just tea, thanks," said Bindyl, pouring himself a cup.

"Liz is going on a journey today," Gideon said.

"I know," said Bindyl. "That's why I am up here. Where are we going?"

"We?" asked Gideon. "How did you know that Liz was going anywhere?"

"Jesse," said Bindyl, rolling his eyes.

"Had another visit?" asked Gideon.

"Yes," said Bindyl.

"I think she is going to leave here around 7:00 p.m.," said Gideon.

"And I will be waiting," said Bindyl.

Chapter Fourteen

At 6:45 p.m. that evening, Gideon and Bindyl went looking for Elizabeth.

They entered the main castle and met her as she was running down the stairs.

"Bindyl!" she said, sprinting downward. "What are you doing here this time of the evening?"

"I am going with you," he said, following her. "Jesse said that we are going to Silbury Hill today."

Elizabeth stopped, turning to face him. "You know, you don't have to come with me everywhere I go. I can manage by myself."

"You know I have to go with you. Please don't make this difficult, Elizabeth. If you leave me behind, it may be bad for me."

Elizabeth turned away from him and continued down the stairs.

When the three reached the castle entrance, Gideon kissed Elizabeth goodbye.

"Look after her, Bindyl," he said.

Elizabeth looked down her nose, as Gideon shrugged, smiled, and walked away to find his parents.

When Elizabeth and Bindyl reached the cottage, Grandma Rose was in the kitchen, drinking a cup of tea.

"Good evening, Gran."

"Good evening, you two," said Grandma.

"I'm going to change my clothes, Gran. I'll be back in a minute,"

"Would you like a cup of tea, Bindyl?" asked Grandma.

"Yes please," he said.

When Elizabeth returned to the kitchen, Bindyl was human size and drinking his tea.

"Okay, here's the plan," Elizabeth said. "Where we are going, there won't be many people, but I want you to stay small and stay close to me. I don't want to have to go looking for you."

"We should only be gone an hour or two," said Elizabeth, gulping down her tea.

"Be careful," said Grandma.

"We will, Gran."

Bindyl followed her out to the car. "Can I stay human size so that…"

"HEY LIZ, wait a sec."

Elizabeth saw her friend Andre out of the corner of her eye. She turned to Bindyl, who was clearly visible in his human size.

"Get in the car," she said.

Bindyl opened the door and jumped into the passenger seat, closing the door quickly.

"Who's that?" Andre asked, peering around her.

"A friend of Gran's. What a nice surprise. What are you doing here, Andre?"

"I came to see you because Mavis is organizing a small hunter-jumper competition next weekend," said Andre. "I wondered if you would like me to put your name on the list."

"Can I give you a call during the week? I'm not sure what I am going to be doing, and I'm in a bit of a hurry. Gran's friend has to be at the railway station, so I will talk to you later, okay?"

"Okay, Liz, I'll go and see Grandma Rose while I'm here," Andre said, turning onto the pathway that led to the garden.

Elizabeth watched him disappear around the other side of the house, and got into the driver's seat.

"Get invisible, Bindyl," she said.

"But I have to shrink down to do that," he protested.

"I don't want any more close calls, please get invisible now!" she insisted.

Bindyl shrank down, disappearing to all but Elizabeth, looking at her disapprovingly as he did so.

They had been heading towards Marlborough for a few minutes, when Elizabeth turned the radio on. Bindyl began dancing around on the seat.

"Do you like this music?" she asked.

"Never heard this sort of music before, but yes, I like it," he said, bouncing around on the car seat.

"Sit down," said Elizabeth. "You're distracting me."

Bindyl sat down, but couldn't resist moving to the music.

Elizabeth smiled when she looked over at him. He had stood again and had his back to her. He was leaning with his elbows against the door window, his hips swaying to the music on the radio.

It was beginning to get dark by the time they arrived at Silbury Hill.

"This is why we are here?" said Bindyl, staring up at the flat topped hill as he stepped out of the car.

He began running up the side of the hill.

"Bindyl stop!"

Bindyl turned and ran back down. "I thought we had to go up to the top, that's what the riddle says. Doesn't it?"

"Yes," said Elizabeth, "but keep to the path. The hill is riddled with shafts from when they were trying to find out why the hill was here. It's not safe anymore."

Bindyl moved over to the path that wound upwards, and began to climb again, Elizabeth followed close behind.

When they reached the top, she looked toward the required direction, but all she could see was a field. In it, barely visible, was the rising mound of The Long Barrow.

Elizabeth had written down the rhyme and was holding it in her hand. Bindyl was standing beside her, looking out at the countryside.

"I don't have a clue what I'm looking for," she said.

"May I please see the rhyme?" Bindyl asked.

Elizabeth handed him the piece of paper that she had written the rhyme on. Bindyl looked at it then looked out to where it referred to.

"What's that over there?" he asked, pointing to the left.

"That's Long Barrow," said Elizabeth.

"What is it?" he asked.

"The Long Barrow is a manmade structure of rooms, covered over with earth."

"Is it new?" asked Bindyl.

"Goodness me no. It's about five thousand years old," said Elizabeth.

"Are there rocks there?" he asked.

"Yes, there are large rocks at the entrance of the Barrow, around the other side."

"Then that's what the rhyme is saying," said Bindyl.

"How do you know that?" asked Elizabeth.

Bindyl pointed to the rhyme.

"Glorranbow. The letters re-arranged spell Long Barrow," he said.

Elizabeth kissed him on the cheek. "Bindyl, you're an absolute genius!"

"Careful now, you are betrothed to my boss!" he said, with a grin.

Elizabeth was already making her way down the hill. Bindyl followed her down, touching the part of his cheek she had kissed.

At the bottom of the hill they turned left, and followed the road for about four hundred yards. They crossed it, turned right and entered the field through a wrought iron turnstile gate.

The wind that was almost always constant around the area, whipped at their hair and clothing as they walked up the sloped field. A half a mile from the road, they turned to the right and faced the entrance to The Long Barrow.

Small lines of light zig-zagged this way and that, in front of the entrance.

"What's that?" asked Bindyl, pointing to the small flashes of light.

"Fireflies," Elizabeth said.

"They're beautiful," said Bindyl.

Elizabeth entered through the irregular stone entrance and into the Barrow, Bindyl followed her in, glad to be out of the wind.

"It is a bit dark in here, don't you think?" asked Bindyl, looking around him. "It's more than a bit creepy! And a wee bit on the chilly side too."

"Aren't you supposed to be a warrior?" Elizabeth said.

"Yes, and a cold one at the moment!" Bindyl protested.

Elizabeth held up her right hand. "Light our way through the darkness."

About fifty fire flies buzzed into the entrance and formed a ball of light above their heads. The fire flies followed them as they walked.

"That's better," said Bindyl. "Could we have a little heat?"

"Don't be a baby, Bindyl," she said walking on ahead.

They continued towards the back of the barrow, passing empty rooms on either side of them as they went.

"Wait for me, you two."

Bindyl jumped so high, his head almost hit the low roof of the barrow. The two of them turned and saw Jesse standing in the entrance of one of the rooms to the left.

"Hello, Jesse," said Elizabeth. "I must be in the right place again."

"Absolutely, sis," Jesse said, with a grin.

"I think it is downright spooky how he can appear like that," said Bindyl, looking Jesse up and down. "Is he going to do this a lot during our little adventure?"

"I'm afraid so, Bindyl," said Elizabeth. "Come on, I think I see something up ahead."

At the end of the passageway, was the largest room. Elizabeth could just make out a figure in armour, sitting on the floor in the darkness.

He looked up when Elizabeth and Bindyl entered.

The light followed her, illuminating the room. "Who are you?" she asked.

"I might ask you the same question," said the young knight.

He stood, taking off his helmet. "I also might ask how you can see me. I have been roaming these rooms for hundreds of years, and no one has ever seen me before."

"I asked first," said Elizabeth.

"My name is Sir Gareth PenDragon, nephew to King Arthur PenDragon," the young knight said, with an over exaggerated bow.

"What are you doing here?" asked Bindyl.

"I found a mirror in one of my uncle's rooms at the castle," Sir Gareth replied. "My uncle found me with the mirror and told me to stay away from it. He moved the mirror to another part of the castle, but I became intrigued and went looking for it. I eventually found it and decided to examine it. As I looked into the mirror, I saw no reflection looking back at me, only darkness. I placed my hand on the front of the mirror and it began to pull me in. I took my sword from its scabbard and used the hilt to grab onto the edge of the mirror, in an attempt to pull myself out. Alas, the force was too great.

"I let go of the sword and it followed me through. I never discovered how to return. As I wandered through the fields and the woods, I became ill and found my way here. I died here.

"It was then that I found out that I could not leave this place, even in death. If I travel away from here, I end up back in this room.

"I watched as the people of my time came and went. I watched as wars were fought. I watched people die and go on to where ever they go, but I could not go with them. I always seem to end up in this room. I can go to the entrance, and I can walk around, but then I end up here.

"Now it's your turn. What are you doing here?"

Elizabeth stepped forward and took a good look at this young man.

"My name is Elizabeth Ghenestone. The mirror that you stepped through, was it called the Mirronstep?"

"Why, yes it was. I clearly remember my uncle calling it by that name. Did you by chance come here with a rhyme given to you by a monk whose head was detached from his body?" Sir Gareth asked.

"Yes," said Elizabeth.

"If you tell me the rhyme, then I have a riddle for you," said Sir Gareth.

"Who told you the riddle?" asked Elizabeth.

"That, I cannot say," said Sir Gareth.

"He talks even funnier than you," said Bindyl.

"Bindyl,"

"Yes, Elizabeth?"

"Shut up."

"Yes, Elizabeth."

"Liz, don't be mean," said Jesse.

Elizabeth gave him a sideways glance.

Jesse shrugged. "I know, sis. Shut up, Jesse,"

"Thank you," she told them both.

Elizabeth told the young knight the rhyme that the headless monk had told her.

"I will give you the riddle," said Sir Gareth, "only if you give me your word that you will send me back to my time if you succeed in your quest."

"I will try to help you if I find the Mirronstep," she said.

"Very well," said Sir Gareth. "You must remember the riddle, and I cannot help you with the answer."

"I'm listening," Elizabeth said.

"Go to where the saint's reside.
Where gallant Lords in death abide.
Where dedications to the soldiers of Wiltshire were placed.
After war and death took them in haste.
William, the earl awaits you there.
Don't wait too long to stand and stare.
The beams are high and the roof is stone.
But on the ground is where it is found."

"How wonderful, I have no idea what that means," said Elizabeth.

"We solved the last rhyme, didn't we?" said Bindyl.

"Yes," she said, feeling exasperated.

"Then we will solve this one too."

"If I find the Mirronstep," said Elizabeth. "I'll come back here, Sir Gareth. We'll see if we can send you through it and on to where you are supposed to be."

"That would be appreciated, my lady," said Sir Gareth.

Elizabeth and Bindyl turned to leave.

"My lady," Sir Gareth said.

Elizabeth looked back at the young Knight.

"Would you please leave the light? It gets so dark in here at night."

"Of course," she said.

"This room is lit, to see the way. It's not to leave but wait and stay," Elizabeth said, as she waved her hand at the ball of light above their heads.

"When you want the light, say 'light my way and reveal.' The fire flies will come in and give you light. When you want it to go out, just say 'out', and the fire flies will go away until you need them again."

"Thank you, my lady."

Elizabeth and Bindyl passed by Jesse, who slowly vanished as they exited the Long Barrow, and made their way to the car.

"You can stay human size," Elizabeth said. "It's dark now. You'll be less likely to be seen."

Bindyl sat in the passenger seat beside Elizabeth. He looked out of the window on their way home to Oaklade.

"Bindyl?" asked Elizabeth.

"Yes?"

"Do you know why you have to help me?" she asked.

"No," came his quick reply, "do you?"

"No," she answered.

Bindyl turned his head away from her. "I have just lied to her," he thought, trying to hold back tears.

"Bindyl, are you all right? Are you crying?" she asked.

Bindyl wiped his eyes, keeping his gaze away from her. "I still miss Zoe, and from time to time, the pain becomes too much to bear."

"That was not a lie," he thought. "I miss Zoe every day of my life."

"I'm sorry, Bindyl. I know how much you loved her."

When they reached Oaklade, Bindyl got out of the car. "I am going back down to Kimadrian, are you coming, Elizabeth?"

"No," she said. "I think I'll stay up here for tonight. I'll see you tomorrow."

Bindyl disappeared across the back lawn and into the darkness.

When Elizabeth stepped through the back door, she was surprised to see Grandma Rose still up.

"How did it go?" she asked.

"Well, I have another riddle," said Elizabeth.

She wrote it down and handed it to her.

Grandma read the riddle and shook her head. "Hmm, I have no idea what that could mean."

"The book and the mirror that Thalios gave me are doing strange things, Gran. The mirror keeps showing me images like the church in Highwell. And the book seems to be putting pictures on the blank pages when I discover the next part of the quest. I'm betting it has more pages now. I think it's a sort of journal of events."

"Is the book in the Realm?" asked Grandma.

"Yes, it's hidden. I'll have a look at it tomorrow when I return.

"I'm tired, dear. So I think I'll turn in," said Grandma. "Will I see you in the morning before you go down to the Realm?"

"We could have breakfast together before I go?" Elizabeth suggested.

"I would like that. Good night," said Grandma.

After Grandma had gone to bed, Elizabeth washed the tea things and went to bed herself.

Chapter Fifteen

Elizabeth woke the following morning and made her way down the hall.

"I love it down in the Realm, but I sleep so much better in my own bed," she thought, as she opened the kitchen door.

Grandma turned as she entered. "Would you like a cup of coffee?"

"Love one, please," she said, sitting at the table.

"I thought I'd make homemade doughnuts to go with our morning coffee."

Elizabeth sipped her coffee and nibbled on a doughnut as she re-read the riddle Sir Gareth had given her.

"These doughnuts are delicious, Gran," Elizabeth said, taking another one.

"Thank you, dear, but don't eat too many. You still have to get into a wedding dress soon."

Elizabeth laughed. "I promise not to eat too much sugar before I get fitted for the dress."

Grandma sat at the table and took a doughnut. She broke a piece off and dunked it in her coffee, then popped it in her mouth.

"I looked over the riddle again when I got up this morning," she told Elizabeth between bites. "I'm quite sure you have to go to another church."

"Any ideas on which one?"

"There are so many churches around here," said Grandma. "Most of them have some kind of nobility buried somewhere in their grounds, they also have dedications to our fallen soldiers."

"You're right. I could be searching for years."

"There is a clue in the riddle that we are not picking up on," said Grandma.

"We know it's in Wiltshire," said Elizabeth. "Does that narrow it down a bit?"

"No!" said Grandma Rose, laughing.

"What about the church in Oaklade," Elizabeth suggested.

"It won't be a church in this town," said Grandma. "We live in the county of Gloucestershire. Oaklade is right on the edge of the two counties. Only when you reach Highwell are you in Wiltshire."

"Is there any way the information in the churches could spill over into another county, since they are so close?" asked Elizabeth.

"No," said Grandma. "The clergy were, and still are very specific about the boundaries regarding the parishes."

Grandma Rose thought back to when her brother, Stephen was alive. "You know, your great uncle Stephen used to live in Highwell. He was in the army during the Second World War. I still have some of his memorabilia. I'll look through it and see if I can get any clues for you."

Elizabeth cleared the table and began washing the dishes.

"Thanks, Gran," she said, as she stood at the kitchen sink. "I wish I could have known Uncle Stephen. I heard mum talk about him quite often."

"Your mother was still fairly young when he died, but he used to adore her," said Grandma.

"You miss him don't you, Gran."

"Yes. I have watched quite a few of my family die; some of old age, others like your uncle Stephen, taken too early."

"I still have plenty of cousins around though," Elizabeth said, with a smile. "I don't know how you remember them all, but I know you do, from all the cards we get at Christmas."

"When it's time for me to send Christmas cards, it takes a bit of effort, but I don't mind."

"I'm going down to the castle now, Gran," Elizabeth said, when the dishes were finished. "I'll see you a bit later."

She kissed her grandma on the cheek and left the cottage.

Chapter Sixteen

Elizabeth made her way through the castle and went to her apartment. She took the mirror and the book out of the cupboard, sat at her desk and opened the book. She looked into the mirror, but only saw her reflection. Then she opened the book

"Just as I suspected," she thought.

She saw a drawing of herself on one of the pages. She was standing on the top of Silbury Hill with Bindyl beside her. The picture on the next page was also new. It was of Sir Gareth. He was sitting on the floor of the large room in the Long Barrow, just the way he had been when they first saw him.

Two knocks on the door, and the muffled sound of Gideon's voice, turned her attention away from the book.

"Come in," she called back.

He entered the room, closing the door behind him.

"Grandma Rose is asking for you," he said, eyeing the book on her lap.

"Is she ill?" Elizabeth asked, feeling panic rise in her.

"No, no," said Gideon, "she said something about an uncle of yours. Stephen I think she said his name was. She said that she had found out some interesting things about him that you might want to know. Did you find anything else in that book?"

Elizabeth felt a pang of relief. "It's some sort of journal I think, but I'll go through it more thoroughly later. I think I'll go up and spend the night with her. I'll come back to the Realm in the morning."

"I'll come with you to the entrance," said Gideon, taking her arm.

Elizabeth entered the cottage from the back door.

"GRAN, ARE YOU HERE?"

"I'm in here, come in and see what I've found," she heard her grandma say, from down the hall

When Elizabeth reached the bedroom, Grandma Rose was seated at the table by the window. She had four or five biscuit tins full of old photos and paperwork, open on the top.

"Sit down and let me show you what I've found," said Grandma.

Grandma Rose handed Elizabeth a photo of a man in an army uniform.

"He looks like you, except for the red hair," said Elizabeth.

Grandma laughed. "Red hair runs in the family,"

"Yes," said Elizabeth, absently touching her own locks. "Is this Uncle Stephen? He looks a lot younger than the other photos I've seen."

Grandma nodded. She smiled remembering happy times, and handed Elizabeth two medals he had won for bravery during the Second World War. On one of them, it said the words 'Wiltshire Regiment'.

"As your uncle and I got older. We would spend more and more time together, talking about the past," said Grandma. "I vaguely remember him telling me that the Wiltshire Regiment was based in Salisbury."

Elizabeth looked at the picture of her uncle, then back at her Grandma.

"So?" she said.

"There is a cathedral in Salisbury," said Grandma. "I called the office of the clergy there. On the wall there are plaques with dedications to the soldiers of the Wilts and Dorset Regiment. They say that there is an effigy of Sir William Longspee, Earl of Salisbury in the south nave aisle. Say the riddle again."

"Go to where saints reside.

Where the gallant Lords in death abide.

Where dedications to the soldiers of Wiltshire were placed.

After war and death took them in haste.
William, the Earl waits for you there.
Don't wait too long to stand and stare.
The beams are high and the roof is stone.
But on the ground is where it is found."

"I'll go and have a look around tomorrow," said Elizabeth.

"If you are going to go to Salisbury cathedral, I suggest you get a room in the centre of town," said Grandma. "Wait until the cathedral is closed for the night. When it's dark, you can use your powers to get in.

"I'm going to bed now. I've been looking through this stuff for hours and I'm tired. Are you going to stay here tonight?"

Elizabeth nodded. "I'll go down to the Realm in the morning and let Bindyl know we're going on another trip."

"Have you found out why you have to take Bindyl with you when you go on these trips to find the Mirronstep?" said Grandma.

"No, but Jesse says I have to take him."

"I'm a bit concerned about Bindyl roaming around up here," said Grandma. "Be careful, Elizabeth.

"I will, good night, Gran," she said, kissing her grandma on the forehead.

***

Gideon was not in his rooms when Elizabeth arrived at the castle the next morning.

"My apologies, my lady," said his butler. "I will send for him. I think he is in a meeting with his highness."

She took a seat by the window, looking out over the gardens. Gideon arrived a few minutes later.

"Good morning, Liz," he said, pulling her up from her seat and kissing her on the forehead.

"Good morning. Have you seen Bindyl today?" she asked.

"He's in the guard room," said Gideon. "He has been staying there instead of going home. I keep meaning to ask him why he's here all the time, lately. I think it might be because he's afraid you are going to go on one of your trips to find the Mirronstep without him."

"Actually, I'm here to come and get him so we can go to Salisbury Cathedral," said Elizabeth.

"Let's go down and find him," said Gideon, taking her hand.

They found Bindyl in the sleeping quarters of the barracks.

"You stayed here again last night, didn't you," said Gideon.

"I just thought that if I had to go anywhere with Elizabeth, it would be better if I were here instead of out in the country," said Bindyl.

"See Liz, I told you that's why he has not gone home," said Gideon.

"We have to go on a journey today and we will probably be gone overnight," Elizabeth told him.

"Where are we going?" Bindyl asked.

"To Salisbury cathedral, so pack a bag. We won't go into the cathedral until its dark."

"I'm so glad that we are going to another church!" said Bindyl, stuffing some clothes into a leather bag.

"I'm sorry Bindyl, but I think the riddle says I'm supposed to go there. Look on the bright side, we may find the Mirronstep there."

Bindyl laughed. "What is it you humans say about holding your breath?" he said, as he slung his bag over his shoulder.

"If we leave now I can book a room. If you like, we can buy you a hat so we can hide those lovely ears of yours, and walk around the town. You know, do a bit of sightseeing until it gets dark."

"Sounds a bit more entertaining than the last time I went to a church," said Bindyl.

Gideon went with them as far as the castle grounds and ordered a coach.

He watched as the carriage hurried away.

"Be safe, you two," he said, under his breath.

Elizabeth and Bindyl came out of the tree. They made their way over the bridge, through the gate, and around the side of the cottage to the car.

"Can I be human size on the way, so I can see out of the window?" Bindyl asked.

"All right, but don't get out of the car with those clothes on. You'll get us both arrested."

Bindyl grew to human size, opened the passenger door and got in.

It took about an hour to get to the outskirts of Salisbury.

"You should shrink down before we look for a hotel," said Elizabeth.

When they reached the town centre, Elizabeth parked the car.

"You stay here. I need to book a room," she told Bindyl.

She made her way into the main town, and entered the Inn. "Do you have a room available for one night please?"

"Yes, Miss. Would you like a bathroom included?" asked the desk clerk.

"Yes, please."

"That will be fifty five pounds, please, Miss," said the desk clerk.

Elizabeth handed him the money and he handed her a key.

"Just go up the stairs to your left. It's the third door on the right," the desk clerk told her.

"Thank you," said Elizabeth.

She went back to her car and pulled her overnight case out of the back seat. Bindyl picked up his bag and followed her to the hotel.

Elizabeth climbed up the stairs with an invisible Bindyl close behind. She unlocked the door and Bindyl entered the room ahead of her. Elizabeth closed the door and put her case on the bed.

"We can go for a walk if you want to. I packed some human clothes for you," she said.

"I can stay small," said Bindyl.

"And I will be walking along the street, talking to myself," said Elizabeth.

"Oh, yes. I never thought of that," said Bindyl.

He grew to human size and reluctantly changed into the clothes Elizabeth had packed. While he was changing, she went down to the gift shop and purchased a hat for him.

"No point in showing off those pointy ears," she told him, pulling the hat onto his head.

They walked through the streets of Salisbury. After they stopped and ate lunch, they went to the cathedral and looked around the outside.

"There are no graves in the cathedral grounds," said Bindyl. "I thought all churches had graveyards?"

"They can't put graves in the ground here," Elizabeth told him. "The cathedral was built a long time ago, on a flood plain. If they buried bodies near the cathedral, they would wash up to the surface with the first good rain storm,"

"Ugh!" said Bindyl, pulling a face.

Elizabeth laughed. "Don't worry, Bindyl, there are no bodies buried around here."

When they arrived back at the room, Elizabeth ordered some tea and fruit. When she turned on the T.V. to watch the evening news, Bindyl became very upset, and ran behind the couch.

"What's wrong?" she asked.

"There are people inside of that box. How do they do that?" he said, peeping around the arm rest.

"It's just a picture, made by electricity coming through a wire in the wall," Elizabeth explained. "Didn't Gideon ever tell you about our television at the cottage?"

"NO!"

Elizabeth tried to stifle a giggle. "Come on, Bindyl. Don't be such a baby. Just because you've never seen something before, doesn't mean it's going to harm you. Get out from behind that couch, soldier, and watch this telly!"

Bindyl sat down on the floor behind the couch.

"All right, but you don't know what you're missing," she said.

After about five minutes, Bindyl worked up enough courage to come out.

He stood for a while, looking at the T.V. set.

A few minutes later, he felt comfortable enough to sit on the couch. It didn't take long for him to be totally mesmerized by it.

Every now and then, he would look behind the T.V., hoping to catch whoever it was, on the screen, running from the machine.

"Bindyl, stop it! There are no people behind the television. The picture comes through an electrical line that is plugged into the wall."

"I do not believe you!" he said. "It is one of your spells isn't it. Come on, Elizabeth. You can tell me. I won't tell anyone."

"No, it's not," she said.

Bindyl would have none of it. Every few minutes, he ran behind the T.V.

"Oh well," she thought. "At least it's keeping him busy."

When Elizabeth had purchased Bindyl's hat, she had also bought a book about the cathedral, containing maps and photos. She found pictures of the Wiltshire and Dorset dedications on a wall in the main nave. There was also a picture of an effigy of William Longspee, the Earl of Salisbury.

Elizabeth felt a pang of excitement. "Perhaps my search is over, and the Mirronstep is somewhere in the cathedral," she thought. "We'll find out tonight."

At the stroke of midnight, Elizabeth and Bindyl set out to the cathedral.

"It's deserted," said Bindyl, following Elizabeth along the street.

"Salisbury is a very popular tourist attraction, but just about everyone has gone home now," she said.

The two of them made their way across town until they could make out the cathedral spire. When they entered the grounds, Bindyl sat on a bench by the gate. Elizabeth headed towards the main entrance. She was about to enter the alcove, when she heard voices.

She moved quickly around to the other side of the alcove, and out of sight to whomever the voices belonged to.

Two volunteers who had been working late, were on their way out of the cathedral. The older of the two gentlemen put a long heavy wooden bar across the double doors, locked it in place and put the key in his pocket. He exited the alcove, catching up with his fellow volunteer.

He had just stepped onto the pathway, when Elizabeth moved and accidentally kicked a stone lying on the gravel where she stood.

She ran her right hand from her head downward toward her feet. She disappeared as she whispered the words "hide in plain sight."

The gentleman turned suddenly. He walked to the side of the alcove and looked to where the noise was. He was standing only inches away from Elizabeth.

"Everything alright there, Bert?" asked the younger volunteer.

Bert looked up, shrugged and turned back towards his friend.

"Yes, but I think I'll have someone look at that window there," he answered, pointing to the window above Elizabeth's head. "I think it might be coming loose."

The two volunteers stepped onto the pathway and out into the street.

Bindyl had moved unseen, past the two gentlemen and was standing by the door. When they were out of sight, Elizabeth entered the alcove.

"Why don't you try to come with me?" she asked Bindyl.

"I know I won't be able to enter, so it's no use trying," he said.

"How do you know?" she asked.

"I just know I am supposed to be outside. Don't worry Elizabeth. I will be fine out here."

She smiled at him and turned towards the main entrance.

She approached the double doors and closed her eyes. The bar across the doors dropped to the ground. The door to the right creaked, as it slowly opened.

Elizabeth entered the cathedral. The lighting outside shone through the stained glass windows just enough, so she could see her way around in the dimness. She looked up at the sculpted ceiling.

"It seems so much bigger at night," she thought.

She entered the centre of the aisle, and turned left. On the wall facing her were the plaques dedicated to the Wiltshire and Dorset Regiment of the British Army.

She gently touched each one of the plaques, running her finger down the list of names, wondering if her uncle was among them. As she touched the last one, the plaque moved to one side. Sticking out from behind it was an old discoloured piece of paper. She carefully pulled the paper from between the wall and the plaque, and unfolded it. She could barely make out the brown writing that read, 'You may want to go and have a chat with the Earl.'

Elizabeth looked around, trying to get her bearings, so she could find the effigy of the Earl of Salisbury.

As she was holding the paper, it dissolved in her hand, running through her fingers like sand. It left a thin layer of dust at her feet, on the flagstone floor.

Elizabeth made her way towards the nave. She turned, heading along the south aisle, until she came to the effigy of Sir William Longspee, Earl of Salisbury.

"Am I supposed to say something?" she said quietly.

She looked from side to side, feeling a bit foolish as the sound of her voice echoed down the aisle.

She stepped closer to the effigy. "Uh, my name is Elizabeth and I am supposed to come and talk to you."

She stepped back, scanning the effigy from the head to the toes and back again, when a creaking sound came from the stone figure lying supine on its resting place.

Slowly, the right arm of the figure moved to the chest, pulling at the shield on the effigy's body. As the shield broke free, the Earl slowly began to sit up. He moved his legs over to the side of the stone slab and placed the shield beside him.

"Hello, Elizabeth. What do you require of me?" the Earl asked.

"How do you know my name?" Elizabeth asked.

"I have been waiting for you," the Earl replied.

"But I…. Never mind. I am looking for the Mirronstep," she said, stepping back a few paces.

"Ah, the Mirronstep," said the Earl. "I remember it well. The druids gave it to the monks hundreds of years ago, to look after. The monks hid it somewhere else for a while. Then they brought it here, but the cathedral floods from time to time. The monks were afraid that the Mirronstep would be damaged, so they moved it."

"I don't suppose you would happen to know where it is?" she asked.

"The monks told me to give the searcher of the object a message."

"I'm listening," she said, with a sigh.

"To Malmesbury where the Kings lie still,
You will travel at your will.
King Athelstan's tomb awaits you there.
But be careful what you speak.
The reflection of you staring back.
Will put you on the proper track.
And give you what you seek," he said.

The Mirrorstep

"It's at Malmesbury then?" Elizabeth asked.

"Who knows," said the Earl. "It has been moved countless times over many, many years. Perhaps it is there, perhaps not, but I do know you are supposed to remember the riddle and say it to the right person, when the time comes."

"Well, thanks for the rhyme. I'll do my best to remember it, and I'll put it with the others," she said.

She glanced down the nave. When she looked back, the Earl of Salisbury was once again a stone effigy of what was once a man.

She turned back towards the entrance and had only taken a few steps, when she heard the Earl's voice echo through the air.

"Be careful Elizabeth, you have taken something from the cathedral. The gargoyles won't like that."

"If you mean the paper behind the plaque, I didn't take it. It turned to dust!" she said.

No sooner had she heard the Earl's voice, when two strange looking creatures appeared from far back in the cathedral. They had long noses, big eyes and one horn coming out of the top of their heads. Bat-like wings flapped behind them. In front of their wings, were long bony arms with clawed hands.

They bounded down the nave aisle towards her, on legs that resembled a dog.

Jesse appeared and ran towards them with his arms flailing above his head. The gargoyles flew up, and over the top of him, continuing towards Elizabeth. Who, by this time had seen enough and was running full tilt towards the west doors. Just as she reached them, she threw her shoulder against the doors, bursting out of the cathedral. The gargoyles followed.

Bindyl was standing directly in front of the entrance. He threw his dagger at the first gargoyle to fly out. It hit the gargoyle squarely in the chest, sending it crashing to the grass. As it landed, it faded away, leaving only Bindyl's blade.

The second gargoyle came shooting out. It stopped in mid- air, eyeing Bindyl, who was standing in front of Elizabeth. It hesitated for a moment, looked up, and flew upward into one of the spires. It perched on the ledge, and turned to stone.

"Thanks Bindyl! I tried to chant magic, but it didn't affect them."

Jesse walked out of the cathedral. He closed the doors behind him, and turned to Elizabeth. "That was close, Liz."

"Yes, it was," she said, "If it hadn't been for Bindyl, I think I might have been killed."

Bindyl had sat back down on the grass. "Well, now I know I'm good for something on this journey," he said, sarcastically.

"Get over yourself, Bindyl," said Jesse.

Bindyl eyed Jesse and at first he felt anger. Then he laughed. Jesse began to laugh too.

Elizabeth looked at the two of them. It had been years since she heard Jesse laugh.

"It's time to go," she said.

Bindyl and Jesse both looked at her at the same time.

"See you later," said Jesse, disappearing.

"Come on, Bindyl. Let's get out of here before we're discovered."

Chapter Seventeen

Elizabeth woke at 6:00 a.m.

Bindyl was still asleep in the bathtub. She picked up the phone and asked room service for a double ordering of tea and toast for breakfast.

When the waiter arrived with the food, he gave Elizabeth a strange look.

"I thought you ordered for two?" he said, looking for another person.

"I ordered two of everything. I didn't say that I had ordered for two," said Elizabeth.

The waiter put the tray down on the table by the window. "Bit hungry are we, Miss?" he asked, looking Elizabeth up and down.

Elizabeth ignored his remark.

"Seems to me," said the waiter, "that those of us who have nice slim figures, won't have them for long, if we eat enough for two people."

"It seems to me," said Elizabeth, looking directly into the waiter's eyes, "that if the hotel waiter is ill mannered enough to make comments about the eating habits of the guests. He may lose his job. Therefore, he should keep his comments to himself!"

The waiter made a hasty retreat to the door, letting himself out with no tip.

The noise woke Bindyl. He came out into the room yawning and stretching.

"Did you sleep well," she asked.

"Yes, thank you. And you?"

"Like a baby. Would you like some breakfast?"

"What is for breakfast?" Bindyl asked.

"Toast, honey and hot sweet tea," said Elizabeth.

Bindyl sat down at the table and Elizabeth poured some tea.

"Time to disappear, Bindyl," said Elizabeth, after the morning meal.

Bindyl shrank down, following her out of the room and down the stairs. He stood beside her, while she paid the bill at the front desk.

Grandma Rose was in the kitchen when they returned.

"How did it go?" she asked.

Bindyl sat at the kitchen table. "May I have a cup of tea please,Lady Rose?"

"But of course, Bindyl. We will all have one," said Grandma.

Elizabeth took a seat opposite Bindyl.

"Well, now I have to go to Malmesbury."

Grandma Rose smiled.

"Don't be so smug, Gran."

"I told you that it may not be as easy to find the Mirronstep as you thought," said Grandma. "How do you know you have to go to Malmesbury?"

"Because the Earl of Salisbury told me so."

Grandma couldn't help but laugh. "He's a little old to be giving advice, isn't he?"

"By all accounts, Elizabeth said he was a stony old codger," Bindyl said, with a giggle.

They all burst into a fit of laughter.

"Bindyl has apparently learned some slang words during his time in the Human Realm," said Grandma.

"Seriously, Elizabeth. What do you have to do now?"

"I don't know what to do yet. I need to do some more research. Bindyl and I are going down to the Elven Realm. Would you like to come with us?"

"No thanks," said Grandma. "I have some chores I need to attend to, but you two go on. Give Gideon my regards."

Chapter Eighteen

Bindyl and Elizabeth left to go down to the Elven Realm. When Grandma Rose was sure that they had gone, she bathed and drove herself to an appointment she had made with her doctor.

She sat in the waiting room until Doctor Andrews' nurse called her.

Grandma Rose followed the nurse into the Doctor's consulting room.

"The doctor will be with you in a minute," said the nurse.

Grandma Rose sat, looking around the walls at all the diplomas and awards. A minute or two later, Doctor Andrews came in and sat down behind his desk.

"I have the results of your x-rays and blood tests, Rose. I'm sorry it took so long, but I wanted to be sure of the result."

"Why do I feel so tired all the time?" asked Grandma.

"It is as we suspected during your last visit. There is a problem with your heart."

"Oh," said Grandma, feeling a little panicked by his answer.

"Your heart is not working as well as it used to," said Dr Andrews.

"Is there a cure?" asked Grandma.

"No, but with medicine and proper care, you could live for a good few years. You will need to be careful with your diet, and not expose yourself to any undue stress."

"I understand," said Grandma.

"I will write you a prescription," said Dr Andrews, scribbling on his pad. "You will need to take these every day. If your symptoms become worse, call here, and I'll come to see you."

"Thank you," said Grandma, taking the prescription from him.

"Remember Rose, no stress."

Grandma Rose left the doctor's office and went to the local pharmacy. She filled the prescription and drove home.

As soon as she arrived back at the cottage, Grandma called the family attorney, who was aware of the Elves.

"Good morning. Benson, Hyde and Brace-Girdle?" a voice on the other end of the phone, said.

"This is Rose Humphries."

"Hello Mrs Humphries. I hope you are well," said the voice.

"I am, thank you. I would like to make an appointment to see Mr Xander Benson."

"Could I ask you the nature of your appointment?" the voice inquired.

"Yes," answered Grandma. "I would like to talk to Mr. Benson about my Will."

"Very well, Mrs Humphries. Would tomorrow at 10:00 a.m. be convenient for you?" asked the voice.

"Yes," said Grandma. "Yes, it would. Thank you."

"See you then. Goodbye," said the voice.

Grandma Rose hung up the phone.

"It's time to make preparations for Elizabeth and Jesse. Just in case anything should happen. It's also time for a nice cuppa," she thought, reaching for the teapot.

Chapter Nineteen

Bindyl held the door to the carriage open for Elizabeth to step down. She followed him up the steps to the castle entrance.

"I'm not staying," said Bindyl. "I'm going to get my things and go home to take a bath and rest for a while."

"That sounds like a good idea to me," said Elizabeth. "I'll see you when you get back."

She sprinted up the stairs to her rooms. After she had bathed and dressed, Elizabeth thought about looking at the book again.

"No," she said to herself, "I think, I need a break. If I start looking through that book, it'll give me more clues and another sleepless night! Tomorrow, I'll be the chosen one. Today I'm going to be Elizabeth Ghenestone."

As she was drying her hair, she looked down into the garden. Merlyn and Charlie were playing on the lawn. Merlyn looked up. When he saw Elizabeth, he flapped his wings and managed to fly up to the window. He hovered there for a few seconds to show Elizabeth how good he had become at flying. Elizabeth clapped and smiled at him.

Merlyn was so excited about hovering; he forgot what he was doing and began to fall. Elizabeth leaned forward, watching him as he plummeted towards the ground. He managed to get control of his wings just before he hit. He looked up at Elizabeth, with the equivalent of a Dragon grin. She smiled back and waved. Charlie looked up, waving a paw.

"I think I'll go down and spend a few minutes with the two of them before I go to find Gideon," she thought.

As she entered through the garden gate, she was immediately met by Merlyn, who promptly jumped up, knocking her to the ground. He began licking her face and making happy chuckling noises. Charlie, who thought it was funny, jumped onto Merlyn's back. The three of them were wrestling around on the grass having fun, when Elizabeth heard a familiar voice.

"That is very unbecoming for the future queen of Kimadrian," Gideon said, standing with his hands on his hips.

Charlie looked at Elizabeth, Elizabeth looked at Merlyn and they all looked at Gideon, who realized too late, that he was in trouble. The three of them were on him in an instant. They wrestled him to the ground and began tickling him.

Up in the King's private quarters, Queen Paulina and King Morvand were looking out of the window.

"It has been a while since things were so light hearted around here," the King said, with a smile.

Chapter Twenty

"It's a beautiful morning!" thought Grandma. "The medicine Dr. Andrews gave me must be working. I slept so well last night. I think I'll go and see Jesse."

After breakfast, Grandma travelled to Kimadrian, and made her way down to Vandrayven's rooms.

She sat beside Jesse, taking his hand. "You look well today."

He didn't respond.

She had been with Jesse for a couple of hours, when Vandrayven put his hand on her shoulder. "Why don't you take a break, Lady Rose. I am going to get something to eat and would like some company."

Grandma turned to the nurse. "Will you let me know if there is any change?"

The nurse nodded. "As always, my lady."

Grandma accompanied Vandrayven up to the dining room.

"Thank you for the break. It was much needed, Vandrayven. I think I'll go and see Elizabeth," Grandma said, after lunch.

"Give her my regards," said Vandrayven, excusing himself.

When she reached Elizabeth's rooms, Gideon answered the door.

"Gideon?" said Grandma. "I wasn't expecting to see you here."

"It's all right Grandma," he said, standing back to let her in. "I know I'm not supposed to be alone with Elizabeth. Gilda has been here most of the morning. I'm helping Elizabeth with her research."

Elizabeth was at her desk. "Hello Gran. Have you had lunch?

Gilda has just gone down to order some for us."

"I had lunch with Vandrayven," said Grandma. "How is the research coming along?"

"Every time I go somewhere, the book records it," said Elizabeth, handing it to her.

Grandma opened the book. There was a drawing of a piece of paper with writing on it and another picture of the stone effigy of the Earl of Salisbury. There was the rhyme that the Earl had given Elizabeth, and a picture of a gargoyle. On the next page, there was a picture of Malmesbury Abbey.

"But you haven't been to Malmesbury Abbey," said Grandma.

"The book gives me a little bit more than I have done each time," said Elizabeth.

"When are you leaving?" asked Grandma.

"I think Bindyl and I will go tomorrow night."

***

After Bindyl, bathed, ate some food and rested for a while, he called Seth into the house, to give him instructions.

"Might I ask how long you will be gone sir?" asked Seth, after Bindyl had told him his duties.

"I am not sure. I may be gone for a few days, or I may be home tomorrow. If you need me, send someone with a message to the castle."

"Very well, sir," said Seth.

With his bags packed, Bindyl saddled his horse and made his way back to the castle.

***

Elizabeth decided to look at the little mirror, after Gideon and Grandma left. As she stared into it, Malmesbury Abbey came into view. She opened the book to see the picture of Malmesbury Abbey was now accompanied by a descriptive map of the entire building.

She put the book and the mirror in a bag along with a few other things for the journey. She ran down the stairs as Bindyl was running up them.

"I was just coming to see if you had returned," she said.

"What's the plan?" he asked, following Elizabeth down to the main entrance.

"We are going to Malmesbury. I'll check us into a hotel, like the last time."

When they reached the cottage, Bindyl changed into human clothes and Elizabeth drove them as usual. They reached Malmesbury around 5:30 p.m.

"Shrink down," said Elizabeth.

"But I thought I didn't have to do that, if I look human?" Bindyl protested.

"I don't want to pay for two rooms," said Elizabeth.

"Miser," Bindyl remarked, sulkily.

Elizabeth checked them in to a small hotel close to the Abbey.

She made her way up to the room with Bindyl following behind her.

"Do you think we will find the Mirronstep tonight?" he said.

"I don't know," Elizabeth replied.

"I don't have anywhere to put my dagger, in these clothes," said Bindyl.

"You'll find somewhere to put it," said Elizabeth.

"What?" said a gentleman who was passing her on the stairs. "Did you say something?"

"A… I said watch your footing. I think one of the stair rods is loose. The carpet moved when I stepped on it," said Elizabeth.

"Thank you for your concern. I will watch where I walk," said the gentleman.

"You didn't say that," said Bindyl.

"Stop talking to me," Elizabeth whispered. "He couldn't see you."

"Oh, so he thought you were a bit… strange?" laughed Bindyl.

Elizabeth ignored him.

Once in the room, Bindyl sat down and glued himself to the television. Elizabeth went downstairs to see if she could find a book on Malmesbury at the gift shop. While she was there, she picked up a bar of chocolate, and decided to get a bar for her grandma, too, as a gift. She found a book on the history of

Malmesbury Abbey. She paid for the items and made her way back to the room

While Bindyl was watching the television, Elizabeth sat at the table by the bay window and read the book. As she was reading, she opened the chocolate bar, broke a piece off and popped it in her mouth.

She was browsing through the pages, when she noticed Bindyl staring at her.

"Is there something wrong?" she asked, returning his gaze.

"What are you eating?" he said.

"Chocolate," she replied.

"What is chocolate?" said Bindyl.

"You've never had chocolate?"

"No, I don't think so," he said.

"Well, come here and have a square," said Elizabeth, breaking a piece off and handing it to him.

Bindyl looked at it carefully then put it into his mouth. He stood for a moment letting the chocolate melt onto his tongue.

"This is delicious," he said, "May I please have a bit more?"

Elizabeth broke off another piece.

"You don't have anything like this in the elven realm?" she asked, as she handed another square to him.

He shook his head, intent on enjoying his new discovery.

While Elizabeth was reading her book, Bindyl ate the rest of her chocolate and her grandma's too.

A few minutes later, she heard him being violently sick in the bathroom. She rushed in, to see if he was all right.

"I don't think I like your chocolate very much after all," he said, looking pale.

"I think that you probably ate too much of it," said Elizabeth.

She made Bindyl a bed on the floor of the bathroom.

"I think your chocolate has poisoned me," he said, holding his stomach.

"Oh, I think you'll be better after a nap," she said, and went back to her book.

Elizabeth smiled to herself, as she heard him groaning.

"That'll teach him not to be so greedy," she thought.

"Well that was interesting," she said, after thumbing through the pages of the book. "I think I'll take a bit of a nap until the sun goes down."

Elizabeth woke Bindyl at two in the morning.

"How are you feeling?" she asked

"I feel quite well, thank you," he said.

"Are you sure? I don't want you coming with me if you are feeling ill," she said.

"I don't feel ill. I think I vomited up most of that sweet stuff you gave me."

Elizabeth looked him up and down. "Well, you don't look as pale as you did before you went to sleep."

"We should go," Bindyl said, trying to avoid any further conversation regarding his gluttony.

The two of them quietly left the hotel.

They walked through the deserted streets until they reached the iron fence that surrounded the front of the Abbey. The gate was open, allowing them onto the grounds.

Bindyl slowed down, then stopped. He went over to the grave stones on the right hand side of the pathway and put his hand on one of them. Elizabeth, who was walking ahead of him, stopped and turned.

Bindyl looked to see Jesse standing on the pathway. Jesse beckoned him to come back to the pathway and pointed to the archway.

As Elizabeth made her way along the path, she noticed the remains of a stone wall attached to the church, to the right of the graveyard. It had three arches that looked as though they were windows at one time, but were now bricked in.

"This was my dream," Bindyl said, looking at Jesse.

"Yes, this is where you are supposed to be," said Jesse.

Bindyl looked along the pathway, trying to see into the entrance where he had seen the ghost of the young boy in his dream. When Elizabeth saw him looking past her, she turned to see what he was looking at.

"You can follow Elizabeth to the door of the Abbey, but don't go any further, Bindyl," said Jesse.

"I don't want to go to the archway, thank you," said Bindyl, remembering his dream.

Jesse motioned for Elizabeth to keep going towards the door. Bindyl stepped back onto the pathway and followed her.

When Elizabeth reached the stone arch that led to the entrance of the Abbey, she saw a little boy dressed all in white. He was sitting on the bench, on the left hand side, just inside the archway. He turned to her when she reached the entrance. The young boy's face was white, matching the rest of him.

His hair was short and wavy.

"He has the face of an angel," Elizabeth said.

"That's not how I remember him," Bindyl muttered.

When the ghost of the young boy stood, Elizabeth could see the door through his body. He looked around her at Bindyl and waggled his finger at him, shaking his head.

"You do not have to tell me twice, ghost," Bindyl said, backing away.

"You go ahead," said Bindyl. "This ghost and I have met before. He is telling me that I cannot go into the Abbey, so I will just wait here."

Elizabeth turned back to the young boy.

"Do you have a riddle for me?" he asked.

"His voice. It's beautiful," thought Elizabeth, "As though he's singing."

Elizabeth said the riddle to him. He nodded and turned to the door. He put his hand on the metal ring and turned it clockwise. He looked back at Elizabeth, motioning for her to go with him.

The boy led her through the Abbey until they reached another door. As they approached, it opened by itself. The boy and Elizabeth made their way through the church, and continued into the oldest part of the Abbey. Time and weather had done its part on this ancient building, and it was now a shell. The windows above the walls were still there, but no longer had glass in them and the roof had long gone. The walls were covered in stone patterns and carvings, pitted and blackened with age.

The boy led her around the side wall that Elizabeth had noticed on the way in. When she first looked at it, the wall was just stone, slowly, the arches from the other side of the wall appeared.

Hung within each of the three arches embedded in the stone wall, was an ornate, full length, oval shaped mirror,

Elizabeth took the hand mirror out of the bag she had been carrying.

The Mirronstep

"This one looks just like those," she said. "But I thought there was only one Mirronstep. Why are there three of them on the wall?"

The ghostly boy moved to the first of the three mirrors. As he approached, the mirror's reflection darkened. The boy stood in front of it, looking into the frame. His reflection disappeared, only blackness replaced it. He went to the second mirror and it did the same thing, as did the third.

He turned to Elizabeth. "Only one of these mirrors is the real Mirronstep. You must pick the right one."

"But why are there three, and how am I supposed to know which is the real one?" she asked.

"Because the druids have decided that if the mirror gets into the wrong hands, it could destroy the world. They knew someone would come looking for it eventually, so they decided that only the person with the right answer would be able to use it."

He snapped his fingers and a scroll appeared in his right hand. "This is a contract. Please read it aloud so that I might know that you understand it," he said, handing the scroll to her.

She unrolled it, and held it up.

"You must decide which mirror to use.
If you pick the wrong one, all of them you will lose.
So use your head, and in truth you will see.
The real mirror before you, and learn what could be.
To unfold the future, it will be foretold.
To step into the mirror, you must be bold.
If your soul is pure, you will be safe.
If your intentions are evil, you will meet with a wraith.
To unfold the past, you may go through.
If you meddle with time you'll be stuck, it's true.
Be cautious of what decisions you make.
Or you won't come back through the timeless gate."

When she finished reading, her signature appeared at the bottom.

Elizabeth looked at the boy. "I didn't agree to anything."

The ghostly boy looked down his nose at her. "If you didn't want to abide by the contract, you shouldn't have read it. You can leave now and your signature will disappear from the scroll."

"No," she said. "I've come this far. I can't give up now."

The boy turned to her and held out his arm with a flourish, as though introducing his audience of one, to a fabulous magic trick.

"All three mirrors are identical, but only one will send you back, or forward in time," he said, solemnly. "Choose carefully, Elizabeth, the humans and the elves are depending on you."

Elizabeth approached the wall, eyeing the first mirror, then on to the second and the third. She stepped back.

"Elizabeth?"

"Bindyl, is that you?"

"Yes," he said, "I am on the other side of this wall."

"How did you know where I would be?" she asked.

"Jesse brought me here. He told me to wait until I heard your voice."

"Where is Jesse now?" said Elizabeth.

"I'm here, Liz."

She turned, looking for her ghostly companion, but he had disappeared, and Jesse was now standing where the boy had been.

"Why did you put Bindyl on the other side of the wall?" she asked.

"The higher powers have forbidden him from coming in," said Jesse. "They didn't say that he couldn't be on the other side of the wall. Talk to him, Liz, he may be able to help you solve the riddle with the mirrors."

Elizabeth approached the wall.

"Bindyl, I have three mirrors in front of me," she said. "They all look exactly the same, but only one of them is the true Mirronstep. Do you have any idea how I might choose the correct one? If I make the wrong choice, all of them will be destroyed."

"Bindyl? Are you there?" she said, after a few seconds.

"Elizabeth, do you remember when we went to the Long Barrow and met with Sir Gareth?" asked Bindyl.

"Yes," said Elizabeth.

"Do you remember what he said about trying to get back out of the mirror by using the hilt of his sword?"

"Yes."

"Why don't you look at each mirror? There may be a nick in the side where the hilt of his sword hung onto it."

"Yes!" she said.

Elizabeth went to the first mirror and looked into it. Her reflection disappeared as the mirror went dark. She ran her hand over the gilded pattern around the edge of it, careful not to put her hand on the glass. It had no marks or nicks on the pattern.

She went to the second mirror and ran her right hand around the edge from right to left. Just to the bottom left of the mirror, she noticed a notch on the inner edge of the bottom part of the pattern, on the right hand side. Elizabeth looked closer. There was a definite indent. She went to the other mirror and felt around the edge. It was smooth, no nicks or notches in it.

"There is a notch in the filigree pattern, on the side of the second mirror," she said.

"Are there any notches in the other two?" asked Bindyl.

"Not that I can see or feel."

She stood back, looking at the mirrors, reluctant to pull one off the wall.

"Elizabeth, you have to make a decision," Bindyl said, after a minute or two.

"I know. Just... give me a second."

She turned to Jesse.

"I can't help you, Liz. I'm not allowed to. Bindyl's idea was a really good one though, don't you think?"

Elizabeth looked into her brother's face. He smiled, nodding at the mirrors.

She went to the mirror with the nick in it and pulled it off the wall. The two remaining mirrors shimmered for a second, before fading away into nothing.

"Oh, thank goodness!" Jesse gasped.

"Thank you for the vote of confidence, dear brother."

"Liz! I'm just relieved, that's all. I never really had a doubt that you would pick the right one."

Elizabeth turned away from her brother. "Bindyl, are you still there?"

"Yes," he replied.

"Meet me at the entrance. We're going home."

Elizabeth tucked the mirror under her arm and made her way

back through the Abbey, Jesse following behind. He disappeared as she exited through the Abbey entrance.

Bindyl was waiting for her by the door. She held it up.

"Is it the right one do you think?" he said.

"The boy said if I picked the wrong one, they would all disappear, so I must have the right one. Come on, let's get our things from the hotel room. We're going home tonight. I'm not putting this in our room. Someone might see it and know what it is."

"Very sensible," said Bindyl.

As they made their way along the path, Elizabeth noticed that the three arches had re-appeared on the graveyard side of the wall.

When they reached the car park, Elizabeth opened the boot and put the mirror underneath a blanket.

"Bindyl, you stay here and keep watch."

She hurried up to the room, packed their things and gave the concierge the key.

"Bit of an odd time to be checking out miss," he said, with concern. "I hope everything is all right."

"I've had a family emergency and need to leave straight away."

"Well, drive carefully, miss."

They arrived back at the cottage just as the sun was coming up. Elizabeth grabbed the Mirronstep and carried it into the house.

She gently knocked on Grandma's door.

"Elizabeth?"

"Yes Gran. Can you get up and come to the kitchen? I have something to show you."

Grandma Rose got out of bed. She went into her bathroom and splashed her face with cold water. When she reached the kitchen, Elizabeth was making a pot of coffee. Bindyl was sat at the kitchen table. On the table beside him was a blanket with something underneath it. Grandma Rose looked at Elizabeth.

Elizabeth nodded and smiled.

Grandma lifted the blanket.

"It's beautiful," she said, putting her hand out to touch it.

"Don't!" said Elizabeth.

Grandma Rose pulled her hand back, startled.

"I'm sorry Gran, I didn't mean to frighten you, but that thing is dangerous and I don't want anything to happen to you."

"Sorry," Grandma said, "I should be more careful. I'm still half asleep."

Elizabeth took the Mirronstep off the table and propped it up against the wall with the mirror facing inward.

"Sit down Gran," Elizabeth said, putting a cup of coffee in front of her. "This will wake you up a bit."

"Bindyl, I want you to go to Stonehenge with Grandma and contact Thalios.

"Gran, I want you to park by the road so that he can jump the fence. Bindyl, go to the Heel stone. You know the big stone we came out of to get to Avebury when we regenerated the Grymlons. Stand close to it and call his name, ask him to meet me down in the Elven Realm. Don't say anything else. As soon as you get back here, I want you to meet me at the castle. I have to get down to the Realm now. I want to get this mirror to a safe place so I can't go with you."

"I'll get dressed," said Grandma.

Bindyl, when you get to Stonehenge, shrink down before you get out of the car," said Elizabeth. "Just in case someone should stop and ask Gran what she's doing there. She can say her car has broken down or something."

"Don't worry about us," said Bindyl. "We will be back before you know it."

Elizabeth picked up the Mirronstep.

Bindyl followed her out of the back door and watched her walk along the garden path. She turned and waved to him just before she entered the branches of the willow tree. Ten minutes later he and Grandma Rose were on their way to Stonehenge.

Elizabeth carried the mirror under her arm, through the corridors of the castle. When she reached Gideon's rooms, she knocked on the door, and was greeted by a sleepy manservant.

"My goodness, miss, is there an emergency?" he asked, rubbing his eyes.

"I need to speak to the prince straight away," she said.

The manservant stood back to let her in. She went to Gideon's office and placed the mirror on his desk.

Gideon came out of his bedroom, yawning. "Who is it, Wynford?"

"It is Miss Elizabeth, your highness. She is in your office."

"Go back to bed, Wynford. I think I know why she is here."

"Would you like me to wake Gilda, Sir?" Wynford asked.

"No, no. Just go back to bed," said Gideon.

Elizabeth was sat by the window when Gideon entered his office. He saw the blanket on his desk, and knew immediately what it was.

"Where is Bindyl?" he asked.

"He and Gran have gone to Stonehenge to contact Thalios. I came straight down here."

Gideon lifted a corner of the blanket. When he saw the Mirronstep, he turned to Elizabeth.

"You did it!" I can't believe it, you actually found the Mirronstep."

"What now?" he asked, sitting at his desk.

"Now I will try to find Renmar, but first you and I will go and wake your father."

Chapter Twenty One

Gideon, Elizabeth, and Vandrayven were sat in the King's office. The Mirronstep had been placed on a table by the wall.

"We will call upon the elviron for a meeting to arrange for your journey," said the King.

"No," said Elizabeth, "I don't think you should tell the elviron just yet. I don't trust them. I think I should just go ahead and make the search for the Grymlons."

"But I gave my word to King Kalidryd. He and I agreed that if you found the Mirronstep, I would let him know," said the King.

"I don't want you to tell him yet," Elizabeth insisted. "I have just spent days risking my life to get the Mirronstep. I would like some say in how the events unfold. If the elviron are aware that we now have it, and I fail in my task, they may try to get their hands on it for their own use.

"I would like the chance to try to save the Grymlons before you tell them. That way, if I succeed, the elviron will be able to live the way they used to, hundreds of years ago."

"She does have a point, father," said Gideon.

"Very well," the King agreed. "I will give you three days to try to accomplish your task. After which, I will inform King Kalidryd that we have the mirror."

"I've been up most of the night," said Elizabeth. "I would like to go to my rooms and rest for a bit. My grandma and Bindyl will come here as soon as they get back from Stonehenge."

"We will meet later this afternoon and work out a plan," said the King.

Elizabeth left to go to her rooms, taking the Mirronstep with her. She cast a spell, rendering all the items invisible, stretched out on her bed and fell asleep.

It was early afternoon when Elizabeth woke to find Merlyn was asleep on the pillow beside her. She sat up when her maid knocked then entered.

"I'm sorry to disturb you, miss, but your grandma said to tell you that she is here and will meet you in Lord Vandrayven's rooms."

"Thank you," said Elizabeth.

"Will that be all, my lady?"

"Yes," said Elizabeth. "I'll go and see her in a bit."

The maid curtsied and left.

Elizabeth bathed, dressed and went down to Vandrayven.

Jesse was sleeping peacefully and Grandma was holding his hand. The nurse sat patiently in the corner of the room, as usual.

Elizabeth gently tapped her grandma on the shoulder. Grandma Rose placed Jesse's hand on his chest and got up from the chair. She followed Elizabeth out of the room and the two of them made their way to the dining area.

"Did everything go all right Gran?"

"Bindyl did as you asked," said Grandma. "It was still early, so no one saw us. He has gone home for a day or two, since you don't need him anymore."

"Now we will just have to wait," said Elizabeth.

The two of them took a seat at a table. Elizabeth asked one of the servants to bring them some lunch. They ate in silence, each of them preoccupied with their own thoughts.

Grandma Rose finished her food and stood. "I'm going back up to the cottage. I have some errands to do."

"I'll see you later, Gran," Elizabeth said, also leaving the table to look for Gideon.

On her way to the barracks, she was stopped by one of the guards. "Gideon is with his parents, my lady. He asks that you meet him in the main library."

The guard saluted and went on his way.

She entered the library, as Queen Paulina was leaving.

"We must meet soon, for afternoon tea," said the Queen, embracing her.

"I look forward to it," said Elizabeth.

She curtsied, politely as the Queen exited the library.

"Are you well rested?" asked the King.

"Yes, thank you," Elizabeth said, taking a seat next to Gideon.

"Gideon and I were wondering if you were going to take anyone with you on your travels?" asked the King.

"No," said Elizabeth, "I hadn't planned on taking anyone. I think I'm supposed to go alone."

"I could come with you, if you want me to," said Gideon.

Elizabeth smiled at her handsome prince. "As much as I would love your company, I still want to go alone."

Bindyl entered the library unannounced.

"Please forgive the intrusion, your majesty," he said, politely, "but I have a message for Elizabeth."

"I thought you had gone home for a couple of days," said Gideon.

"I did," said Bindyl.

"What's the message?" Elizabeth asked.

"I have to come with you."

"I thought you were only supposed to go with me to find the Mirronstep," she said.

"I went home to the farm," said Bindyl. "I decided to get a little sleep. So I lay on my bed and stretched out. I was looking forward to relaxing for the next few days. I fell asleep quickly. Along with the sleep came Jesse in a dream, again. He said that I have to go with you."

"Why?" Elizabeth asked.

"I'm not allowed to tell you."

"You've said that before," said Elizabeth.

"I know. I wish you would trust me."

"I do trust you, Bindyl, but I thought your job was finished."

"I don't want to go with you, but I don't have a choice," said Bindyl. "Let me know when we are to leave and I will be ready."

He bowed to the king, before turning and leaving the three of them.

"I wonder why he has to go with you?" said Gideon.

"I don't know," said Elizabeth. "I'll try to use the Mirronstep first thing tomorrow morning. I would like you to be there with me, Gideon, just in case."

"I'll be there," said Gideon.

"I still have some research to do," said Elizabeth, "so if you will both excuse me, I should get started."

The king stood. Elizabeth curtsied as he left the room.

"Can I do anything to help, Liz?" asked Gideon.

"No, just be with me when I go through the mirror. Will I see you for supper?"

"Of course," he answered, kissing her on the cheek.

As soon as Elizabeth had closed the door to her living room, she took a seat and put herself into a light sleep. Jesse appeared in the room a minute or so later.

"You called, sis?" he asked, as he sat down in the easy chair opposite to her.

"Why does Bindyl have to come with me through the Mirron-step?"

"Because he has been told he has to do so," said Jesse.

"That's not good enough, Jesse."

"Well, that's all you are going to get from me."

"Jesse, I'm starting to wake up," said Elizabeth.

"I know, sis," Jesse replied, beginning to fade away. "Remember, I won't let anything happen to you."

Elizabeth awoke feeling disgruntled and tired. She climbed up on the bed and fell asleep.

When she woke, she ordered some tea from her maid. She cancelled the spell that hid the Mirronstep from sight and got to work.

When she opened the book, she noticed it too, had been busy.

"There are so many more pages now," she thought, thumbing through them.

As Elizabeth read the new information, she discovered directions on how to use the Mirronstep.

"So the little mirror is the way back," she said, reading the instructions aloud. "When I step through the Mirronstep, I am to have the little mirror with me to open the doorway back to where I came from. It says here that all I have to do is think of where I want to be, and as I step through the mirror I will go there."

The Mirronstep

"Time to give it a little test drive," she said, putting the Mirronstep on the floor.

She grabbed the little mirror and put it in her pocket. As she stepped onto the Mirronstep, she closed her eyes and thought about standing by the Heel Stone at Stonehenge.

Elizabeth felt dizzy and a little sick for a few seconds. When she opened her eyes, she found herself standing just outside of the stone ring.

She was about to walk to the Heel Stone when she noticed a figure standing by it. Elizabeth ducked behind the stone she was next to, peeping around it to see who it was.

"It's me!" she whispered, as she watched herself standing at the stone.

"I was here when I tried to contact Thalios," she thought, looking back to the car park.

A blue car was parked alone. Elizabeth could make out the figure of her grandma.

"I need to leave here, now!" she said, taking the small mirror out of her pocket. Elizabeth touched her fingers to the glass and felt the same uncomfortable sensation as before.

"I'm back in my room at the castle in Kimadrian," she thought.

Elizabeth opened her eyes just as she popped out of the Mirronstep and onto the carpet in her room. She landed on her backside on the floor.

She looked up as she hit the carpet, noticing a figure in white, standing in front of her.

"What do you think you are doing?" Thalios asked.

Elizabeth picked herself up and smoothed out her pullover.

"I was just testing it."

Thalios stood at the window for a moment looking out, before he turned to face her. "Sit down, Elizabeth, and listen very carefully to what I have to say".

She took a seat on the couch.

"You will need to be in a specific place and time for you to be able to save the elviron set of Grymlons." Thalios said.

Elizabeth glanced at the mirror as it lay on the floor. "But I went to Stonehenge, just by thinking about it. If I can do that from here, why can't I go to where Renmar was?"

"The Mirronstep took you to Stonehenge, because you had already been there," said Thalios. "To find Renmar you may have to be where he was when the event happened. If you miss the mark, even by a few seconds, it probably won't work. You must either be in Distardrian, and try to get to Renmar before he steals the Grymlons, or you will have to find out where Renmar went when he travelled up to the human realm. You will have to stop the vampire attack and get the Grymlons away from him. In either case, you will have to be right there when it happens.

"If you fail, you must get back through the Mirronstep as soon as possible. Do not stay in the past for one second longer than you have to, or you may change the future in a way other than desired.

"I wonder if you grasp the importance of what I'm telling you," he said, looking into her eyes.

"How do you know how I'm supposed to be right there, if I don't know when 'there' was?" she said, returning his gaze.

Elizabeth stopped talking. She looked at Thalios, who had a confused look on his face.

She shook her head. "I'm not quite sure what exactly I just said."

Thalios looked at her sternly at first. "I could not have said it better myself," he said, with a sudden chuckle.

The two of them spent the next couple of hours researching history and paperwork that the elviron had given them.

"As I see it," said Elizabeth. "We have two options. One is your suggestion, to try to stop Renmar before he reached the Human Realm. That means I will have to travel to Distardrian. Or two, find out where Renmar came up to the Human Realm."

"I agree," said Thalios.

"I think I'll try to be waiting at the entrance to the Human Realm," she decided. "That way, I won't have to reveal to the elviron that I have the Mirronstep. The problem is, there is no information about where he came up. I could go to Uffington and try to retrace my steps."

"Could you have perhaps come up near the White Horse at Uffington?" said Thalios.

"There is some reference to it in the archives, in the druidic council room, where I came by the artifacts I gave to you," Thalios replied.

"You didn't tell me that when you gave them to me," said Elizabeth.

"I didn't really think you would find the Mirronstep," admitted Thalios.

"Thanks for your vote of confidence," Elizabeth said, sarcastically. "Where is the entrance?"

"At the foot of the White Horse, carved in the hillside, is a small white mound of earth, called Dragon Hill. The story tells of how St. George slew the Dragon on that spot. There are white chalk marks where the Dragon's blood was spilled. They say nothing will grow there, even to this day."

"I know the story, Thalios. As do most kids around here. I've been there. My dad took Jesse and I there when we were kids."

"The entrance used to be at the edge of the mound," Thalios continued. "The elviron sealed it when Renmar was attacked by the unknown beast. They feared that the beast would find its way down to the Elviron Realm.

"Take the Mirronstep there and use it near where Renmar came up through the earth. I will come with you to protect the Mirronstep while you are gone."

"When would you like to go?" Elizabeth asked.

"No time like the present. If Bindyl is coming, perhaps Gideon should come, too," Thalios said. "Keslyn and I will meet you at your grandma's at dusk."

"I'll send word to Gideon and see you then," said Elizabeth, "Oh, and Thalios?"

"Yes Elizabeth?"

"Don't hide anything else from me?"

"Yes, Elizabeth," Thalios replied, feeling a bit uneasy.

Elizabeth found Gideon with the king, and outlined the plan.

"I will go and find Bindyl," said Gideon. "We'll meet you in the reception area downstairs."

Chapter Twenty Two

Elizabeth waited.

Bindyl was the first to arrive.

"Where is Gideon?" she asked.

"He sent a message with a guard, for me to meet you both here," Bindyl replied.

He stared out of the window while they were waiting.

"He looks upset," Elizabeth thought, watching him gaze out into the courtyard.

Gideon arrived a few minutes later.

"Oh, the guard found you. Good."

Bindyl continued to stare out of the window.

"Is anything the matter, Bindyl?" he asked.

"No," said Bindyl, not turning around.

"He's sulking because he has to come with me," said Elizabeth.

"That is not true!" Bindyl said, rather loudly.

"Oh yes it is," she shot back. "You have to come with me, so get used to it and let's get a move on."

"I for one am glad Bindyl is coming," said Gideon. "As much as Bindyl is complaining, I know he wouldn't hesitate to protect you if there were trouble."

Bindyl ignored them both.

Elizabeth left the reception area. Gideon fell into step beside her.

"I have a potion here from Vandrayven," he said. "If I am to travel with you two, then I would like to look as human as possible. I have some for you too, Bindyl."

"I can't wait to take it," Bindyl muttered. "I just love looking like a human."

"Good," said Elizabeth. "You can take it when we get to Grandma's."

Bindyl followed behind the two of them.

On their way to the cottage, Elizabeth told Gideon about the gargoyles.

"They are so awfully ugly, and fast. I thought I was done for when I ran out of the cathedral doors, but Bindyl killed the one behind me without hesitation. Tell Gideon what you said about the Earl."

"I told Grandma the Earl was a stony old codger," said Bindyl, sheepishly.

"You are beginning to pick up a human sense of humour," Gideon said, with a laugh.

Elizabeth noticed that Bindyl's mood seemed to lighten a little, when Gideon laughed at his remark.

Thalios and Keslyn were already waiting for them when they entered through the back door of the cottage.

"I'll drive us," said Elizabeth.

Gideon took the potion to make him look more human. Bindyl grew to human size and did the same.

"How do I look," said Gideon.

Thalios eyed the two elves. "You could pass as human, if one didn't look too close."

When all were seated in the car, Elizabeth put the Mirronstep in the boot.

Bindyl and Gideon sat in the back with Keslyn between them. Thalios sat in the front with Elizabeth. Grandma Rose opened the gate and Elizabeth drove through. She slowed down a little to wave at Grandma as she passed her. They drove to Faringdon and then on to Uffington. It was getting dark by the time they arrived. Elizabeth parked the car at the Woolstone Hill car park, and they made their way to Dragon Hill. Above them was the chalk figure of the white horse, almost luminous in the coming darkness.

Gideon stayed at the foot of the hill. Elizabeth, Bindyl, Thalios and Keslyn climbed up onto the mound.

"This is definitely where Renmar came out of the ground," said Elizabeth. "I thought it looked familiar."

Elizabeth took the mirror and placed it on the grass a few feet away from the barren spot. Thalios stood a little way off from her with Keslyn at his side. Elizabeth thought about an elf coming up out of the ground. She closed her eyes, feeling in her pocket for the small mirror. She motioned for Bindyl to hold her hand as they stepped onto the Mirronstep.

Elizabeth opened her eyes. Bindyl was standing beside her. Renmar was laying a little way off from them.

"He looks dead," she thought, but then he got up and with some effort, made his way to the spot on the ground. He pulled open the concealed door and jumped through it, closing the door behind him. Elizabeth and Bindyl ran over to where he had been.

"Did you see him holding a bag?" she asked Bindyl.

"No. I take it you didn't follow him back to this spot," he said, still looking to where Renmar had disappeared.

"No, one minute I was following him out of Uffington, the next I was watching him go inside his house. I know which direction he came from so I'll retrace his steps. You look around here," Elizabeth said.

Bindyl circled the area.

Elizabeth walked almost to the road.

"I didn't see anything out of the ordinary," Bindyl said, when she returned.

"We could go into Uffington and look around," Bindyl suggested.

"I don't somehow think that would do any good," said Elizabeth.

"Let's look around a bit more."

"Bindyl, I think we're too late," she said, after a few minutes. "Let's go back."

He grabbed her hand.

Elizabeth put her hand on the little mirror. They popped back out of the Mirronstep, in front of Thalios.

"Well?" he asked.

Elizabeth sat on the grass for a moment, trying to catch her breath. Bindyl stood, brushing the grass off his backside.

"We were too late," she said. "We went through just as Renmar was jumping into the entrance to the Elviron Realm. There was no sign of the Grymlons."

Thalios approached the edge of the mound. "Renmar should have had the Grymlons with him. We know the druid ran from him. He should have had the Grymlons with him up until the moment he went back down to the Elviron Realm. Where could they have gone? You have to try again."

Elizabeth nodded. She closed her eyes and formed a picture in her head of the elviron coming up through the ground. As she was thinking this, she grabbed Bindyl's hand again and walked into the Mirronstep.

Elizabeth and Bindyl appeared close to the entrance of the Elviron Realm, and waited for ten minutes.

Bindyl paced back and forth impatiently, but nothing happened. Finally, he put his hand on her shoulder. She pushed her hand into the mirror and they popped back out of the Mirronstep again.

They both landed on the grass.

Thalios knelt down to her.

"Anything?" he asked, helping her up.

Elizabeth shook her head. "What do we do now?"

"We go back to the Elven Realm. We contact the elviron and you and Bindyl must go to Distardrian," replied Thalios.

Elizabeth picked up the Mirronstep and began making her way down the mound. Bindyl went on ahead to join Gideon down below. Thalios and Keslyn followed her.

Just as Elizabeth was about to climb down the hill, she heard a sound. She turned around, but only Thalios and Keslyn were behind her.

"Did you hear that?" she asked.

"Hear what?" said Thalios.

Elizabeth turned to Keslyn.

"Did you just snort?"

Keslyn shook her head.

"I heard a sound like snorting," said Elizabeth.

"We must leave now," said Thalios.

"Why? What's wrong?" Elizabeth asked.

"I don't know, but I definitely think that we should leave this place," said Thalios.

The three of them scrambled down the hill.

"Is everything all right?" asked Gideon, when they reached him.

"Come on, let's get out of here," said Elizabeth, as she passed the two elves.

"If Elizabeth wants to leave this place. Then it probably isn't safe to stay," said Bindyl, not needing to be told twice. He hurried to catch up with them, Gideon following closely behind.

They practically ran to the car. Elizabeth had the engine running and was ready to leave before all of them were seated. Thalios was holding on to the Mirronstep. Elizabeth placed the Mirronstep in the boot. They sped away from the hill as fast as Elizabeth could drive. No one said anything for a few minutes.

Finally, Gideon spoke up. "Why did we leave in such a hurry?"

"Elizabeth heard something," said Thalios.

"What?" asked Bindyl.

"Something snorted at me back there," she said.

"So we ran away because of a snort? Oh, well then, we had every reason to make a quick escape," said Gideon.

Thalios, who was sitting in the front seat turned and looked at Gideon.

"You would do well to listen to any sense of danger that Elizabeth feels. It may one day save your life, young elf!" he said, with distain.

"I am sorry Elizabeth," said Gideon.

Elizabeth ignored him.

There was very little conversation on the way home.

When they arrived at the cottage, Elizabeth parked the car and went into the house.

"Any luck?" asked Grandma, when Elizabeth entered through the back door.

"No," said Elizabeth. "I'll have to go to Distardrian and try again there. I'm going back down to the Elven Realm. Will you be all right?"

"I'll be fine, dear," replied Grandma. "Just keep me posted."

Chapter Twenty Three

The carriage pulled up to the front of the castle entrance and dropped them off.

"I'm going to the barracks to get some rest," said Bindyl.

Gideon made arrangements for Thalios and Keslyn to stay in the guest quarters of the castle and turned in for the night.

Elizabeth went to her rooms and got ready for bed. She sat in the easy chair and put herself into a sleep trance. It only took a minute or two before Jesse appeared.

"Where were you tonight?" she asked.

"My presence was required elsewhere at the time you were on Dragon Hill," he said. "How did it go?"

"Not well," said Elizabeth.

"Tell me what happened?"

Elizabeth told Jesse of the night's events.

He shook his head. "Be careful Elizabeth, it may not be safe in Distardrian."

"Will you be making an appearance this time?" she asked.

"Oh yes."

"I'll see you soon then," said Elizabeth.

"Yes. You should wake and go to bed," said Jesse.

Elizabeth woke from her trance, as Jesse faded away.

She climbed up onto the four poster bed and fell asleep.

***

Elizabeth, Bindyl, Gideon, King Morvand and Vandrayven sat around the table in the main library.

"I will send for King Kalidryd," said King Morvand. "We will outline our plan for Elizabeth and Bindyl to go to Distardrian to use the Mirronstep."

"I don't think we should tell him that I have already tried to find Renmar," said Elizabeth.

"I agree," said the King. "It may cause a bit of tension, if the elviron think we are trying to do this behind their backs."

King Kalidryd arrived the next morning with Drewmannus. After secretly bringing them into the castle, all of them met in King Morvand's office.

When everyone was settled, Elizabeth entered the room with the Mirronstep under her arm.

She put it down on the table and removed the blanket.

King Kalidryd gasped. Drewmannus, who was beside him, bent over and reached out to touch it.

"Don't!" said Elizabeth.

The wizard drew his hand back.

"Where did you find it?" King Kalidryd asked.

"That's not important," said Elizabeth. "I think I need to be in your Realm to make it work."

Drewmannus looked at King Kalidryd. "How do you know that you have to be in our Realm to use it?"

"Because she tried to use it in the Human Realm and it didn't work," Thalios said, entering the room. "I apologize for being late."

It had been many years since an elviron had seen a druid. King Kalidryd and the wizard dropped down on one knee.

Elizabeth leaned sideways, into King Morvand. "Why are they doing that?" she whispered in his ear.

"Druids were just as important to the elviron once, as they are to the elves," he replied quietly. "When the elviron changed, the druids stopped communicating with them for fear of being infected."

Thalios approached them, waving his hands. "Get up, get up! There is no need for that," he said.

Thalios moved around the table, taking a seat next to Elizabeth.

Keslyn hissed at the two elviron as she passed by.

The Mirronstep

"Be quiet Keslyn," Thalios said, as he leaned back from his chair, putting his staff against the wall.

Keslyn sat on the floor beside him, looking at Drewmannus out of the corner of her eye.

"How long have you had the Mirronstep, Elizabeth?" asked King Kalidryd.

"I wanted to try it out to see if it really worked," she answered. "I thought that if I could get your Grymlons back while I was testing it out, we would save some time."

"You never had any intention of stealing it, did you?" asked Drewmannus.

King Kalidryd put his hand on the wizard's shoulder. "Drewmannus simply means that you should have contacted us as soon as you found the Mirronstep. That is what we had agreed upon."

Elizabeth looked directly into the wizard's eyes. They stared at each other for a few moments.

"Did her eyes just turn orange?" Drewmannus thought, dropping his gaze. "She has a temper, best not make her angry."

Elizabeth turned away from the wizard. "I have no intention of stealing the Mirronstep."

She turned to Drewmannus again and smiled, "If you want to look normal again, you funny looking little wizard. You are going to have to trust me."

King Morvand stood. "Elizabeth!!"

Drewmannus glanced up at her, then looked down at the table and kept his gaze there.

King Kalidryd also stood, realizing that the meeting could turn into something disastrous, if he didn't control his wizard. "I apologize, Elizabeth. Drewmannus is a little nervous about the Mirronstep."

Ignoring the king's excuse, Elizabeth addressed the meeting.

"The plan is for me to go to Distardrian and go into the castle. I'll use the Mirronstep to go back and try to stop Renmar before he steals the Grymlons. If this is not acceptable, I could try to do it from here, but I think I'll be more successful in Distardrian."

King Kalidryd and Drewmannus exchanged glances.

"I think that would be agreeable," said King Kalidryd.

"Elizabeth will leave for Distardrian with my son and Thalios first thing in the morning," said King Morvand.

"We will leave now to make preparations for your visit," said King Kalidryd.

King Morvand called two guards to take King Kalidryd and Drewmannus to their carriage.

"I'm going down to see Jesse," said Elizabeth.

***

Elizabeth gazed into Jesse's face as she held his hand.

"I'm just going to sit here with you for a bit," she said aloud. "I don't know if you are aware of me, but I feel better when I'm near you."

She sat for an hour before leaving for the Human Realm. When she reached the cottage, Elizabeth got into her car and drove to Uffington. She parked the car, climbed up to Dragon Hill, and stood, listening for a moment. Then she sat on the flat topped mound and crossed her legs. She closed her eyes feeling the wind, as it whipped at her hair.

"I know you're here," she said.

"You are brave for a maiden," a soft voice answered, so faint it sounded like the breeze. "We shall meet, but not today."

Elizabeth sat as still as stone, waiting for something to happen. After a few minutes, she realized that whoever, or whatever was there with her, was now gone. She stood, brushed off her jeans and went back to her car.

"Whatever that was back there, knows me," she thought, as she drove. "Now all I have to do is find out what, or who it is."

Elizabeth stopped in Faringdon, an old picturesque market town close to Highwell. She went into one of the quaint little restaurants in the centre of the town. The waiter took her to a seat by one of the windows looking out onto the old town hall.

She ate a leisurely lunch, enjoying a sense of solitude for a while. She sat and watched as the people went about their daily business. A little while later, she looked at her watch.

"I should get back," she thought.

The Mirrorstep

She paid for her meal and drove back to the cottage, then made her way back down to the Elven Realm.

Grandma Rose and Gideon were waiting for her when she reached the castle.

"Where have you been?" asked Grandma Rose. "We have been frantic, looking for you."

"I needed to think about some things. So I thought a little drive in the country would do me good," said Elizabeth.

"Well, in the future, could you please tell someone where you are going," said Gideon. "You cannot just leave like that. You are the future queen. You could have been kidnapped."

Elizabeth looked at Gideon and laughed. "I promise I will inform someone if I go anywhere, just in case I get abducted by aliens or something."

"Don't be sarcastic, young lady," said Grandma Rose. "You have a responsibility to Gideon and me. Don't be so thoughtless."

"I'm sorry, Gran. It didn't occur to me that I would be missed so quickly. I won't disappear without letting someone know again."

"I understand the pressure you're under," said Grandma. "I'm not too sure that I wouldn't have done the same, had it been me."

"I don't know about you two, but I'm hungry. I suggest we eat an early supper and retire for the night," said Gideon

Chapter Twenty Four

Elizabeth sat in her rooms, closed her eyes and listened to the silence. Charlie was asleep at the bottom of her bed, Merlyn on the pillow next to hers.

She glanced over at them noticing how peaceful they looked. "I so love my little friends. They ask so little and give so much," she thought.

She got ready for bed, climbed up onto the mattress, careful not to disturb them, and fell into a peaceful sleep.

The next morning, Elizabeth, Gideon, Bindyl and Thalios met with the King and Queen for breakfast.

"We should give the impression that everything is normal by going on with our duties, that way, you are less likely to be missed while you are gone," The King suggested after the morning meal. "Your mother and I will say goodbye now."

Gideon kissed his mother on the cheek. "I will come and find you, as soon as I get home."

Queen Paulina hugged him. "Please be careful, and look after Elizabeth."

"I'll guard her with my life, mother."

Thalios found Keslyn playing in the garden with Charlie. He sat down on one of the stone benches that lined the pathway.

"I am going to leave for a while. I want you to stay here and spend some well-deserved time with Merlyn."

"I would like that," Keslyn pushed into his head.

Keslyn and Charlie ran off to find Merlyn.

Grandma Rose hugged Elizabeth. "Come and see me when you return. Don't let those nasty elviron intimidate you."

"I won't, Gran.

"You can go," Bindyl told the driver of the carriage. "Gideon and I will drive today."

"Are you sure, sir?" the driver asked. "I know the way. The king has given me instructions."

"I know we can trust you, but I think this would be a good time for you to take a day or so off," said Bindyl, "but thank you for volunteering."

"Very well," the driver said.

They travelled through Kimadrian and across the border to Distardrian.

Not far from the border, King Kalidryd had arranged for them to stop at The Hornet's Nest Inn, to eat and rest for the night.

The innkeeper, an older elviron, was waiting by a table to serve them.

"What can I get for you today?" he asked. "King Kalidryd sent some supplies here just for you."

"Just some bread and cheese, and some ale, please," said Gideon.

"It's not very busy," said Bindyl, noticing they were the only customers. "Where is everyone?"

"The king asked that I close my establishment for the night, so you would not be... a disturbed," the Innkeeper informed him.

They ate in an uneasy silence. At the end of their meal, Elizabeth strolled around the room, curious about how the elviron lived.

"It's horrible here!" she said, as she looked at the dirty floors and walls.

"Keep your voice down, Elizabeth!" said Thalios. "King Kalidryd is trying to be courteous. Don't be a brat."

"I don't like it here either," said Gideon.

"Me either," said Bindyl.

"We could just keep going," said Gideon.

"But you have had no rest," said Thalios.

"I am not tired," said Gideon. "I have a bad feeling about this place. I don't want to spend the night here, that's for sure."

"I can take over driving the carriage for a while, give Bindyl a rest," said Gideon.

"I would really like to keep going, if it's okay with you, Thalios," Elizabeth said.

Thalios nodded in agreement.

"It's agreed then," said Gideon. "Barkeep, please have a change of horses ready for us. We have decided to continue our journey."

"Very well my lord," the elviron bar keeper said.

Fresh horses were harnessed to the carriage and the group went on their way.

"Well," said the elviron Innkeeper, as he watched them disappear down the road. "The king paid me well to close my establishment down. But now they have gone, I can open up and make even more money."

Gideon and Bindyl took turns driving the carriage through the night. When they arrived at the castle in Distardrian, they were greeted at the back of the castle by Drewmannus and two elviron guards.

"We weren't expecting you until noon," one of them said.

"We decided to keep going," said Thalios, helping Elizabeth exit the carriage.

They were led through the castle to King Kalidryd's private rooms. He stood when they entered.

"Welcome," he said, with a polite smile.

He ushered them into a room that had somewhat been cleaned up.

"You look exhausted," he said to Elizabeth. "You must all be tired. I suggest you rest for a while before you attempt to find Renmar."

"Good idea," said Gideon. "I for one, am more than ready to sleep."

"I will have my servant show you all to somewhere you can rest for a while," said King Kalidryd.

The servant returned a few minutes later, and was about to take Thalios to his room, when Elizabeth stopped him. "Will you look after the Mirronstep while I sleep for just a bit?"

"Of course," said Thalios. "The elviron won't come near me. They are too afraid of the druids."

Elizabeth was escorted to a room down the hall. She closed the door, putting her bag on the floor, and went over to the bed.

"Ugh! These covers are filthy."

She found a fairly clean spot on the floor. Threw her sleeping bag down and got into it.

It seemed that she had only been sleeping a few minutes, when she felt someone touching her on the shoulder.

Instinctively, she grabbed the hand and turned it backwards, pulling it towards her as she did so.

"You know, if I were really here, that would hurt... a lot," said Jesse, waiting for Elizabeth to release his hand.

"What are you doing here?"

"Thalios is asleep and someone has stolen the Mirronstep," said Jesse.

"Who? Wait, Jesse, don't go!" Jesse was fading before her eyes.

"Tell me who has the Mirronstep!" Elizabeth shouted, as he faded away completely.

Pushing the sleeping bag out of the way, she jumped to her feet, and ran to the door of her room. She turned the handle, but it was locked.

She stood back from the door and waved her hand. "Open!" she commanded in a loud voice.

The door flew open. Slamming hard against its hinges.

"I don't know where Thalios is!" she thought.

Elizabeth closed her eyes and thought about him. "Show me," she said.

The room faded and she could see Thalios fast asleep on the floor in another part of the castle. She looked around the room he was in, until she saw a door.

"Open!" she shouted.

Elizabeth raised both of her arms then held them out, shoulder length. She closed her eyes and bowed her head.

"Pull the arm that leads to Thalios," she said.

Her right arm tugged her along the corridor, until she came to an open door.

Elizabeth ran inside. Thalios was on the floor with a blanket over him. She knelt down by his side. The blanket that had been covering the Mirronstep was behind him. Elizabeth lifted it, already knowing that it was gone.

"Thalios, wake up!"

He stirred and opened his eyes. When he saw Elizabeth kneeling over him, he put his hand on where the Mirronstep had been resting.

"Where is it?" he said.

"It's been stolen."

Thalios struggled to his feet, reaching for his staff. "Who could have done this?" I would have awoken if anyone had come into the room."

"Not if whoever was in here used magic," said Elizabeth.

Thalios looked down at Elizabeth.

"Drewmannus!"

"I think so," she said.

"But why? What would he have to gain by stopping you from helping all the elviron?"

"I don't know, but I'm going to find out," she said.

"You go and find Gideon and Bindyl and wait for me here. I'm going down to where the Grymlons used to be kept. I think that's where Drewmannus has taken the Mirronstep."

Thalios hurried down the hallway.

Elizabeth ran in the other direction and down the stairs, as fast as she could.

She approached the door and waved her hand, it slowly opened. Inside the room, placed evenly around the wall, were five round tables, empty now for many a year. In the middle of the room, Drewmannus had the Mirronstep on the floor and was bent over, looking into it. Elizabeth crept into the room and came up behind him.

"What are you doing?" she said.

Drewmannus reeled around, wide eyed.

"I said, what are you doing?" she repeated.

"How did you find me?" he asked.

"I'm the chosen one, remember?"

"I am going to go to the future, and I, Drewmannus, am going to rule Distardrian instead of that cowardly king of ours. If you succeed with your plan, I will no longer be needed and I cannot allow that."

The Mirronstep

"Drewmannus, the king will always need you," Elizabeth said, trying to calm him. "You didn't have to steal the Mirronstep. We must work together now. We're so close to solving this, and all of you can lead the lives that you were meant to.

"King Morvand still has use for Vandrayven. In fact, Vandrayven has more work than he can handle. Don't ruin it for yourself and everyone else, not now. Besides, there is danger in the Mirronstep if you don't know how to use it."

"Why am I so afraid of her," he thought, pushing down an overpowering urge to fall to his knees, and ask her forgiveness for stealing the magical mirror.

Elizabeth looked into his eyes. Just for a moment, she thought she had changed his mind. Suddenly, he leapt into the mirror.

Without thinking, she jumped in behind him. They both popped out of the Mirronstep, into a room, but in a different part of the castle.

Part of the outside wall was missing and Elizabeth stepped back, suddenly realizing that a good portion of the floor was gone.

She instinctively put her hand to the pocket of the shirt she was wearing. It was empty.

"The little mirror is in the pocket of my jacket," she thought. "What will we do now?"

"I don't understand," said Drewmannus, a little bewildered by his surroundings. "The castle is in ruins. If this is the future, then where am I?"

"It looks as though it's been this way for a long time," Elizabeth said.

She went to the door and out into the hallway, and began walking along the corridor. Drewmannus followed her.

As they were walking, she felt Drewmannus touch her arm.

"Elizabeth," he whispered.

"What?" she asked.

I don't think we are alone," he said, looking past her to the corridor ahead.

Elizabeth turned to where he was pointing. Standing in the hallway in front of them was the figure of some sort of demon. It was covered in a brownish grey robe. Although a cowl covered its misshapen head, large pointed teeth came into view as it smiled at

them. The demon was holding a scythe. It was staring at Drewmannus, as it began to head towards them.

"What is it?" Drewmannus said.

"It's a wraith," said Elizabeth.

She grabbed the wizard's sleeve and began to drag him along
the hall, and then down a staircase.

"Come on, Drewmannus. He's going to try to kill you!"

Drewmannus, suddenly realizing that he was going to have to
run for his life, followed Elizabeth downwards; the wraith staying
on their heels. They continued down, until they were back at the
room where the Grymlons used to be kept.

Elizabeth ran into the room with Drewmannus close behind
her, slamming the door shut. She grabbed furniture and began
pushing it up against the door.

"Help me," she said.

Drewmannus helped her push a large wardrobe and some
heavy tables up against the door.

"What is that thing and why is it following us?" he asked.

The wraith pounded on the door.

"I told you. It's a wraith. The contract for using the Mirronstep says there will be a wraith waiting for you if you're not pure of
heart. I've used the Mirronstep more than once, so I don't think it's
after me, do you?"

Drewmannus shook his head. "What do I do?" he said, backing up against the wall.

"I don't know," she said.

The pounding on the door stopped, as the air in front of Elizabeth began to shimmer. The wraith appeared in front of her. As
he raised his scythe to strike her, she instinctively put her arm over
her head to protect herself.

Jesse suddenly appeared. "Do not touch her," he said, standing
head to head with the wraith.

Jesse held up his hand, produced a scythe of his own and
raised it. The wraith lowered his scythe and bowed his head. He
disappeared for an instant. Reappearing a moment later, in front of
Drewmannus, who was cowering on the floor.

The wraith grabbed Drewmannus by his robe. Elizabeth waved
her hand at the wraith and said, "Sleep."

The wraith turned to her, then back to Drewmannus.

"Your magic won't work, Elizabeth, that's why I'm here," said Jesse.

"Can you help him, Jesse?"

"No!" Jesse replied.

The wraith pulled Drewmannus off his feet. A sweeping sound from the scythe stopped, as it connected with Drewmannus' head. The severed head flew across the room, spraying the wall with blood as it hit. Elizabeth watched in horror, as the head bounced off the furniture stacked up against the door, it came to rest on the floor with a sickening thud. A headless Drewmannus stood for a few seconds, his hands flailing in the air, as though searching for his head, before his body crumpled to the floor.

Elizabeth stood in the middle of the room, frozen with fear. The wraith turned and walked towards her. When it reached her, it stopped. She looked up into his face, seeing only blackness where his eyes should be. The wraith seemed to return her gaze for a moment, before he moved around her. The air shimmered once more, as the wraith disappeared.

Elizabeth dropped to the floor.

"I think I might have a heart attack if that thing returns," she said, turning to Jesse, only to find that he had gone.

She sat on the bare floor for a minute or two, alone in someone else's time.

"Get out of here!" was the first thought that came into her head.

She got up and began pulling the furniture away from the door. She ran up the steps and out through the main entrance.

Elizabeth kept running until the castle was in the distance, stopping to catch her breath only when she was sure it was safe.

She sat down by a tree. "I'm stranded here. I'm tired and hungry, and I have nowhere to go."

"I must calm down," she thought, feeling panic in her chest. "I know. I'll call a Pennar! Perhaps they survived whatever happened here."

Elizabeth knelt down and called Pennarius' name into the ground and waited.

"It might take a while for him to get here from the badlands," she thought, closing her eyes.

"If he comes, I'll ask him to take me to the Elven Realm, if there still is an Elven Realm. I'll just rest here for a few moments," she thought, trying to stay awake.

Chapter Twenty Five

Elizabeth's consciousness surfaced with the realization that she was no longer alone. When she opened her eyes, a black Pennar with a golden mane and tail was standing in front of her.

"Who calls my father's name?" the pennar asked.

"My name is Elizabeth, I..."

"I know who you are," said the pennar. "You and I met many years ago. How did you get here?"

"I came through a device that can take one backwards or forwards in time," said Elizabeth. "Why do you ask?"

"Oh, no reason," said the pennar, not looking Elizabeth in the eye. "My father told us many stories of you when we were young."

"What is your name?" asked Elizabeth.

"Lizzy, after you."

"I'm flattered," said Elizabeth. "How is Pennarius?"

"We are blessed with long life, but he is old now, not long for this world I fear."

"But he was fairly young when I knew him," said Elizabeth. "How much farther into the future have I come."

"Oh, I would say about seventy or so years," said Lizzy.

Lizzy stood patiently, waiting for Elizabeth to decide what to do.

"Will you take me to Kimadrian?"

"Yes," said Lizzy. "Jump up on my back and we will be there in no time."

Elizabeth hopped onto the pennar's back and they flew off into the clouds. When they reached the Kimadrian border, Lizzy landed.

"Do you know the way to the castle in Kimadrian?" Elizabeth asked.

"Yes. I have been there many times," said Lizzy. "Pennarius used to take us there and show us where you lived. He even took us to Humadria and showed us the entrance to the Human Realm. No one guards it anymore, and no one lives at the castle. In fact, there aren't many elves or elviron left."

"In that case, would you take me to the gates of Humadria?" asked Elizabeth.

"Of course," said Lizzy.

They flew across Kimadrian, over the village of Kimadria and over the top of the castle, until they reached the gates of Humadria.

Lizzy landed in front of them.

"Thanks for the ride," said Elizabeth. "Give my regards to Pennarius."

"I will," said Lizzy.

Elizabeth watched as she rose into the air and flew away, When Lizzy was no longer visible, she opened the side door and headed up into the dark streets of Humadria.

It was deserted as she walked upwards through the town. The shop fronts were mostly dark. Elizabeth could see the shadow of an elf moving around inside, here and there, but it was mostly abandoned.

She came out of the willow tree, looking across the bridge to Willow View Cottage. The garden was overgrown with grass and weeds. The roof of the cottage had a hole in it, and the white washed walls were peeling and dirty.

Elizabeth stepped across the bridge, and through the gate. As she made her way along the path, she noticed the garden seat was still there. She turned the corner and knocked on the back door. There was no answer. She tried the door handle, and to her surprise, it was unlocked. When Elizabeth entered the kitchen, it was dusty, abandoned. It was obvious that no one had lived there for a long time.

"Anyone home?" she called, knowing she would get no answer.

She made her way down the hall to her grandma's bedroom, opening the door slowly, wondering what she would find. She looked around the room. One of the window panes was broken. A small strand of ivy had pushed its way in through the hole and was creeping along the floor.

Grandma Rose's bed still rested against the wall. Elizabeth moved it out of the way and felt for the switch. The door slid open and she entered the secret library. All the books were still there. She tried the light switch, but it didn't work.

Elizabeth went back to the kitchen. She found a candle and a box of matches. She returned to the library, and lit the candle. She spilled a few drops of the candle wax on a chair and put the candle in the middle.

"I wonder if there's anything in here that can help me find my way home," she thought.

She moved farther into the room, trying to adjust to the dimness, when she accidentally kicked a small box laying on the floor. She picked it up and dusted it off. The box had ornate carvings all over it. She opened the lid and something jumped out, running into the corner of the room.

"Who's there?" she said, startled.

"It's just me," the little creature said.

"Who is me? Come out of there, so I can see you."

The creature stepped forward into the light.

"Who are you? And how on earth did you fit into this box? asked Elizabeth.

"My name is Tweekawokagy, I am a Pooka. The box is mine. It's magic. You can call me Tweeka, everyone else does. Who are you?"

"My name is Elizabeth."

"Oh, so you are Elizabeth, eh," said Tweeka. "You are the one who disappeared and never came back."

"What a strange looking little thing you are," Elizabeth thought.

She stood for a moment, looking at the creature. She noticed he stood about a foot high, with brown hair all over his body. He was wearing a hat that spiralled at the top. His long, pointed ears peeped out from either side. A pair of black and white checked shorts covered the lower half of his body. Below them were sturdy, hairy legs. He looked like a rabbit, but he was slimmer than a rabbit. He had a long pointed nose, and pointed front teeth.

"I went through a mirror into the future, and now I can't get home," said Elizabeth.

"I can get you home," said Tweeka. "I will have to go with you, but I can get you back to your time."

"How can you do that?" she asked.

"It's magic, he said.

"I like magic," Elizabeth said. "What do we have to do?"

"You have to take me to where you came through the Mirronstep. From there, I can take you home to your time."

"How do you know about the Mirronstep?" Elizabeth asked.

"I know the Mirronstep, because I made it," said Tweeka.

"You made the Mirronstep? I thought the druids made it."

"No, I made it and gave it to the druids. In return they gave me a very long and happy life."

Tweeka began dancing around the room, singing to himself as he did so.

"Will you take me home now?" said Elizabeth.

"I most certainly will," said Tweeka, "on one condition."

"What would that be?" asked Elizabeth.

"When we get back to your time, you have to put me back into the box."

"I can do that," said Elizabeth.

"It may not be that easy," said Tweeka.

"Why not?" asked Elizabeth.

His pointed teeth became prominent as he smiled, "Because I might not want to go back into the box."

"Well, I won't force you," said Elizabeth.

"Then I won't help you."

Elizabeth thought for a moment. "I can get you back into the box."

"How?" Tweeka asked.

"You'll see," said Elizabeth. "Come on, let's get moving."

She knelt down, lifted him up, and put him in the crook of her arm. She picked up the box and opened it. There was a book in the bottom. She picked it up and read the title. 'Instructions on how to get Elizabeth back to her time.' She put the book back in the box.

"Why is there a book about me in the box?" she asked Tweeka.

"You know, I could explain that, but it would probably take more time than you would like. So I think you should just trust me and take me to where you came through the Mirronstep."

"I should take the box with me," she said.

"You can leave it here," said Tweeka. "It will still be where you left it when you return."

"But I'm going backwards in time, not forwards," said Elizabeth.

Tweeka looked at her and displayed his teeth again.

"Okay, I get it," she said. "I'm not going to ask you to try and explain. I don't think I would understand anyway."

She blew out the candle and put the box beside it, on the chair by the door.

Elizabeth closed the door and put the bed back where she had found it. She closed up the room and left the cottage with her new friend.

She went around to the front of the cottage and stood by the gate.

"Where is all the traffic," she said, looking left and right. The road that passed the cottage used to be rather busy, now there's no traffic at all."

Elizabeth looked down at the Pooka under her arm. "What happened?" she asked.

"When you didn't come back, the Grymlons died," said Tweeka. "Everything turned bad and rather quickly. The elves became sick and a lot of them died. The elviron got just as sick and most of them died too. The seasons changed in the Human Realm. That messed up the plants and a lot of the animals died. Everything that is left now, has become pretty good at surviving, but the world is nothing like it was when you left. That's why I must help you get back to your time, so that you can put things right again."

Elizabeth felt tears well up in her eyes. She decided not to ask any more questions, afraid that she might lose control of the fear that was tightly pushed down inside of her.

She turned away from the road and went around to the back of the cottage. With the little Pooka still under her arm, Elizabeth walked over the bridge and into the Willow tree. The two of them made their way down to the gates of Humadria.

Once they were into the Elven Realm, Elizabeth called for Lizzy. A few minutes later she flew into view.

"Hello Tweeka," said Lizzy.

"You know him?" Elizabeth said.

"Why yes, we have met several times over the years. That is, until someone manages to get him back in the box," said Lizzy.

"But the box was in my grandma's house," said Elizabeth.

"I can make the box be wherever I want when I am inside of it," said Tweeka.

Elizabeth jumped up onto Lizzy's back. Tweeka sat in front of her, and they flew to the castle in Distardrian.

Lizzy dropped them at the wall of the castle and flew away. Elizabeth and Tweeka made their way to where she and Drewmannus had appeared.

"What do we do now?" asked Elizabeth.

"You must take me to where you stepped into the Mirronstep when you were here," said Tweeka.

Elizabeth ran down the steps, until they reached the room where she had followed Drewmannus into the Mirronstep.

"There was a wraith here," said Elizabeth.

"Don't worry about him," said Tweeka. "I put him in the contract to stop bad people from moving around in time. The wraith was waiting for the wizard. His heart was not pure and he was doomed as soon as he stepped into the mirror. It has gone now."

Elizabeth stood where the Mirronstep had been. Tweeka stood in front of her. "Take my hands and close your eyes. Try not to fall, as this may feel a bit odd."

Elizabeth leaned over, grasped the Pooka's little hands and closed her eyes. She felt as though she was riding on a roller coaster. When the motion stopped, the Pooka let go of her hands and she opened her eyes.

"Are we back?" she asked.

"Yes," Tweeka said.

Elizabeth looked down. By her side was the Mirronstep. She picked it up and the two of them left the room where the Grymlons once lived.

The Mirronstep

As they were leaving, Thalios and King Kalidryd came hurrying towards them. Thalios looked down at the little Pooka, then back to Elizabeth.

"We have been looking everywhere in the castle," he said. "The king sent guards looking for Drewmannus and the elves, and I went looking for you. This is the last place we were coming to," said Thalios.

Elizabeth looked down at Tweeka.

"Only minutes have passed here," he said.

"Tweekawokagy, what are you doing here?" said Thalios.

"Does everyone know about this little creature except me?" said Elizabeth.

"Tweeka was put into a box and hidden by the druids hundreds of years ago. He escapes now and then, but your grandma has always managed to get him back in," said Thalios.

"He made the Mirronstep," said Elizabeth.

"That is true," said Thalios.

"Then why didn't you ask him about it instead of making me look for it?" said Elizabeth.

"I told you," said Tweeka, "the druids took it from me when I made it. I never saw it again until today."

The king, who had been standing behind Thalios, stepped forward. "Where is Drewmannus?"

"Drewmannus is dead," said Elizabeth.

King Kalidryd became suddenly alert. "How did he die?"

"Drewmannus stole the Mirronstep and went through it without considering what he might find there," said Elizabeth.

"What did he find?" asked the King.

"He found a wraith, and it killed him," said Elizabeth. King Kalidryd sighed. "We have been together for many years. I will miss him. Did he say why he went through the Mirronstep?"

Elizabeth looked at the elviron king and thought, "I hate what you stand for, but I know you're trying to right the wrongs of hundreds of years."

"He was going to try to save the elviron," she said.

"He was trying to do something good?" said King Kalidryd.

"Yes, for all of you," she said.

"Good," said the King, turning away and walking down the hall. "Good."

Thalios turned to Elizabeth. "Liar," he said, quietly.

Elizabeth shrugged. She picked Tweeka up and followed the king.

When they reached the main hall, the two elves came running up behind them.

"Are you all right, Liz?" said Gideon, grabbing her by the hand.

"I'm fine. We just had a little adventure," she said, looking down at Tweeka and smiling.

"Who is this?" said Bindyl.

"This is Tweekawokagy, he is a Pooka," said Elizabeth.

"Nice to meet you," said Bindyl.

"You, too," said Tweeka.

"Is anyone hungry?" asked the King.

They all looked at one another, wondering what sort of food the elviron would have to offer.

"It's all right," said King Kalidryd. "I have had some food brought in, that will be palatable to you. I think that you will be pleasantly surprised."

"Well, I don't know about the rest of you, but I am starving," said Gideon.

"Me, too," said Elizabeth.

King Kalidryd led them to the main dining room, which had not been used in years.

It had been cleaned up and a table was standing against the back wall, full of breads, assorted fruits and vegetables,

"If you will excuse me," said King Kalidryd. "I have some matters to attend to."

Tweeka jumped up onto the food table and filled up a plate. He jumped down, grabbed the plate and sat in the corner of the room to enjoy his food.

"Well, what happened?" asked Gideon.

"Drewmannus jumped into the Mirronstep before I could stop him," said Elizabeth, between bites of food.

"And you followed him in?" said Thalios.

"I had to," said Elizabeth. "He had no idea what was going to happen to him."

"What did happen?" asked Bindyl.

"Well, he went through and I followed," said Elizabeth. "When we reached the other side, I asked Drewmannus why he went into the Mirronstep, when I had asked him not to."

"What did he say?" asked Thalios.

"He.....,"

"Your majesty," Thalios said, loudly, as the king returned. "Back so soon?"

"He said," Elizabeth repeated in a quieter tone, "that he wanted to be the first to go through, to see if he could help me stop Renmar from stealing the Grymlons."

Thalios looked from Elizabeth to the king.

"Oh," said Bindyl. "Perhaps you and I should go into your adventure in greater length, a little later."

"Good idea," said Elizabeth, smiling at the king.

"Where did you find him?" asked Gideon, looking over at Tweeka.

"In a box, at Gran's," Elizabeth said.

"He's a cute little thing," said Bindyl, waving at him.

The food was cleared away and everyone sat down to form a plan.

"What should we do now?" asked King Kalidryd.

"I want to go back down to the room where the Grymlons were," said Elizabeth. "That's where Renmar took the Grymlons. I remember what Renmar looked like. If I can put a clear enough picture in my mind. I may be able to find him before he lost them."

"I think that's an excellent plan," said Thalios.

"First though, I would like to try and rest," said Elizabeth. "I was only gone from here for a few minutes. A whole day passed by when I went forward in time."

"Perhaps after your ordeal, it might be a good idea if all of you rested for a while," said King Kalidryd.

"I will have the Mirronstep with me this time," said Elizabeth.

"I'm not tired. I'll stand guard at your door, so you can get some rest," said Gideon.

Tweeka had been sitting in the corner, watching all that went on with great interest. "Can I come and rest with you in your room?" he asked Elizabeth.

"Absolutely," she said, picking him up and making her way along the hallway.

Elizabeth reached her room, closed the door and put Tweeka down on the floor. She knelt down and straightened out her sleeping bag.

Tweeka stood in the middle of the room and closed his eyes. The little box he had jumped out of, appeared on the floor.

"How did you do that?" asked Elizabeth.

"Magic," said Tweeka.

He began pacing back and forth across the room.

"What's wrong?" asked Elizabeth.

"I have to go back into the box," said Tweeka.

"Then do so, and thank you for all your help."

"I don't want to go back in the box," he said.

"What if I go into the box with you?" said Elizabeth.

"Why would you?" said Tweeka.

"You said that the druids have given you a long and happy life. So show me your life, Tweeka."

"Well come on then, let's go," Tweeka said.

"Close your eyes. He told her, "I don't want you to feel sick."

She took his hand and closed her eyes, and together they stepped into the box.

Elizabeth opened her eyes and looked around. Tweeka let go of her hand and danced across the purple grass. The sky was green and the flowers were browns and blues.

"Well, do you like my home?" said Tweeka.

"It's a bit different than mine," said Elizabeth.

"Yes it is, but if you don't like it, you can change it," he said.

"How?" asked Elizabeth.

"Just think of what you like and it will happen," said Tweeka.

Elizabeth closed her eyes and thought about the sky being blue and the grass being green. She opened her eyes and everything was just as she had thought about.

She closed her eyes. "Toby, my favourite horse is here with a saddle and a bridle, ready for me to ride." When she opened them, there he was.

Elizabeth laughed. "Can I stay here with you for a little while?"

"Of course," said Tweeka.

He began to run off, hesitated and turned. "I'll be back in a few minutes. You go ahead and have fun."

Elizabeth watched Tweeka disappear into the distance.

She sat down and ate chocolate ice cream. She rode Toby at a gallop across the fields. She imagined that she could fly, and she did.

A little while later, Tweeka returned. "It's time for you to go home now. You need your rest."

"Unfortunately, you're right," said Elizabeth.

"Now that you know of me. If you need me, just open the box. You'll find it on the chair at your Gran's house," said Tweeka.

Elizabeth knelt down and hugged him.

"Thank you," she said. "How do I get out of the box?"

"Close your eyes and imagine that you are back in the room," said Tweeka.

Elizabeth closed her eyes. When she opened them again, she was back in the room and the box was gone. She got into her sleeping bag, put the Mirronstep beside her and fell asleep.

A little while later, Elizabeth woke. She sat up and put her hand down by the Mirronstep to make sure that it was still there.

As she stood, stretching the sleep away, someone knocked on the door.

"Come in," she said.

Gideon entered with a cup in his hand. "Would you like a cup of tea?"

Where did you get that?" she said.

"I brought it with me, just in case you wanted a cup of that tea that you like to kill for."

Elizabeth took the cup, sipping the tea. "I knew I loved you for some reason."

Gideon laughed. "Come on Liz, Thalios is waiting for you down in the room where you and Drewmannus went through the Mirronstep."

"What about the king, and you and Bindyl?" she asked.

"Only Bindyl will go with you. Thalios will stand guard by the Mirronstep, and I will be outside the door, to make sure no one else tries to steal it again."

Elizabeth finished her tea. She picked up the Mirronstep, and they went down into the base of the castle. Bindyl and Thalios were already waiting for her.

King Kalidryd stood outside the door. "I think I will wait here with Gideon."

Elizabeth put the Mirronstep on the floor and took Bindyl's hand. Together, they stepped into the mirror.

Elizabeth and Bindyl opened their eyes, looking around the room.

"The Grymlons have already been taken. We may have just missed him. If we hurry, we might catch up with him," said Elizabeth.

With one hand on his dagger, Bindyl cracked the door open and peered outside.

"No guards, come on," he said.

They turned and headed towards the dungeons.

"I know the way," said Bindyl.

They made their way through the dimly lit hallway, past the guard room and out through the door to the side.

"Where do we go from here to get to the Human Realm?" Bindyl asked.

The entrance to Dragon Hill is by that wooded area over there," said Elizabeth, pointing to a patch of trees about fifty feet away.

"That close?" said Bindyl.

They entered the trees and found the large oak. Elizabeth pushed on the base and a door appeared. They entered the tree, and she found the torch and lit it. Bindyl followed her upwards along the corridor. They continued until they came to a roof. Bindyl stopped, but Elizabeth kept going. As she touched the roof, it opened up and they could see the stars. They stepped up onto the grass, right by the spot where the Dragon was supposed to have been slain.

Renmar was nowhere to be found.

"Come on," said Elizabeth. "If we just missed him, he's on his way into town to find the druid."

Bindyl grew to human size and they hurried towards Uffington.

The Mirrorstep

When they arrived it was late and the streets were empty. The local tavern was still open and they peeped into the window.

"There are some people in there, but none in druid's robes," said Elizabeth.

Bindyl turned, hearing voices from around the back of the building. They crept to the edge of the wall and looked around the corner.

Renmar was there with a bag slung over his shoulder.

A tall man in white robes was talking to him.

"That's Alomer," Elizabeth said.

"He doesn't seem to be very happy to be talking to Renmar," said Bindyl.

"That's because he knows Renmar's been bitten by a vampire," said Elizabeth.

Alomer suddenly backed away from Renmar and began walking towards them.

"Quick," said Elizabeth. "Alomer is leaving!"

They ducked behind a bush, as Alomer stormed passed them. Renmar staggered after him. Then stopped, leaning against the tavern wall.

"He looks exhausted," thought Elizabeth, as she watched him stagger down the street.

Bindyl suddenly turned on his heel, and Elizabeth turned to see what he was looking at.

Standing behind them, was an old woman.

"You cannot save the Grymlons," she said.

"Who are you?" asked Bindyl.

"My name is Lydia, said the old woman, looking at Elizabeth. "You and the elf can come and go through the mirror as much as you please, but you will never succeed in saving the Grymlons."

"Why not?" asked Elizabeth.

The old woman cackled, showing rotten, browned teeth.

"Because they are not meant to be saved," she said.

"Then we are all doomed," said Bindyl.

"Not true," said the old witch. "You must go and see the Dragon," she said.

"What Dragon?" said Elizabeth.

"George's Dragon," she replied.

Elizabeth and Bindyl looked at one another. They both turned to where the witch had been standing, but instead of the old woman, a small grey hare stood where Lydia had been. It nodded to them both before hopping away into the darkness.

"There's no point trying to save him now. If what the old witch said is true, if we try to save him, we may be tampering with time," said Elizabeth, "let's go back to the Mirronstep and see if Thalios knows what the witch meant."

They made their way back to Dragon Hill, and down into Distardrian.

When they returned to the castle, Elizabeth held onto Bindyl's hand. She touched the small mirror in her pocket with her other hand. They popped out of the Mirronstep and fell onto the floor. Thalios helped them up.

"What did you find out?" he asked.

"We met with an old witch," said Bindyl.

"She said her name was Lydia," said Elizabeth.

"Lydia Sheers?" said Thalios.

"Do you know her?" asked Bindyl.

"I know of her," Thalios answered. "What did she say to you?"

"She said we could not save the Grymlons, and that we were to go and see the Dragon," said Elizabeth.

"What Dragon?" asked Thalios.

"George's Dragon," said Bindyl.

"What does that mean?" asked Thalios.

"I think I know," said Elizabeth. "Bindyl, I have to go to Uffington and this time, you can't go with me."

"But I…" Bindyl started to say.

"No," said Elizabeth. "I must contact my brother. Thalios, we need to go back to the human realm. Bindyl, you can go home."

"Why?" he asked.

"Trust me Bindyl. I think your job is done," said Elizabeth. "Thalios, please come with us. I think I know what happened to the Grymlons, and I think I know why we can't find them. I'm beginning to suspect this whole thing is somehow connected to the Dragon."

Thalios picked up the Mirronstep and they left the room. King Kalidryd and Gideon were still waiting in the hallway.

"We are going back up to the Human Realm," she told the king.

"Things didn't work out, I gather," he said.

"I'm not sure what's going on," said Elizabeth, "but I'm going to find out."

"I will arrange for a carriage to take us to Kimadrian," said King Kalidryd.

"You don't have to come with us," said Elizabeth.

"I want to," said King Kalidryd. "I want to follow any progress you make. They were our Grymlons, after all."

Chapter Twenty Six

Gideon and Bindyl took turns driving the carriage. They stopped at the Hornet's Nest Inn, changed horses and continued on.

When they reached the castle at Kimadrian, Gideon drove around to the back wall.

"King Kalidryd will need a blanket to shield him from the sunlight," said Gideon.

"I'll run in and get one," said Elizabeth.

As she opened the gate, she was greeted by two guards.

"Prince Gideon and I have returned from Distardrian," she told the guards. "We have a visitor with us. Please tell the king we have returned."

"We cannot leave our post, my lady," one of the guards said.

Gideon stepped out of the carriage, Bindyl followed him.

When the guards saw them, they stood to attention, saluting.

"You can go," said Gideon. "Lieutenant Blakely and I will guard the gate until you return."

"Yes, sir," they both said at once.

Elizabeth followed the guards to the back entrance of the royal apartments. She hurried to her room, grabbed a blanket and ran back to the carriage.

King Kalidryd exited the carriage with the blanket over his head and shoulders. Thalios guided him into the castle. Once he was safely inside, the guards were allowed to return to their post.

When Gideon and Bindyl met up with Elizabeth and Thalios in the library, King Morvand and King Kalidryd were already seated.

"We had no luck," Elizabeth said. "I'm going to go up to the Human Realm and travel to Uffington."

"I will come with you to the Human Realm," said King Kalidryd.

"You wouldn't last a day, not in our sunlight," said Elizabeth.

"She is right, Kalidryd," said King Morvand. "Let the girl go and try to find out what is happening."

"I won't let anything happen to the Mirronstep," said Elizabeth.

"I trust you, now hurry back, and let me know how everything goes," said King Kalidryd.

Elizabeth touched the old king's hand, as she looked into his watery blue eyes.

"He seems to have hope in his eyes, instead of the dead fish look I usually see," she thought.

"I could go with you," said Gideon.

"Thank you, but no," said Elizabeth.

"I have come to know that look," said Gideon. "I'll stay here and wait for you to return."

"Thalios, I think I want you to come with me."

"Let's get going, then," he said, heading for the door.

"I'm going to go and see my mother," said Gideon.

"And I'm going to go home and get some peace and quiet," said Bindyl.

I'll walk down the hall with you," said Gideon, following him out.

"Have you ever heard of this Dragon they are talking about, Gideon?" Bindyl asked, as they made their way through the castle.

"Not much, but I don't like what I have heard about it so far. Elizabeth told me that the Dragon used to eat people; women in particular, I think."

"Elizabeth is certainly brave," said Bindyl.

"Do me a favour, Bindyl."

"What is that, Gideon?"

"Marry a female who has no desire for danger."

Bindyl smiled at his friend. "Consider it done."

***

Thalios and Elizabeth arrived at the cottage, and Thalios brought Grandma Rose up to date on the events that had taken place, while Elizabeth went to her room with the Mirronstep. She propped it up in the corner of the room and waved her hand. It shimmered for a second or two before disappearing.

She sat in the easy chair by the window. "Okay, now for Jesse," she said, closing her eyes. A minute or so later, he appeared.

"What can I do for you, sis?"

"I want you to release Bindyl from his obligation. I don't know why you are making him accompany me, but I think this little adventure is almost over. I am going to see a Dragon and Bindyl can't be there."

"I think you're right," said Jesse. "I'll go and see Bindyl and tell him that his task is finished."

Jesse was about to go, then he turned to Elizabeth.

"Be careful, Liz."

Elizabeth looked at her brother. "When this is over, what happens to you?"

"I don't know, but I think it might be all right. Get some rest, Liz. Don't worry about me," said Jesse, becoming more and more transparent as he spoke.

"I hate the way it makes me feel when I have to contact him," she said, climbing onto the bed and falling fast asleep.

Grandma Rose came into her room a few minutes later. She unfolded the blanket placed at the foot of Elizabeth's bed, covered her with it, and went back to the kitchen.

"Where is Elizabeth?" said Thalios.

"She's asleep," said Grandma. "Come on Thalios. Let's go for a walk along the river."

"A walk along the river sounds wonderful." Thalios held out his arm and Rose took it.

They strolled out into the garden, went through the gate and over the bridge.

Instead of walking towards the willow tree, they turned left and strolled towards the village restaurant on the riverbank.

Elizabeth slept on, lapsing into a dreamless sleep, giving her mind and body much needed rest.

Chapter Twenty Seven

Bindyl rode through the gate and into his courtyard. His servant put his horse away and Bindyl entered the cottage.

"Please prepare some food," he informed the maid. "I will eat in the living room."

The maid bobbed a curtsy and headed to the kitchen. Bindyl poured himself a glass of wine, sat in his favourite chair and took a long drink. He leaned back, closing his eyes, and dozed off.

A few minutes later, Bindyl opened his eyes to see a familiar figure standing in front of him.

"What do you want now, uncle?" he asked.

"I came to tell you that you have succeeded in your task. I will now be moving on from this horrible place," said Brondly.

"Does this mean I am no longer burdened with your sins, uncle?"

Brondly opened his mouth to say something, but nothing came out. He grabbed his throat, trying to clear it, attempting to speak.

Bindyl sat forward in his chair, watching his uncle struggle.

Jesse appeared beside Brondly. "You were never burdened with your uncle's sins, Bindyl. We knew you would accompany Elizabeth."

Jesse stepped in front of Brondly, moving closer to Bindyl's chair. "We knew that you would have gone with her, with or without your uncle's blackmailing demands. We just wanted to see how far he would go in his wickedness. You did a good job of protecting Elizabeth in a situation where she could not use her powers. I, as her brother, thank you for that."

Bindyl nodded toward his uncle. "What's wrong with him?"

Jesse turned to Brondly. "You didn't think that we have been watching you all this time?"

Fear ran across Brondly's face.

"Say goodbye to your uncle Brondly, Bindyl. He is right. It is time for him to move on."

"Goodbye uncle," said Bindyl.

The room darkened and a faint sound of shrieking could be heard, as Jesse stepped back a couple more paces, wisps of swirling grey mist came up from around Brondly's feet. Four hooded figures rose up from the mist, each one carrying a long chain.

Brondly looked towards Bindyl with wide eyes. He found his voice and screamed, as one of the figures threw his chain outward, wrapping it around Brondly's ankles.

"What are they?!" Brondly shouted, looking down at the chains.

Two of the other figures threw their chains toward him. Each one wrapping around his arms, stretching them outwards, as though on a cross. Brondly's screams were choked off as the fourth hooded figure's chain wrapped itself around Brondly's neck. The hooded figures began to sink into the mist, pulling Brondly down with them.

"They are your transportation," said Jesse.

"Where is he going," said Bindyl. "I thought he was already in hell."

"No, Brondly wasn't in hell. He was at the edge of hell, where the not quite bad enough to go to hell, elves go. A sort of limbo, you might say. Now he's going all the way down," said Jesse.

Brondly managed to pull one of his arms closer, and grabbed at the chain around his neck, loosening it.

"No!" he screamed, "I made a deal!"

"No you didn't," said Jesse. "You tried to bargain with a situation that fate had already put into play."

"But they promised! They said that if I could persuade Bindyl to go with the witch, they would let me go."

"Yes, they did, but you neglected to ask them where they would let you go to," said Jesse. "You assumed when they agreed to let you go: that you would go up. You should have asked which direction you were going, Brondly. They never lie."

Brondly screamed again, trying to pull the chains loose. Blackness filled the ring. The ring faded and the screams faded with it, as the room returned to normal.

Bindyl sat back in his chair. "Is that what I have in store for me?" he asked Jesse.

"No, a lot nicer place is reserved for you, my friend. Now sleep for a while."

"But I'm hungry," said Bindyl, as his eyes closed and consciousness left him. Jesse gently took the glass out of his hand. Placed it on the table beside the chair, and faded away.

Chapter Twenty Eight

Elizabeth sat up and stretched. Grandma Rose peeped her head around the door, as Elizabeth put her feet to the floor.

"Want a cuppa?" she asked.

"Oh, yes please, Gran. I'll be there in a minute."

Elizabeth splashed some water on her face and headed for the kitchen.

"Did you have a good nap?" asked Thalios, sipping his own cup of tea.

"I did, thanks."

"Drink your tea, both of you," said Grandma.

"It's time we got going," said Thalios. "If I drink another cup of tea, I'll bust."

Grandma cleared away the cups and Elizabeth was tidying up the kitchen table, when they heard a scratching at the back door.

Elizabeth opened it and Charlie entered, brushing against her leg.

"What are you doing here?" asked Elizabeth, picking her up.

"I missed you. When are you coming home?" Charlie said, brushing the side of her furry face against Elizabeth's cheek.

"Soon, I have a few more things to attend to here, then I'll come and see you and Merlyn. Try to keep that mischievous little Dragon out of trouble till I get there."

Charlie purred and licked Elizabeth's face. "You promise that you will be home soon?"

"Charlie, why are you so worried?" said Elizabeth.

Charlie stopped purring. "I just feel a bit scared for you, that's all."

"You? Charlie the Brave?" Elizabeth said, with a grin. "Go back down to the Elven Realm and look after Merlyn."

"Tell Keslyn I am going with Elizabeth, and I will return soon," said Thalios.

Charlie went to the door. Elizabeth followed her and let her out.

"I'd like to come with you if you would let me," said Grandma.

"No!" both Elizabeth and Thalios said, at the same time.

Grandma Rose let out a laugh. "Very well then, it's agreed. I stay here."

"Sorry, Gran. It's just that we need you here. Someone will have to let the others know if anything goes wrong."

"Legend says, that Dragon has killed many women, Elizabeth, don't add yourself to the list," said Grandma.

"I won't, Gran. You worry too much."

Thalios followed Elizabeth out to the car.

"Do you know anything about this Dragon?" she asked.

"I know some of the story," said Thalios. "You know - about George slaying the Dragon and saving the maiden, who was offered to the Dragon to save the rest of the town. St George's day falls on the 23rd of April. There are so many stories about this man. There are stories in many countries about the same man slaying a Dragon in each one. Are you sure that Lydia Sheers said George's Dragon?"

"Yes," said Elizabeth.

By the time they reached the car park, on the hill of the White Horse, it was fully dark.

"I'll stay down here and keep watch," said Thalios.

Elizabeth climbed up the slope to Dragons Hill.

She reached the mound, sat down in the middle of it and closed her eyes, falling into a light trance.

After a minute or two, she opened her eyes to the sound of snorting.

"You are a very brave maiden to summon me. I have eaten many young maidens in my time," said the Dragon, now crouched directly in front of her.

"You are welcome to try and take a taste of me," said Elizabeth. "Although, I don't think you will find me very appealing."

She stood, avoiding the heat from the Dragon's breath,

"I suspect that you may be right," said the Dragon.

"Aren't you supposed to be dead? Didn't George slay you?" Elizabeth asked, walking back and forth in front of him.

"It is true," said the Dragon. "A valiant soul did despatch me to a place other than here, but I am a Dragon. I have obligations to both good and evil, and I do not answer to the same rules as humans. Do you have a question for me?"

"A few hundred years ago, an elf by the name of Renmar came up into the Human Realm with a set of five orbs," said Elizabeth.

"Yes, you mean the Grymlons. You must be the human girl in the prophesy."

"You know about me?" she asked.

"I do. In fact I have been waiting for you to call me," said the Dragon.

"How do you…? Never mind. Renmar was attacked by something. He went back down to the Elven Realm, but left the Grymlons here."

"This is true," said the Dragon. "The elviron was here and he did leave the Grymlons. You are also correct about him being attacked. The creature that attacked him has long since ceased to exist, but I think the elviron must have fought courageously for his life. I noticed that his wounds were quite extensive."

"What happened to the Grymlons?" said Elizabeth.

"I ate them," said the Dragon.

Elizabeth stopped, turning to the Dragon. "Why?"

"Because I was supposed to. I knew that Renmar would be coming up here with the Grymlons. Fate took a hand in those events. I was the one who arranged for the creature to attack him, so that I could eat the Grymlons."

"Why didn't you attack Renmar?" Elizabeth asked.

"Renmar and I came to an agreement. I persuaded him to give me the Grymlons and caused a lapse in time so that no one would know what happened. He went down to the Elviron Realm without them, in the hope that he would not be punished, if his superiors could not prove that he had taken them."

"They killed him for his crime," said Elizabeth. "That's why he never mentioned you, he didn't remember."

"I know," said the Dragon.

"You could have just killed him up here," said Elizabeth.

"That was not my task. I was instructed only to eat the Grymlons. I was to arrange for Renmar to be disabled in some other manner so as not to interfere with future events."

"Told by whom?" Elizabeth asked.

"I am unable to say."

"There were two sets of Grymlons," said Elizabeth.

The Dragon stared into her eyes. "This I know."

"What is your role in all of this, Dragon? You play a part in the Grymlons existence don't you," said Elizabeth.

"You are correct."

"What do I have to do to save the Grymlons that are left?" she asked.

"You cannot save the other set of Grymlons because they are not meant to be saved. I want you to bring them to me."

"If I let them die, the humans and the elves will be doomed," said Elizabeth.

"Not if you do as I tell you," said the Dragon.

"I'm listening," said Elizabeth.

"You must go and get the remaining set of Grymlons and bring them to me. You must let me eat them. You will also bring with you two containers that are air tight and waterproof."

"What then?" Elizabeth asked.

"Then, we shall see," said the Dragon, turning and looking down at Thalios. "Go now and follow my instructions."

Thalios, who had been watching the Dragon intently, turned away from his gaze.

The Dragon turned his attention back to Elizabeth. "When you return, don't bring the druid with you. He is constantly trying to get into my mind. It is very irritating," he said. "Leave now and do as I ask. If you do this thing, you will see something wonderful happen."

Elizabeth watched as the Dragon flapped his wings noiselessly, disappearing into the darkness.

She climbed back down the hill to Thalios. "Did you manage to read anything from him," she asked.

"He was mostly blocking his thoughts, but I did sense that he was sincere," said Thalios.

"What do you think will happen if he eats the other Grymlons?" said Elizabeth.

"I do not have the slightest idea," said Thalios.

The drive back to the cottage was quiet.

Elizabeth and Thalios entered the cottage through the back door, finding Grandma in the kitchen.

"How did it go?" Grandma asked.

"I will let Elizabeth tell you all about it," said Thalios. "I am very tired and would like to rest."

"I've made up the bed in the spare room," said Grandma. "We will see you in the morning."

"Thank you for your hospitality," said Thalios, as he left the kitchen.

Elizabeth took a seat at the kitchen table.

"Did you meet the Dragon?" asked Grandma.

"Yes. He ate the elviron set of Grymlons all those years ago. Now he wants to eat the remaining set. He says he's supposed to. According to the Dragon, the events that happened all that time ago, are tied to everything that is happening now. Are there any references to him in any of your books?"

"Not that I have ever read," said Grandma. "Over the years I have thumbed through just about all of the many books in that room. I don't ever remember any reference to a Dragon eating the Grymlons."

"Well, I am going to take the Grymlons to him," said Elizabeth. "I don't see any other way to stop what is happening to them. I'm tired, Gran. I think I'm going to go to bed now. We'll go down and explain everything to King Morvand in the morning."

"Sleep well, dear," said Grandma.

Thalios left early the next morning, and went down to the Elven Realm. After Grandma had made breakfast, they followed him down.

When they reached the castle, Grandma went to Jesse's room and Elizabeth looked for Vandrayven.

When she arrived at his laboratory, he was nowhere to be found.

"Do you know where Vandrayven is?" she asked Mac, Vandrayven's pet bird.

"No," Mac said, "but if you look into the crystal ball. You'll know what to do."

Elizabeth crossed the room, to a large glass ball perched on an ornate silver pedestal.

"Where are you, Vandrayven," she said, looking into the ball.

Smoke swirled around the inside. When it cleared, she could see Vandrayven in some sort of cave. As he became visible, he turned and looked at her.

Vandrayven raised his hands above his head, moving them in circles. He vanished from inside of the glass ball and appeared beside her.

"Where were you?" she asked.

"Visiting some friends," he said, straightening his robes. What can I do for you?"

"I have been instructed by the Dragon to have two bags made," said Elizabeth. "They are to be waterproof and air tight."

"That old Dragon is dangerous," said Vandrayven, as he went to his workbench.

"He doesn't scare me," said Elizabeth.

"You are becoming a little arrogant, young lady," Vandrayven said, as he cast his spell to make the bags.

"You're the one who taught me," said Elizabeth.

"A little too well, I fear," said Vandrayven, handing her two bags. "I hope these will work."

"Thanks, Vandrayven. I will see you when I get back," she said, heading for the door.

"Be careful!" he shouted, as she closed the door behind her.

Chapter Twenty Nine

"Where is the Mirronstep?" asked King Kalidryd, as he sipped Elven tea with King Morvand.

"I told you, I don't know where it is," the King replied. "Elizabeth took it with her."

"Are you sure you haven't hidden it somewhere?"

King Morvand breathed a sigh of relief when Elizabeth and Thalios walked in on the conversation.

"King Kalidryd thinks I have the Mirronstep and I am hiding it."

"King Morvand says that you have the Mirronstep," said King Kalidryd.

"I do," she answered.

"I want to see it," demanded King Kalidryd.

"No. The Mirronstep does not belong to any of us. Besides, it can't help us with the Grymlons."

"How did you find that out?" said King Kalidryd.

"I met with a Dragon who informed me that he ate your Grymlons. Renmar gave them to him. He wants the Elven set of Grymlons, so he can eat those too."

"What?" said King Morvand.

"You cannot seriously believe him?" said King Kalidryd.

"I most certainly do," said Elizabeth. "The Grymlons are going to die, no matter what. If you can come up with a better idea, then I will gladly hear it, and most certainly consider it."

Thalios stood. "The Dragon spoke the truth. I believe he is connected to the Grymlons in some way. Let Elizabeth take them to him and trust her."

The two kings looked at one another.

"Do we have a choice?" asked King Kalidryd.

"No," said Elizabeth. "I'm going to take the Grymlons to the Dragon. You can try and stop me, but I wouldn't recommend it."

"Very well," said King Morvand. "Do what you must."

"What will happen to the Mirronstep?" asked King Kalidryd.

"That will be for the druids to decide," said Thalios.

"That will be for me to decide, not the druids," said Elizabeth. "I'm going to find Gideon. You can discuss the Mirronstep all you want. You won't change my mind."

Elizabeth and Gideon found Keslyn, Merlyn and Charlie.

"I think a walk around the royal gardens would be a fun thing to do, don't you Liz?" suggested Gideon.

Merlyn and Keslyn ran across the lawn.

"Wait for me," Charlie shouted, scampering after them.

"When I went to live with my gran five years ago, I never imagined that I would be escorting two Dragons and a talking cat, through a very large garden, kept by elves," Elizabeth said, watching them.

"You really told my father that you are going to take the Grymlons no matter what?" said Gideon.

"I have made the decision," said Elizabeth. "I'm the guardian and I'm going to take the Grymlons to the Dragon."

Gideon laughed. "I never thought I would see the day, when a girl would tell the King of Kimadrian what to do."

"I didn't tell him what to do. I told him what I was going to do."

"My parents want to have supper with you and your grandma," said Gideon.

"I'd like that," said Elizabeth. "I'll go to Dragon's Hill tonight, after we've eaten."

"I don't want you to go alone," said Gideon. "Didn't that Dragon eat maidens, or something when he was alive?"

"He won't eat me," Elizabeth said, grinning. "I'm too tough."

"He would most certainly be biting off more than he could chew," said Gideon.

Elizabeth made to playfully hit him in the arm. Gideon grabbed her and wrestled her to the ground, tickling her.

The Mirronstep

Thalios, King Morvand and King Kalidryd were up in the King's rooms talking, when they heard the laughter. All three of them went to the window and looked down onto the large expanse of lawns, fountains and hedges.

They watched, as Elizabeth and Gideon rolled around on the grass.

"Bit unroyal, don't you think?" said King Kalidryd.

"We have a saying, up in the Human Realm," said Thalios.

"What might that be?" asked King Morvand.

"Those who play together, stay together."

"I like your saying," said King Morvand, looking down at the future King and Queen of Kimadrian.

King Kalidryd joined them for dinner, which was a first for all of them. He was particularly interested in making conversation with Elizabeth.

"I know we elviron are an odd looking lot. We envy the elves. I hope one day in the future, we can be restored to our former selves."

"That might happen, if you don't try to stop me doing what I'm supposed to," said Elizabeth.

"We have waged war with the elves long enough," said King Kalidryd. "I, for one, want us to live in peace together."

He stood, tapping his fork on his wine glass.

"To future peace between our Realms," he said, raising his glass.

Everyone stood.

"To future peace," they all said, drinking from their glasses.

"It's time for me to leave," Elizabeth whispered, into Gideon's ear.

"Yes," he said, standing. "Please excuse us. I would like to help Elizabeth prepare for her journey,"

"Of course," said King Morvand.

Elizabeth and Gideon climbed the steps of the tower, where the Grymlons were kept. Gideon moved the circles around on the door until it opened.

When she entered the room, the Grymlons rose off their pedestals, turning in the air as though waiting for instructions.

She held up the bag and the Grymlons hovered towards it, dropping into the bag, one by one.

"They have lost some of their light," she said.

Gideon frowned. "I noticed that too."

"I don't just see their dimness," said Elizabeth. "I feel it. It makes me sad that I have to feed them to the Dragon. I feel as though I'm dooming old friends."

Gideon put his arm around her. "Come on. Let's get going."

A carriage was waiting at the castle entrance.

Gideon kissed Elizabeth goodbye. "I'll see you tomorrow," she told him.

He watched as Elizabeth, Grandma, and Thalios got into the carriage.

Charlie and Merlyn were up on the balcony above, looking down on them as they drove away. Elizabeth looked up and waved to them all.

"Do you think it will be the last time we see her?" said Charlie.

"She'll be back," Keslyn pushed into Charlie's head.

"I hope so," said Charlie, beginning to purr loudly.

***

Elizabeth led the way, as the three of them exited the willow tree and made their way across the bridge and through the gate.

"The flowers seem to have lost a bit of their colour," said Grandma

When they reached the split in the pathway that led to the other side of the cottage, Elizabeth turned to her grandma.

"I'll be back before you know it, Gran."

Thalios handed her the bags. "Be cautious."

"I will, I promise," she said.

Grandma and Thalios watched as Elizabeth drove through the open gate. Grandma closed it behind her. They watched the car until it was out of site.

Grandma turned to Thalios. "Would you like a cup of tea?"

Thalios took her arm. "I would love one."

Chapter Thirty

Elizabeth drove to Uffington with the Grymlons in the back of her car. As she wound her way through the countryside, her heart was pounding and she could feel a light coating of sweat on her skin.

She parked the car, and climbed to Dragon's Hill.

"I'm here with the bags, as you asked," she said, standing in the middle of the mound.

She turned to a gentle beating of wings.

"You have returned," said the Dragon as he landed behind her. "You are indeed a brave maiden."

Jesse materialized beside her. "Don't get any ideas, you overgrown lizard," he said, waggling his finger at the Dragon.

"So we meet again, spirit," the Dragon said, bowing.

"You know Jesse?" Elizabeth asked.

The Dragon nodded.

Elizabeth turned to her brother. "You certainly do get around, Jesse."

"Do you think you are the only one doing work for the future, Liz?"

"If you knew that I had to meet this Dragon, all you had to do was tell me," said Elizabeth.

"I can be with you and defend you, Liz, but if you make the wrong decision in any of this, I'm not allowed to change it in any way."

"All right, Jesse! I get it. It's a bit annoying, though, when you get all profound on me."

"Do you have the Grymlons?" the Dragon asked, stepping from

one foot to the other.

"Yes," said Elizabeth.

"Well, please give them to me."

Elizabeth stepped forward with the bag and opened it. The Dragon put one of his front claws inside. He groped around, until he managed to get hold of one, and popped it in his mouth.

"He's enjoying this," Elizabeth thought.

After he had managed to get the last one down, he let out the most enormous burp. "Oh my! Please excuse me!"

Jesse looked at Elizabeth and rolled his eyes.

"A Dragon with manners!" she said, trying to hide a giggle.

"Please hand me one of the bags," said the Dragon.

Elizabeth handed him one of the custom made bags. He snorted a huge flame into it, closing it quickly. Then the Dragon began to cry. Thin spirals of smoke twirled upwards from the bag as the Dragon opened it again and let one of his tears fall in. He closed it quickly and did the same with the other bag.

He handed them back to Elizabeth. "Bury one of them in Distardrian and the other in Kimadrian."

"How much time do I have?" she asked.

"You have about a week before the magic dies, just in case you are not clever enough to get the task done straight away," the Dragon smirked.

"How will I know where to bury them?" she asked, ignoring his remark.

"You will know," said the Dragon.

As Elizabeth turned to walk to the edge of the hill, the Dragon came up behind her.

"Liz, watch out!" Jesse shouted.

Elizabeth, already sensing danger, stepped aside as the Dragon snaked a claw at her back, missing her by an inch.

"You ass!" she shouted, raising her hands to strike him down with magic. "Daggers in the night, rain down and strike!" she yelled to the night sky...

The Dragon looked up, visibly relieved when nothing came showering down.

"Ha-ha. You think your magic will work with me? I am hundreds of years old. Nothing can harm me."

"I can."

The Dragon and Elizabeth turned.

"Thalios, how did you get here?" said Jesse.

"You, druid?" the Dragon chuckled. "And just how do you think you can achieve that?"

Thalios stood staring at the Dragon. The Dragon stared back.

"What are you doing in my head, druid?"

"I am going to show you what you fear most. I am going to let you know that I can give you that fear, Dragon."

Elizabeth and Jesse watched as the eyes of Thalios and the Dragon remained locked in a gaze. Suddenly, the Dragon took a step back. He dropped down on all fours like a dog that had been whipped by his master.

Thalios shook his head as though coming out of a daydream.

He approached the now cowering Dragon.

"What did you think you would achieve by killing the one person who can save both our worlds."

The Dragon dropped his head. "It is in my nature."

Thalios pointed a crooked, but demanding finger at the Dragon's face. "I command you to go back from whence you came. Your purpose here is done."

The Dragon backed away, slowly beating his enormous wings. He rose into the air, and flew off into the night.

"I will meet you at the car," said Thalios, beginning to walk down the hill.

"I'll be right behind you, Thalios," Elizabeth said, turning to Jesse.

"Time to go home, Liz."

"Don't go, Jesse."

"I have to go now, Liz and I'm not sure what happens next."

"I'm afraid I won't see you again. I'm beginning to get used to you and Thalios using those old timey big words like whence, and hence and such."

Jesse smiled at her as he began to fade. "You always were a big baby when it came to saying goodbye."

Elizabeth suddenly felt the cold night air on her skin. She turned, running down the mound.

Thalios was in the passenger seat when she reached the car park.

"How did you get here, Thalios?"

"Druids and dragons are the business of druids and dragons, young lady. If you would kindly drop me at your grandma's. I can get home from there."

When they returned to the cottage, Grandma was sitting in the kitchen.

"Thalios, back so soon?"

"He was at Dragon's Hill," Elizabeth said, putting the bags on the kitchen table.

"Well, Dragons and druids are very connected," said Grandma, putting two cups of tea on the table. "Those bags look quite full. What's in them?"

"Dragon's breath," Thalios informed her.

"Why Dragons breath?" said Elizabeth.

"It is the most magical substance ever known," said Thalios.

"What are you supposed to do with them?" said Grandma.

"The Dragon told me to bury one of the bags in Distardrian and the other in Kimadrian."

"Then you must do as he says," said Thalios.

"In the morning," Elizabeth said, "I'm so tired, I could sleep for a week."

"Can you keep the bags safe until tomorrow?" he asked.

"I think I can manage that," she said, gathering them up, as she left the room.

Grandma and Thalios looked at each other.

"Would you like to stay the night in the guest room again, Thalios?"

"If it's not too much trouble, yes I would," he said. "I think I will go down to the Elven Realm with Elizabeth in the morning."

"I think that would be a good idea," said Grandma.

Grandma Rose stood on the pathway the next morning and waved goodbye, as Elizabeth and Thalios disappeared into the willow tree.

When they reached the castle, Elizabeth looked for the king. Instead, she found the king's aide.

"Please tell King Morvand that I wish to speak with him on a very important matter."

"May I tell him what that matter is?" the aide asked.

"No," said Elizabeth.

"Very well, my lady. I will inform the king. If you can tell me where I can find you, I will send a servant."

"I'm going to the officer's quarters to look for Prince Gideon. You can reach me there," she told him as she walked away.

Gideon was in his office at the barracks with Bindyl. When Elizabeth entered his office, he went to her and put his arms around her.

"How did it go, Liz?"

"It was well… interesting. I have asked for a meeting with the king. I think King Kalidryd should be here too. Bindyl, I want to thank you. I don't think I could have reached this far without you."

"Is all of this almost over?" said Bindyl.

"I think so," Elizabeth said, "I still have a task to perform, but I don't think it will be difficult."

"Let's all meet for lunch," said Gideon.

Bindyl stood. "I would like that. I should go to work now, though. "I will see you both in a couple of hours."

"Where is your dad?" said Elizabeth. "I don't usually have to go through his aide to see him."

"I don't know. Let's go and see mother, he might be with her."

Queen Paulina had just finished her tea when Elizabeth and Gideon arrived.

"Do you know where father is?" asked Gideon.

"I think he is looking for you. He has a surprise for you both," said the Queen. "I will tell my maid to let him know you are here. In the meantime, can I interest you both in a cup of tea?"

A few minutes later, the King arrived with Vandrayven and a young elviron.

"I would like you two to meet Gilpree, he is going to be Vandrayven's apprentice," said King Morvand.

Elizabeth looked at the wizard.

"King Kalidryd has no wizard now that Drewmannus has gone. He had not yet appointed an apprentice, so I volunteered to train this young… elviron," Vandrayven explained.

"You volunteered to train him?" asked Elizabeth.

"Yes," said Vandrayven. "He can act as a representative in King Kalidryd's absence."

Elizabeth approached the young elviron, who cringed and dropped to his knees.

"Don't do that!" she said. "As long as you don't try to harm anyone or anything, you'll be safe around me."

The young elviron stood, but kept his head bowed.

"I think I should be talking to the cook or something," Queen Paulina said, as she stood. "I will see you all later."

The Queen made a hasty exit, not wanting to be part of the situation in her living room.

"What happened when you went to see the Dragon?" asked King Morvand.

Elizabeth outlined what had happened on Dragon's Hill. While she was talking, she noticed Gilpree never once took his eyes from her, unless she looked his way

"King Kalidryd should be informed," said Thalios.

"I agree," said King Morvand.

A servant was sent to get the elviron king. When he arrived, he was brought up to date on the plan.

"Do you know where in Distardrian you are to bury the bag?" he asked.

"The Dragon told me that I would just know," said Elizabeth.

"I would like to provide you with an escort when you go into Distardrian," said King Kalidryd.

"I was told to go alone."

"Did the Dragon tell you why?" asked King Kalidryd.

"No," said Elizabeth, "but perhaps it's because of the danger. I am, after all, the chosen one and can defend myself from things that none of you can."

King Morvand looked out of the window. He turned when he heard Elizabeth's tone of voice become impatient with the elviron king's questions. It had been raining and the day was cloudy and dim. King Morvand took the elviron king's arm. "Can I interest you in a walk around the royal gardens, Kalidryd?"

"I would be delighted, Morvand. As long as the sun doesn't come out."

"We will walk close to the walls, just in case," said King Morvand, escorting him to the door that led to the outside.

Elizabeth breathed a sigh of relief. "Thank goodness! I thought he would never stop talking."

Vandrayven looked at Gilpree, then to Elizabeth. "Gilpree, why don't you go back down to my laboratory and practice the spells we were working on this morning."

Gilpree bowed to his new mentor and left the room.

Vandrayven waited for the door to close before he wheeled around, grabbing Elizabeth by the arm.

"Hey! What are you doing?" she said, trying to pull away from him.

Vandrayven walked Elizabeth over to a couch by the fireplace and plopped her down on it.

"What did I do to deserve that?" she said, rubbing her elbow.

"You may not like the elviron king, Elizabeth. And to be brutally honest, he simply cannot stand the sight of you, but you will show him respect in front of one of his subjects!"

"I'm sorry. That comment was uncalled for and disrespectful. I'll be more careful in the future."

Vandrayven took a seat beside her. "Elizabeth, you are to be the future queen of this Realm. If you want to be treated with dignity, you will have to change your behaviour. You are not a child any longer. Try to act like the adult you have become."

Elizabeth bridled at his remark. "I get it! I will try my best to be more... adult."

Vandrayven stood and headed to the door, but turned to Elizabeth before he left. "Gilpree is going to play an important role in the future. Perhaps you could help me a little with his training after you are finished with your quest."

"If you think I can help? I would be willing to try."

After Vandrayven closed the door behind him, Elizabeth went to the window and looked down at the two Kings.

"What a strange duo. Never thought I'd see the day," she thought.

Chapter Thirty One

Elizabeth bathed, dressed and headed down into the royal gardens.

She stood for a moment, letting the sunlight wash over her face. She began walking through the gardens, when she suddenly had the urge to lie down on the grass, the way she used to when she was a girl.

Gideon found her face down on the grass with her hands outstretched.

"What are you doing?" he asked.

Elizabeth rolled over, and sat up, grinning. "I'm relaxing."

"The grass is wet, Liz. Look at the front of your clothing."

Elizabeth looked down. The front of her blouse and her jeans were wet.

"It feels rather refreshing," she said, holding out her hand.

Gideon took it and pulled her to her feet.

"I wonder about you sometimes, Liz."

"Don't worry, Gideon. I'm not crazy. I used to lay on the grass a lot when I was younger. I had the urge to do it again today."

"I came to find you," he said. "We are supposed to meet everyone for lunch."

"Good," she said, brushing herself off. "I'm hungry."

After lunch, Gideon left to go to the barracks and Elizabeth headed back to her rooms.

As she got closer to her door she slowed, then stopped.

"Someone is in there!" she thought.

She waved her hand in front of herself and said, "Hidden," becoming invisible.

She crept down the hallway, stopping at her door, which was slightly open. As she slid into her rooms, she discovered Gilpree snooping around.

Elizabeth stood still, watching him as he moved about the room, touching this and that. Occasionally picking up objects and turning them over in his hands.

"I don't think he's here to steal anything. I think I'm going to have a bit of fun with you, you nosy little brat," she thought.

Elizabeth sat down in one of the easy chairs.

"What are you doing here?" she said, still invisible.

The young elviron spun around.

"I said what are you doing here?"

Gilpree was visibly shaking by now. He watched as Elizabeth slowly materialized in front of his very eyes.

He started to run for the door.

"Oh no you don't." Elizabeth motioned with her hand and the door slammed shut. Realizing he was trapped, Gilpree dropped to his knees and began sobbing.

"I believe I asked you a question," she said.

"I… I… was just curious. I mean, you are the all-powerful human and I wanted to see how you did it."

"Did what?"

"You know… all the magic and stuff."

"I don't do it, Gilpree, it's who I am. I am the magic."

Gilpree stared at Elizabeth.

"You are just a young human female, not much older than me. I hope I get out of here alive!" he thought.

"How old are you?" Elizabeth asked.

"Fourteen. I am so sorry for being here without your permission," he said, cowering again. "Will I be severely punished? "

"How long have you been in here?" she asked. "I think you should leave now and go back to Vandrayven before you are missed."

"You are not going to tell him what I did?" said Gilpree.

"Did you take anything?"

The young elviron shook his head.

"Did you break anything?"

"No," he answered.

"Then we'll keep this between us, but if I find you snooping around again, I'll turn you into a rabbit. Do you understand?"

Gilpree nodded his head vigorously.

Elizabeth pointed to the door and it opened. Gilpree backed towards it, never turning his body away from her and not once taking his eyes off her. When he reached the door, he shot out of it like a bullet.

"I think young Gilpree is going to be very trainable," she said to herself, with a laugh.

Elizabeth stood and waved her right hand. "In plain sight," she said quietly.

The Mirronstep and the bags that had been laying on her bed, became visible.

"Gilpree will never know how close he had been to the most powerful objects imaginable," she thought.

Elizabeth woke the next morning to the sound of purring in her ear.

She turned to see Charlie staring back at her.

"Let me out, please."

Elizabeth got out of bed and went to the door.

"No, no," said Charlie, "Out of the window. I have to go… you know."

"Oh, sorry." Elizabeth hurried to open the window.

Charlie jumped onto the ledge and climbed down the wall.

Elizabeth closed the window and got ready to make her journey to Distardrian. She picked up one of the bags with the Dragon's breath inside and placed it in a backpack.

She swept her hand in front of her and watched as the Mirronstep and the other bag disappeared.

She went down into the breakfast room and met Gideon and the king. Grandma Rose arrived after a few minutes.

Elizabeth poured herself another cup of elven tea and took a seat by her grandma.

"How is Jesse?"

"There's no change," Grandma said between bites of toast.

Elizabeth swigged down her tea. "I have to go, Gran. I'll come and find you as soon as I get back."

"We'll be waiting," said Grandma.

Elizabeth turned to Gideon, who was having breakfast with his father.

"Will you walk to the edge of the woods with me?"

Gideon excused himself from the king and took her arm. "Just try and stop me," he whispered in her ear. "I will do anything to spend a few more minutes with you."

"Flatterer," she whispered back.

They left through the back entrance to the castle and into the woods.

Elizabeth stopped at the edge of the trees and Gideon handed her the backpack.

"I would like to go further with you, Liz."

"No," she said, looking into his eyes.

He kissed her gently then she turned and disappeared into the woods.

"Don't look back!" she thought. "If I do, I won't go."

Gideon turned and headed towards the castle.

"One day she will go on one of these quests and she may not return," he thought. "But she is who she is. Nothing can change that.

I never really realized until now, how completely I love her. If anything happens to her, I may not be able to go on. Poor Bindyl, I am only just now beginning to understand how he feels about Zoe."

***

"I don't like it in here," Elizabeth thought, peering into the trees. "I'll be glad to see open space."

At the edge of the woods, she knelt down.

"Pennarius, please come," she whispered.

A few minutes later, she looked up and saw the small outline of a flying horse.

Pennarius landed noiselessly in front of her.

"How may I be of assistance to you, Elizabeth?"

"If you could take me to Distardrian, it would be appreciated."

"May I ask why?" said Pennarius.

"I have to take something there."

"Where in Distardrian?" he asked.

"I think we should start by going into the middle of the Realm and then see what happens."

Sometime later, Pennarius landed by a clump of trees.

"This is about as in the middle as you can get," he said, as Elizabeth jumped down.

"Thanks. Will you wait?" she said.

Pennarius lowered his head and looked into her eyes. "Of course,"

Elizabeth began to walk straight ahead. She continued for about a half a mile.

"I have absolutely no idea what I'm supposed to do," she thought. "I know. I'll sit down and eat something: take a bit of a break."

She sat against a tree, and opened her backpack, pulling out some cheese and berries.

"I wonder what I'm supposed to co next?"

As she reached down to pick up her bottle of water, something touched her hand.

"What the?" she said, pulling her hand back.

Standing by her bottle was the smallest person she had ever seen. He was about six inches high and dressed in yellow leggings with a bolero style top. A green pointed hat sat at an angle on his head.

"Who are you?" she asked.

The little man looked up at her, giving her a most engaging smile.

"My name is Tanji. I am here to guide you to where you will go to bury the bag you're carrying."

"Who sent you?"

"No one sent me," Tanji replied. "We have been expecting you for a long time. We were beginning to think you would never solve the problem and find us."

"Us?" said Elizabeth.

"The pixies," said Tanji, moving his arm in a circle.

Dozens of pixies appeared out of the grass, gathering around her.

"How enchanting," she thought, as she watched them, watching her.

They began pulling at her clothes and shoes. A few of them went to the bag and began to open it.

"Hey, stop that!" she shouted.

When Elizabeth raised her voice, the pixies ran for cover like little ants.

"It's alright. I didn't mean to scare you. I won't hurt you. Come on out."

Slowly, the pixies re-appeared. Tanji climbed up on a stone near Elizabeth.

"Are you ready to go now?" he said, looking up at her.

"I will be in a few seconds," she said, gathering her things.

"Will you carry me please? We will get there quicker if you do."

"I can put you in my pocket," said Elizabeth, "but what about the others?"

"Oh don't worry about them. I'm your guide."

She gently picked him up, placing him in her pocket. His little head popped out of the top, and he hung on to the stitched edge.

Tanji turned to his fellow pixies. "Go home and wait for word the job has been done," he shouted.

Elizabeth watched as the pixies seemed to dissolve into the grass.

"Which way?" said Elizabeth.

"That way," He said, pointing to the right of her.

Elizabeth began walking in the direction Tanji had indicated. They had not gone very far when he tugged at her jacket.

"What?" she asked.

"Now go that way," he said pointing to the left.

Onward they went.

"You can stop now," said Tanji.

Elizabeth pulled Tanji out of her pocket and placed him on the ground.

He dragged a line in the dirt with his foot. "Dig here."

Elizabeth began to dig. She dug down about a foot, pulled the bag out of her pack and put it into the hole.

Tanji stood, watching her with his hands on his hips, nodding and smiling as she filled in the hole.

"Pick me up and take me back where we met, please," he said when she was finished.

Elizabeth popped him back into her pocket, and made her way back.

She put him down on the rocks.

"Thank you," he said, running into the grass. "See you soon."

Elizabeth stood for a moment, looking to see if she could follow where he went, but he seemed to fade away.

"Pennarius, please come and get me," she said, into the ground.

Pennarius appeared and took her back to the edge of the woods.

Elizabeth entered the castle through the back entrance. When she reached the king and queen's private rooms, Gideon, King Morvand, Queen Paulina, Thalios and Grandma Rose were deep in conversation.

They turned and looked in surprise when she entered the room.

Gideon went to her. "Is everything all right?"

"Yes, of course. The bag has been buried and I'm ready to take the other one and bury it."

"But we thought that you would have been gone a bit longer than this," said Thalios.

"So did I," said Elizabeth. "It seems that I was expected."

She sat down and told her story to the group, who were both amused and amazed.

"I think I'll go into Kimadrian tomorrow," she said, after some thought. "For now, though. I would like to spend some time with Jesse today."

"Tomorrow will be a good day to bury the other bag," said Thalios.

"I have some business to attend to." Gideon said, kissing Elizabeth on the cheek. "I will see you in a little while."

Elizabeth made her way down into Vandrayven's rooms, and pulled a chair over to Jesse's bed. She picked up his hand and sat for a while, looking at him.

Thalios, Grandma, and the King and Queen were all still sitting around drinking tea and chatting, when Elizabeth returned from visiting Jesse.

Gideon arrived a few minutes later.

"Everything has been arranged," he said.

Everyone smiled with approval.

Elizabeth looked around at all of them.

"What's going on?"

"We are going to see Bindyl," Gideon whispered in her ear.

"Why?" she asked.

"You should take a chaperone," said Grandma Rose.

"Oh, I think we can trust them, don't you my dear?" said Queen Paulina.

The king glanced at Gideon.

"Yes father, I will be the perfect gentleman," Gideon said.

"I think it would be acceptable, just this once, for the two of them to go to Bindyl's. There will be many other elves there," King Morvand said, with a nod of approval.

While Elizabeth and Gideon were on their way to Bindyl's, he was busy receiving the invited guests.

"Your early return is nice, Liz. It has made it possible for the party to begin sooner," said Gideon, as the carriage made its way to the Blakely residence.

"How many people will be there?" she asked.

"Friends of Bindyl and myself, and hopefully your friends too now, Liz."

"I've already met most of your friends, haven't I?"

"Well yes, but these are friends whose parents are courtiers and dignitaries across the Realm. Father would like you to meet them as well. You know, get connected so to speak."

"You mean to get them used to the fact that you are marrying a human," Elizabeth said, staring out of the carriage window.

"Yes. For those who might oppose our marriage, it may make it easier for them to accept you once they know you."

"To know me is to love me, right Gideon?"

"But of course. What about you is there not to love? That is, once one knows you." Gideon replied with a sheepish grin.

***

Bindyl mingled among the guests in the now crowded farm house.

"What's this little celebration for?" asked Kedrick, as Bindyl passed by.

"Prince Gideon and Elizabeth Ghenestone are to be married soon," Bindyl told him. "I thought it would be nice to introduce Elizabeth to some of Gideon's friends."

"Yes, most of us knew Zoe, but not many of us have met with the human girl," said Kedrick.

"Her name is Elizabeth," Bindyl reminded him.

"I didn't mean any disrespect. It's just that we elves would be more comfortable with an elven queen," said Kedrick.

"I didn't know there was such an opinion in the Elven Realm," said Bindyl.

"Elves talk," said Kedrick. "I think you are doing a very wise and diplomatic thing for Prince Gideon and his bride to be. It is most certainly a more relaxed atmosphere away from the castle. The more the elves get to know Elizabeth, the more they may warm to a human queen."

"That was the idea," said Bindyl, who turned, as a hand rested on his arm.

"The Prince is here, sir," one of the servants informed him.

"Let me know what you think of our new guest," said Bindyl.

Kedrick smiled and raised his glass.

Gideon helped Elizabeth down from the carriage, and they entered Bindyl's house.

Elizabeth turned to Gideon. "I feel a little nervous."

He grabbed her hand and gently squeezed it. "Don't be Liz. Just be you and they will love you."

Gideon and Bindyl watched Elizabeth as she mingled among the guests. She smiled and made small talk, taking care to speak with anyone who required her ear.

"She's positively glowing," said Bindyl.

"Yes she is," said Gideon. "I think she will make a wonderful queen. Don't you?"

"I think it was very wise of the king to suggest a union between the future King of Kimadrian and one of the most powerful beings alive."

"But I love her," said Gideon. "I think I would have married her no matter what."

"Yes, how fortunate you are, Gideon, that you have love in your life."

"I'm sorry, Bindyl. I didn't mean to be insensitive."

Bindyl smiled. "I will always miss her, but I am happy for you."

Gideon looked into his best friend's sad face. "There is another love out there somewhere, just waiting for a tall, dark, handsome elf."

"I don't want another love. At least not at this point in my life," said Bindyl.

"Still, one day perhaps," said Gideon.

"No more talk about me. This party is for you and Elizabeth," said Bindyl. "Go with her and mingle. Enjoy yourself."

Gideon stepped up beside Elizabeth, gently touching her elbow to let her know he was there. As she turned to look at him, Bindyl saw love in her eyes.

"I miss you, Zoe," he thought, as he watched them. "I miss you so much."

Grandma Rose was waiting when Gideon and Elizabeth returned to the castle.

"Grandma, what are you doing here? It's late."

"It's Jesse," said Grandma. "I think you should come, Elizabeth."

She followed Grandma Rose towards the staircase that led down to Jesse's room, feeling sick with worry, with each step down she took.

Vandrayven met them at the door. "Come in. I have tried everything I know. Perhaps you might give it a try."

Elizabeth sat down by Jesse's bed. He was as white as chalk and he was sweating profusely. Elizabeth took his hand. His palms were slippery with sweat. He opened his eyes. When he saw her, he managed a brief smile.

Elizabeth started to cry and turned to Vandrayven. "Is he dying?"

"I think he might be," Vandrayven said, quietly.

Elizabeth touched Jesse's cheek with the back of her hand.

"How long has he been like this?" she asked.

The nurse stepped forward. "It began this morning. It hasn't become any worse, but he has not improved either."

"I have a feeling that when I took the Dragon's breath to Distardrian, it did something to him," said Elizabeth.

"How?" said Grandma.

"I don't know."

"Hang in there, Jesse, it's almost over. Try to be strong," she whispered in his ear.

He opened his eyes again and looked directly into hers. He managed enough of a nod that Elizabeth knew he had understood her.

Elizabeth stood. "I am going to bury the other bag now. It'll be light soon. I think if I can get the other bag buried, it might help Jesse."

"How do you know that?" asked Grandma.

"I don't, but I have to try," she said, as she headed for the door.

Elizabeth ran up the stairs. When she reached her rooms, she changed her clothes, grabbed the other bag with the Dragon's breath, and then made her way back down to the entrance.

Grandma Rose was waiting with Gideon at the door.

"I won't be long, Gran."

"I'll walk with you to the castle walls," Gideon said, taking her free hand.

They reached the back wall just as the sun was coming up, he kissed her on the lips. "Are you going to be okay, Liz, it's been a long night."

She smiled up at him. "I feel just fine, not at all tired."

"It's goodbye again then," he said.

"Stop worrying, Gideon. Pennarius will help me."

Once outside the castle, Elizabeth called to Pennarius and he arrived a few minutes later.

"Where do you want to go," he asked.

"I'm not sure, but I think I'll know when we get there," she said.

Elizabeth was about to get up onto Pennarius when she heard a familiar voice.

"Wait, where are you going?"

Elizabeth looked down.

"How did you get here, Tanji?"

"Magic," he said with a grin. "Could I ride on him, too?"

Elizabeth put the pixie in her pocket. "Give Pennarius directions, Tanji."

They had been flying for a half an hour, when Tanji asked Pennarius to land.

"Here," he said, pointing just ahead.

Elizabeth stepped forward to where Tanji had pointed and began to dig. She dug down until the hole was big enough to hold the bag, dropped it in and buried it.

Tanji began jumping up and down and running around as though he had won a huge prize.

"What's the big celebration?" she asked, laughing.

He stopped. "You don't know?" he asked.

"Tanji, what are you talking about?"

Tanji began walking away. He turned back and called to her. "You'll see," he said.

He ran into some tall grass and disappeared.

"Come on Pennarius, let's go back to the castle," Elizabeth said, getting on his back.

When they reached the castle walls, Gideon was waiting.

"Good day to you, Prince Gideon," Pennarius said, as he landed.

"Good day to you too, Pennarius. Thank you for bringing Elizabeth back safely."

"My pleasure as always. I will see you both soon, I hope."

"Thanks Pennarius. Stay safe," Elizabeth said, as he took off.

Gideon watched the Pennar fly off into the distance. Then he turned to Elizabeth.

"All finished?" he asked, as he put his arm around her.

"Yes, I think so. I'm so tired, I can barely walk. How is Jesse?"

"No change I'm afraid. I don't think anyone will miss you if you want to rest for a bit, Liz."

When they reached the door to Elizabeth's room, Gideon opened it. He picked her up and carried her through. He put her on the bed, pulled off her boots, pulled the cover up to her chin and kissed her.

The Mirronstep

"Thank you," she said, closing her eyes.

Gideon left her to sleep and headed to his father's private rooms.

Chapter Thirty Two

"Wake up Elizabeth."

Elizabeth had been in a deep, dreamless sleep. She felt warm and comfortable, and did not want to wake.

"Elizabeth, wake up," the voice said again.

She turned over to see Gideon was standing beside her bed.

"Get up," he said, as he stood by the window.

Elizabeth sat up, and noticed it was dark outside.

"How long did I sleep?"

Gideon turned and faced her. "About two hours."

"But that would make it still daytime," she said.

"Yes," he said, turning back to the window again.

Elizabeth got out of bed and joined him.

"Why is it so dark?"

"It's been this way for about an hour now," Gideon said, peering down at the garden below, "but every now and then you can see some sort of flashing light coming from the direction of where you went to bury the bag."

Elizabeth looked up suddenly as a light streaked into the darkness.

"Oh my!"

Gideon turned to her. "That's why I woke you. It's been doing that now for about half an hour. The flashes started every few minutes or so."

Gilpree had sneaked out of the wizard's laboratory and was watching the spectacle from the ramparts of the castle.

"What are you doing up here?"

Gilpree turned to see a castle guard standing by the entrance to the stairs.

"I was watching the light in the sky," he told the guard, sheepishly.

"Did Lord Vandrayven give you permission to be up here?"

"No," Gilpree said, heading for the stairs.

The guard followed him, making sure he continued down to the wizard's rooms in the basements of the castle.

When Gilpree reached Vandrayven's rooms, Vandrayven was there.

"Have you seen what is happening outside?" Gilpree asked.

"Yes, and I was not aware that I had given you permission to leave these rooms," Vandrayven said.

Gilpree sat at his desk. "I am sorry, master. It will not happen again."

"Humph!" was all Gilpree heard, as he opened one of his books.

Chapter Thirty Three

The elviron in Distardrian were also watching their own light show in the sky. The flashes of light had stopped about the time the ones in Kimadrian had begun. Just about every elviron in the Realm had stepped outside, and were waiting to see what was going to happen next.

As King Kalidryd watched from his window, the sky became a bit less grey.

"What's happening?" he asked his General, who had been watching the spectacle with him.

"I don't know your majesty. Perhaps the spell Drewmannus and the other wizards had cast, to keep the sun out is failing."

The sun slowly peeped out of the greyness. It was hazy at first, then brighter and brighter, until it became a normal sunny day.

The elviron that were outside, ran into their homes, afraid that they would burn.

***

Elizabeth and Gideon watched as the darkness slowly left Kimadrian and the sun came out.

Gilpree was now busy with an experiment Vandrayven had given him to work on.

Vandrayven was going back and forth doing the daily work of a wizard.

"I wish I knew what was happening out there," he thought, as he went about his work. "Although, I'm sure we'll find out soon enough."

He looked up to check on Gilpree's progress, and stopped what he was doing, approaching the young elviron.

Gilpree, who had been engrossed in his work, suddenly felt uncomfortable. He turned to see Vandrayven staring at him intently.

"Is something wrong, master?"

"Gilpree, you should come with me," Vandrayven said, grabbing the young elviron by the shoulder, to a mirror on the wall.

Gilpree looked into his reflection and jumped back in shock.

"But that's not me," he said, turning to Vandrayven.

"Oh but it is, young elviron. Look closer," Vandrayven said, with a smile.

Gilpree approached the mirror to get a closer look at himself. He touched it, still not believing what he saw. Looking back at him was a young dark haired elf. He touched his face, watching himself do so in the mirror. His skin felt smooth. He ran his fingers through the thick thatch of dark hair on his head with wide eyes.

Gilpree turned to Vandrayven. "What?"

"I think I know," Vandrayven said. "You wait here. I'm going to see King Morvand."

He was just about to leave and go upstairs, when Jesse's nurse came running into the room.

"You have to come now!" she said, turning and running back to Jesse's room.

Vandrayven followed her. He took one look at Jesse and left, running up the stairs faster than he had moved in years.

Vandrayven rushed into Elizabeth's rooms without knocking. He stood for a moment out of breath.

"You… you must come… Jesse," was all he could say, trying to catch his breath.

Elizabeth ran past him, sprinting down the steps. When she reached the room Jesse had been in all those years, she suddenly stopped.

"Do I want to go in?" she thought. "I didn't ask Vandrayven what the problem was. What if Jesse has died!"

She opened the door, slowly peering around it.

"Jesse!" she said, rushing towards him.

Jesse was sitting up in the bed, grinning at her.

She threw herself onto him. He managed to catch her just enough that she didn't wind him.

Elizabeth put her arms around him and sobbed. He held onto her until she calmed down enough to be able to speak. "How?" was all she could say.

"I…" he said, grabbing his throat.

Elizabeth turned to the nurse. "He needs something to drink."

The nurse poured a glass of water and gave it to him. "Just sip it. You haven't had much in your stomach for a very long time. You will be sick if you drink too much."

Tears sprang into Elizabeth's eyes again as she watched him take small sips from the glass. "He has lines around his eyes and mouth," she thought. "He has changed so much; so many missed years."

Jesse leaned back against his pillow.

"You're not going to go back to sleep are you?" Elizabeth said.

Jesse put a hand up to his throat and whispered "no," shaking his head at the same time. "I've missed you, Liz."

Vandrayven had sent for Grandma Rose, who entered the room just as Elizabeth had started to cry again. Grandma turned very pale and stood looking at him.

Elizabeth motioned for her grandma to come closer. Grandma Rose went to the bed. Jesse took her hand and kissed it. Grandma gently reached over and put her arms around him.

It was Jesse's turn to cry.

"I've missed you so, Gran," he whispered.

Vandrayven motioned for the nurse to leave. She followed him out and closed the door behind them.

Vandrayven left his basements and hurried up the stairs to the king's rooms. He stopped in front of the door.

"I should slow down a bit," he thought, catching his breath again. "I'm over a hundred years old. I'll have a heart attack if I keep running around like this!"

He burst into the room, unannounced.

"Jesse is awake!" he proclaimed to all present.

Not waiting for a reaction, Vandrayven turned on his heel and left the room.

"Wait," the King shouted after him. "Where are you going?"

Vandrayven held up his hand, as he hurried along the corridor. "One thing at a time," he shouted, not looking back.

King Morvand and Gideon exchanged glances.

"Did he just say that Jesse is awake?" said Gideon.

"I believe he did," replied the King.

They followed Vandrayven down the hall.

The two of them had just reached the bottom of the staircase, when a guard approached them.

"There is someone at the castle entrance asking for Elizabeth, Your Majesty."

"Who is it?" said Gideon.

"Well…, it's a little man."

"What?" said the King.

"What do you mean? A little man," asked Gideon.

The guard bent over, putting out the flat of his hand, indicating just how small the man was.

Gideon looked at his father. "A pixie do you think?"

"One would assume so," said the King, "considering the size."

They followed the guard to the castle entrance. Standing outside, was a pixie dressed in yellow.

"What is your business here?" asked Gideon.

"I am looking for Elizabeth," said the pixie.

"She is busy at the moment," said Gideon. "May I give her a message?"

"No," said the pixie. "If you don't mind, I will wait."

Gideon called one of the guards who had been standing at the door.

"Take…ah?"

"Tanji," said the pixie.

"Take Tanji to the library and make him comfortable, but stay with him," said Gideon.

The king and Gideon continued to Jesse's room.

Jesse was sipping water from a glass when they arrived. Elizabeth and Grandma were sat either side of him.

"I am King Morvand. It is so nice to finally meet you," he said standing at the foot of Jesse's bed.

"And I am Gideon."

"You are the elf that Liz has been talking about?"

Gideon smiled and nodded.

Jesse beamed with happiness. "I can't wait to get out of this bed and begin moving around."

"This is wonderful," the King said. "I will see to it that you obtain all the help you will require to regain your strength, so that you can walk again."

Gideon remembered about the pixie. "Elizabeth, there is a pixie named Tanji waiting in the library downstairs. He says he needs to see you."

"I'll be back, Jesse," said Elizabeth. "I have to see what little Tanji wants."

As she approached the library, Elizabeth could hear strange noises. The guard at the door was peering into the room with a worried look. He turned and saw and sighed with relief.

"What's going on," she asked, as she approached the guard.

He merely nodded towards the library.

Tanji was there, and so were many other pixies. They were running all over the library, picking up books and throwing them on the floor. They were climbing up the ladders that were attached to the sides of the bookshelves and pushing them along, racing along the back wall.

Elizabeth turned to the guard. "Did they all arrive together?"

The guard became wide eyed. He shook his head and shrugged his shoulders. "I don't know where they came from. I only saw the little one in yellow at first. Then suddenly there were dozens of them!"

Elizabeth went farther into the room, feeling irritated at their bad behaviour.

"What is going on here?" she shouted.

The pixies all stopped what they were doing at once. When they saw Elizabeth they seemed to just disappear into the books and furniture.

Elizabeth turned to Tanji, who was sitting quietly on one of the couches.

"Get rid of them, Tanji. They are destroying the library!"

Tanji shouted something. The pixies seemed to come out from everywhere in the room and lined up in front of Elizabeth.

Tanji looked at Elizabeth, waving his hand at them. "They are yours to command."

"Clean up this mess!" she ordered.

The words were hardly out of her mouth before the pixies began running around, picking up books and cleaning up the room. Within seconds, everything was as it was before.

Tanji said something else to them and they made a pixie ladder to the window, opened it, and one by one pulled each other up and out of it.

"Thank you," said Elizabeth.

"My pleasure," said Tanji.

"What do you want?" asked Elizabeth, eager to get back to her brother.

"I came to find you because your task is not finished," said Tanji.

"I don't understand," said Elizabeth.

"Elizabeth Ghenestone, you have to come with me."

"I can't, Tanji, I have more important things to do at the moment."

Tanji looked up into Elizabeth's eyes. "No, you don't! You have a task to perform, and only you can do it. Oh, and you'll need your shovel."

"What am I supposed to be doing?"

Tanji beckoned for Elizabeth to kneel down. She did as she was asked and Tanji whispered in her ear. She looked over at the guard then nodded to Tanji.

"You may leave us and close the door behind you," Elizabeth said to the guard.

"But I have orders from the king not to leave the pixie alone, miss."

"He won't be alone. I'll be with him."

The guard dropped his gaze. "I've heard stories about you," he thought. "King's orders or not, I'm leaving."

"I'll wait outside," he said, backing out of the room, closing the door behind him.

"Now," said Elizabeth. "Explain what you mean by the Grymlons being ready. They were eaten by the Dragon."

Tanji let out an exasperated sigh. "Did the Dragon explain nothing to you?"

Elizabeth shook her head.

"Come with me and you will see what I mean," said Tanji.

"All right. You stay here and don't let your friends back in. I'll be back in a few minutes."

Tanji took a seat on the couch. Elizabeth opened the door to the guard standing outside.

"Go back in there and watch him," she said, "I'm going back down to Vandrayven's rooms to speak with the king, and don't let anymore of his little friends in there."

Elizabeth smiled when she noticed the guard didn't seem too pleased that he had to go back into the library, but he did as he was asked.

When she returned to Jesse, she explained why Tanji had arrived at the castle.

"I have to leave for a while. Apparently, my task is not over."

"That pixie told you so?" asked Gideon.

"Yes. He and I have to leave, but I won't be gone long."

She kissed Jesse on the cheek. "You and I have a lot of catching up to do."

"Yes, I already know where you're going. I'll explain everything to Gran and the others. Hurry back, sis."

"It seems you know more than I do," Elizabeth said, as she made for the door.

She returned to Tanji in the library, relieved there were no more occurrences with his friends, and they left the castle.

"Where are we going?" she asked.

"To Distardrian," said Tanji.

Elizabeth looked towards Distardrian. "It looks different. Not murky and dull?"

Once they were away from the castle, Elizabeth called to Pennarius. He arrived a few minutes later. When Tanji saw him, he jumped up and down, clapping his hands as he did so.

"Are we going for a ride on him again?"

"Yes, so behave yourself."

"Where would you like to go?" Pennarius asked.

Elizabeth turned to Tanji. "Well, where are we going?"

"To where you buried the bag in Distardrian of course."

Elizabeth picked him up and placed him in her pocket. Pennarius knelt down and Elizabeth climbed up onto his back. He took off in the direction of Distardrian.

Tanji was leaning out of Elizabeth's pocket, looking down at the land below.

"Wow what a view!" he kept saying.

"If you fall out, you'll get hurt. Now get back into my pocket," Elizabeth told him.

Tanji moved back into her jacket pocket, but every now and then he couldn't resist leaning forward and looking down.

"It's just ahead. Down by those trees," Elizabeth shouted.

Pennarius dropped down and landed as instructed.

"Shall I wait?" asked Pennarius.

"I think so," Elizabeth said, looking at a large blackened circle on the ground where she had buried the bag. "I don't know what I'm doing here, but I don't want to stay."

Tanji jumped down from Elizabeth's pocket.

"Dig down to the bag," he said.

"But why?" she asked.

"Just do it, please."

Elizabeth took her shovel out of her pack and began to dig.

She found the bag and lifted it out of the hole.

"It feels heavy," she said, opening the top.

She looked in it and gasped. "How?"

Tanji shrugged his little shoulders. "I do not know. I am only a messenger."

Elizabeth knelt down, looking into the pixie's eyes. "A messenger for whom?"

Tanji stared back at her. "I won't tell."

"Okay. Then what do we do with these?"

Pennarius approached them.

"What is in that bag?" he asked.

Elizabeth held open the bag for him to see. He looked down into it and stepped back. "Aren't they Grymlons?"

"Yes," Elizabeth said. "They're a bit smaller than the old ones, but they are definitely Grymlons."

"These belong to the elviron," said Tanji. "We should deliver them, then go to Kimadrian and get the other set."

Elizabeth put Tanji in her pocket and climbed up onto Pennarius. When they reached the castle at Distardrian, Elizabeth approached the gates.

She stopped for a moment watching some elviron who were wandering around outside. She noticed them looking down at their hands. Some of them, touching their faces and looking up, enjoying their newly acquired ability to soak up the sunshine. Some of them smiled at her.

"I never thought I would be a witness to this!" she thought, as she entered the castle grounds.

She was greeted by an elviron guard.

The guard saluted her as he approached. "Please follow me, Lady Elizabeth."

The guard stopped at the door to the king's private chambers.

"If you would please wait, I will let his majesty know you are here."

He returned a moment later.

"Please go in."

The king turned to face her, as the door opened. When he saw Elizabeth he smiled.

"My dear Elizabeth, to what do we owe this honour?"

Elizabeth stared at him.

"He's really rather handsome. Ageing, but handsome," she thought.

The king looked past her to the guard behind. "You may leave us."

The guard bowed, closing the door as he left.

"Would you like some refreshment? We don't have much at the moment. We seem to have only rotten meat in our kitchens, but I'm sure cook could manage something."

"No thanks," said Elizabeth, looking around her at the now clean and tidy room.

"May I ask what you are doing here?" he said.

"I have something for you," she said, holding up the bag so he could see it. "You might want to sit down."

He took a seat, eyeing the bag.

One by one, Elizabeth took out the Grymlons, and placed them on a table. They shone like beacons, changing colours, moving in circles around the table.

"They look like... Grymlons!" the King said.

"That's because they are."

King Kalidryd approached the table. He picked one of them up. "These belong to us?" he said, turning it over in his hands.

"Yes they are yours, but please, put them up high this time: in the sunlight, where they belong."

"I do not know how to thank you," he said putting his arms around her.

"You can start by letting go of me," she said, pulling away.

King Kalidryd quickly pulled his arms back. "Oh, I am so dreadfully sorry!"

Elizabeth let out a laugh. "I apologize for laughing, Your Majesty. It's just that a few months ago, I would have tried to kill you for that."

King Kalidryd turned a little pink. "I forgot myself. It will not happen again."

"A lot has changed, Your Majesty. We will all need to adjust."

"Yes, I agree," he said, turning his attention to the Grymlons again.

"I have to go now. I have another task to perform."

"Yes, yes," said the King. "I quite understand. Do not be a stranger now. Come and visit."

"Will I see you at the wedding?" asked Elizabeth.

"I... I would be honoured."

Pennarius was waiting for her outside of the castle gates. When she walked out into the open countryside, Tanji reappeared from inside of her pocket.

"You kept out of sight," said Elizabeth.

"I do not like the elviron. They have eaten many of my kind over the years."

"They're different now," said Elizabeth.

"I hope so," said Tanji.

Pennarius flew them back to the castle at Kimadrian.

When Elizabeth jumped down she turned to the Pennar. "I have to go inside for a few minutes, and then I will need another ride into Kimadria. Will you please wait for me?"

Pennarius nodded.

Tanji jumped out of Elizabeth's pocket and ran to Pennarius. "I don't want to go with her. I seem to get into trouble in there. Can I stay here with you?"

"If you wish," said Pennarius.

Elizabeth entered through the back gate. When the guards saw her they stood back to let her pass.

When she reached her rooms, she waved her hand and the Mirronstep appeared. Then she went to her bedside cupboard.

"Reveal," she said, waving a hand.

The book and the smaller mirror also appeared.

She looked around to make sure everything was in its place, and chanted the spells that concealed everything, changed her clothes and hurried out of her rooms.

She ran along the corridor. As she turned the corner she slammed head on into Gideon. Both of them landed on the floor.

At first they sat rubbing their heads, and then they looked at each other and laughed.

Gideon got up and helped Elizabeth.

"On your way out again?"

"Yep. Just checking to make sure nothing was missing in my room" Elizabeth said, "where were you going?"

"I was looking for you. One of the guards saw you arrive. I was just coming to see how everything went."

"I have to go," she said. "I want to get this done before the sun goes down, but I promise I'll find you as soon as I get back."

Gideon stood to one side, sweeping his hand, in a 'this way please' gesture.

Elizabeth ran past him, turning to blow a kiss as she bolted down the hallway.

"She never ceases to amaze and delight me," he said to himself, with a grin.

He made his way to the barracks. I'll try to keep myself busy," he thought. "I won't be able to rest easy until she is back safely within these walls, anyway."

Elizabeth hurried out of the castle grounds. When she reached Pennarius, Tanji was sitting between his ears, waving to her as she approached.

"What are you doing up there," she asked with a smile.

"Pennarius let me up here so I could see you coming," he said.

Elizabeth climbed up onto Pennarius, plucked Tanji from the top of his head, and put him back in her jacket pocket.

"Are we going to the spot in Kimadrian where I buried the other bag?" she asked Tanji.

"Yes. I have already told Pennarius where we are going," he replied.

Pennarius took off, flying them across Kimadrian. He circled, and landed, when he saw the patch of scorched earth.

Elizabeth jumped down and began digging in the centre of the singed grass. She pulled the bag from the ground and opened it. Inside, as expected, were five small Grymlons.

Tanji peeped out from Elizabeth's pocket. "Are they all there?"

"Yes they are," she said, jumping up onto Pennarius. "Please take us home, Pennarius. I can't wait to see what happens next!"

Pennarius rose high and flew towards the castle.

After a few minutes Tanji peeped out of Elizabeth's pocket again. "Elizabeth, would you please ask Pennarius to land? This is close to my home."

"Pennarius, Tanji wants us to land," Elizabeth shouted.

Pennarius moved towards the ground, landing by some trees.

Tanji jumped out of Elizabeth's pocket and onto the ground. About fifty pixies appeared out of the grass. They gathered around him. He had performed his task to the letter and the other pixies were cheering him and dancing around, treating him like a hero.

"What an enchanting sight," Elizabeth thought.

Tanji turned to her and waved. She waved back.

"Come on Pennarius, let's go home," she said into one of his ears.

He lifted her up and flew homeward. Elizabeth looked behind her as they flew away from the pixies. They were all standing, looking in her direction, waving.

A few minutes later, Pennarius put Elizabeth down by the back gate of the castle.

"Thank you again," she said.

"I will always be here, if you need me," said Pennarius.

Elizabeth stroked the side of his neck.

"Stay well and safe, Elizabeth," he said, as he took off.

Elizabeth found the King, Queen and Gideon in the king's private rooms. She opened the bag. King Morvand peeped inside. He had the same astonished look as King Kalidryd.

Elizabeth laughed.

"When did you know?" asked the King.

"A little pixie told me."

"The same pixie whose friends wreaked havoc in the main library?" said Gideon.

Elizabeth nodded.

Gideon turned to his father. King Morvand looked back at his son, gently shaking his head to let him know not to say anything about almost throwing Tanji out of the castle.

King Morvand turned to Elizabeth. "Would you like to do the honours? I think it's appropriate since you are their guardian, don't you?"

Elizabeth took the bag. She made her way upwards, through the castle until she arrived at the top of the highest tower. She moved the circular shapes on the door until they all lined up and the door opened.

She entered the round room, put the bag on the floor and opened the top. Elizabeth took a step back, as the Grymlons rose up one by one. The five of them hung in mid-air for moment as though unsure of what to do. Elizabeth stepped forward and gently took the nearest one, placing it on one of the pedestals. The rest of them followed, moving around until they were all in their own spot. She watched, as the one she had placed on the pedestal rose up, and swapped places with another one near the door.

"It's as though they never left," she thought. "Except now they look vibrant and young."

She took one more look around the room and left, locking the door before running down the steps.

When she reached the bottom, Elizabeth turned the corner and stopped. Standing in the foyer were dozens of people.

"What now?" she thought.

The Mirrorstep

Grandma Rose was standing behind Jesse, who was sitting in Elizabeth's old wheelchair. Behind them were Gideon, Bindyl, Thalios, King Morvand and Queen Paulina, Vandrayven, King Kalidryd and Gilpree. Gilda, the chaperone was also there with Keslyn, Merlyn and Charlie, as well as some of the royal dignitaries who had been informed of what had happened. A moment later they began clapping and cheering.

As Elizabeth walked down the last part of the staircase, Gideon stepped forward, took her hand and got down on one knee.

She noticed that he was blushing slightly, as she looked down at him.

"Ladies and gentlemen. Now Elizabeth's quest is over and all is once again as it should be in our realm. I would like to present my wife to be, and future queen of Kimadria."

Cheers and whistles broke out. King Morvand stepped forward and kissed his future daughter in law on the cheek.

"Gideon has very good taste."

The Queen also kissed her on the cheek. "We should get together with your grandma and choose fabric for your gown."

Grandma Rose stepped forward. She said nothing, just put her arms around her precious granddaughter and hugged her really tight.

"There is a buffet and some entertainment in the ballroom," said the King.

Everyone filed out of the main entrance and down the corridor. Zoë's parents were there, and a few other officials.

Elizabeth made small talk for a few minutes. She looked around for Gideon. He had his back to her and was standing chatting with his mother and Thalios.

Elizabeth turned to the glass doors that led out to the expansive gardens. She slowly and politely made her way through the visitors and to the doors, walking out onto the stone patio.

Elizabeth strolled into the gardens and sat down by one of the fountains. There were high topiary formed hedges all around her.

"It's nice to be alone for a minute or two," she thought. "I'll just take a minute, and then I'll go back in."

She sat back in the seat and closed her eyes. She opened them when she heard a rustling in the bushes.

"Hello, Zorgar." Elizabeth peered into the hedge. "How on earth did you get in here un-noticed?" she said into the greenery.

"Hello Elizabeth."

Zorgar pushed his way through the bush until only his head was visible. "I know that the baby Dragon survived. How is my son?"

"Your son? I'm not sure I understand," said Elizabeth.

"Merlyn, my son. I hope he is well?"

"I don't know any Draghorn named Mylan," said Elizabeth.

"Merlyn," corrected Zorgar. "Elizabeth, I know about Merlyn. I have been watching you and the little Dragon for a long time now."

"What do you want, Zorgar?"

"I don't want him to know that he is heir to my throne, Elizabeth. I want him to stay safe with you and anyone else who can take care of him, until I die of old age, then if you wish, you can tell him who he really is."

"I will agree to that," said Elizabeth.

"And I want an invitation to your wedding," said Zorgar.

"Why?" asked Elizabeth.

"I don't want him to know I am his father, but I do want to meet him."

"All right," said Elizabeth, "but you must behave yourself."

"Thank you, Elizabeth."

He backed out of the bushes and around a fern tree. Elizabeth followed him. He quietly made his way along the pathway until he reached the high stone wall. With one graceful jump, he was up in the air and flying across the blue sky.

Elizabeth watched him until he was a dark spec in the distance. She turned and slowly strode back across the lawns towards the castle.

"I'm going to have a little word with Keslyn and Thalios," she thought, as she made her way through the gardens. "No one told me that Zorgar was Merlyn's father. Although, looking back, it makes sense now. Keslyn had tried to hide because Zorgar wasn't just waiting for the egg to hatch. He was waiting for his son to be born. That was why he wanted the egg destroyed. It wasn't just the prophesy. He didn't want to give up his power to his son."

Elizabeth approached the pathway to the glass doors. "A bit barbaric," she thought, as she neared the entrance, "trying to kill your own son to keep the throne, but not too much surprises me about this place. It can be absolutely enchanting with its magic and mystery, but it can also be ruthless in its ways of dealing with conflict."

Gideon met her when she reached the patio.

"Where have you been?"

"Oh, just sitting in the garden. I needed a few minutes of quiet before I faced all of those people."

He kissed her on the cheek before taking her hand and leading her into the room.

"Have you seen Keslyn?" Elizabeth asked.

"She left with Thalios," said Gideon.

"Do you know when they will be back?"

"Thalios said he would be back tomorrow to talk to you about the Mirronstep. He said something about taking it to the druids for safe keeping."

"Interesting that he left without saying anything to me," Elizabeth commented.

"He couldn't find you," said Gideon.

They both smiled politely, as they re-joined the party.

When it was time for everyone to leave, Grandma Rose found Elizabeth. "I'm going back up to the cottage. Jesse is going to need some clothes now he's awake. I'm going to do a bit of shopping for him."

"That's a good idea, Gran. He doesn't really look very good in elven grey."

"Would you like to come with us?"

"No thanks, Gran. I think I'll stay here."

"I'll see you later then," Grandma said, as she turned to leave.

Gideon stepped up behind Elizabeth.

"Good night, Liz. I'll see you tomorrow," he said, kissing her on the cheek.

Elizabeth went to her rooms and took a long hot bath. When she came out of her bathroom, her two new room mates were waiting for her. Charlie was at the foot of the bed and Merlyn was lying on the pillow beside where she slept. They both smiled at her when she entered the room.

"Is this going to be a regular thing now?" she asked.

They looked at one another then back to her, nodding.

"Go to sleep. No messing around," she told them both.

When Merlyn and Charlie had settled down, Elizabeth went to the cupboard by the bed and chanted the spell to make the book and the little mirror appear. She picked up the book and opened it, thumbing through the many pages. The last few had pictures of Sir Gareth, smiling and waving. On one of the pages, a likeness of Elizabeth was standing as though posing for a picture in a beautiful long embroidered gown.

She turned to the last page.

"How strange. Who could those two possibly be," she said, in a quiet voice, as she noticed a drawing of two little girls playing in the castle gardens.

"Oh well, I imagine I'll know when I'm supposed to," she thought, putting the book back in the cupboard.

She chanted the spell to hide the objects and got into bed.

"It's finally over," she thought, as she fell asleep.

Chapter Thirty Four

Elizabeth woke, dressed and took Keslyn and Charlie down to the kitchens.

"Cook, please feed these two and let them out into the back gardens," she said.

The cook looked down at the two of them. "C'mon, you can go out the back door. I'll feed you out there, or you'll get cat hair and Dragon scales all over the place.

Elizabeth left the kitchens and met Gideon and Bindyl in the breakfast room.

"My mother wants you, me, and Grandma Rose to meet with my father," said Gideon, sipping his tea. "She says we should think about setting a date for the wedding."

"I'll go up to the cottage after breakfast and bring my grandma back down."

Gideon turned to Bindyl.

"Elizabeth and I have talked. I would like you to be my best man."

"I would be honoured," Bindyl answered.

Elizabeth noticed he had tears in his eyes.

"Well, I will be getting along," she said. "Gideon, will you walk me out?"

"Of course. Bindyl, don't leave until I return," Gideon said, getting out of his seat.

"Talk to Bindyl," Elizabeth said, as they neared the castle entrance.

"What's wrong?" he asked.

"He's upset, Gideon. Talk to him. He needs someone to talk to about Zoe."

"How do you know that?"

"Because when you asked him to be your best man, he was trying not to cry!"

"I didn't notice," said Gideon. "I'll have a chat with him."

"Good," said Elizabeth. "I'll see you in a bit."

Gideon kissed her goodbye and went back to the main hall.

"Is this going to be too difficult for you, Bindyl? I know how much you still miss Zoe," he said.

Bindyl looked down at his cup. "I am happy for you and Elizabeth. It just brings back memories of Zoe. She so dearly would have loved to be here organizing things for Elizabeth, helping her with her gown, and perhaps talking about marrying me."

Gideon put his hand on his friend's shoulder.

"I am sorry Bindyl,"

Bindyl nodded, they finished the rest of their breakfast in silence.

***

Elizabeth was about to walk out of the willow tree, when one of the guards who was at the entrance touched her arm.

"Don't go out yet, my lady," he said, nodding to a crack in the tree that served as a look out.

Elizabeth stepped back.

Through the branches hanging down around the tree trunk, she could just make out Andre Reese walking to the bridge. She waited until he opened the gate to the garden, before she came out of the tree.

She stood for a moment in the branches, watching him make his way along the pathway to the back door of the cottage. As he turned the corner, Elizabeth stepped out into the open and across the bridge.

Andre had just sat down and Grandma Rose was putting the kettle on when Elizabeth came in through the back door. Both he and Grandma Rose looked up when she entered.

"Good morning, Elizabeth," Grandma said. "We were about to have a cup of tea, would you like some?"

"Yes please, Gran."

Andre moved one of the chairs out from the table so that she could sit down.

Elizabeth looked at him. "He's grown into a handsome man," she thought, as she sat across from him. "He's taller than me now. His pale skin and dark brown eyes are very appealing. His dark hair is nice too, could do with being a bit shorter though. I hope he finds a girl who can make him happy one day soon."

"Where have you been?" he asked.

"I went for a walk along the river. I saw you walk across the field."

"I didn't see you anywhere," Andre said.

"I was on the other side of the Willow tree," she said.

"Oh, did you go to the stables?" he asked.

"No. Just for a walk,"

Grandma Rose boiled the kettle and put some tea into the warmed teapot. She filled the pot with the boiling water and put the lid on. She went to the fridge and got a jug of milk, put the sugar bowl on the table and went over to the counter to get the teapot. Just as she reached the counter, she stopped, grabbing her chest. Elizabeth and Andre looked up just in time to see her hand grasp the counter to stop herself from falling.

"GRAN!"

Elizabeth jumped out of her chair and caught her as she slid down the side of the counter. Andre ran to them both and helped Elizabeth ease her to the floor. Elizabeth looked down at her grandma in disbelief.

"What's wrong with her?" Andre said.

She cradled Grandma Rose's head. "Call an ambulance, quickly!"

Andre reached out to the phone on the kitchen wall and dialled 999. He had a brief conversation with the operator, and hung up.

"The medics are on their way," he said kneeling down beside them. "They said not to move her, but to try to keep her warm and try to keep her calm."

Elizabeth gently put her grandma's head on the kitchen floor. She ran to Grandma Rose's room and grabbed the day blanket and a pillow off the bed, then bolted down the hall with them. She put her grandma's head on the pillow and covered her with the blanket. Grandma Rose opened her eyes and looked up at her.

"My chest feels as though it is being squeezed in a vice," she said, through clenched teeth.

"There's an ambulance on the way, Gran. Try to stay calm," she said, feeling far from calm herself.

A few minutes later, Elizabeth and Andre heard the siren from the ambulance off in the distance. A minute or so later there was a knock at the front door. Andre answered it.

Two paramedics came down the hallway and into the kitchen. One of them knelt down beside her.

"I'm Stephen, Mrs Humphries. "I'm going to open your blouse and listen to your chest."

The medic examined Grandma briefly, while talking to someone on his cell phone.

"We'll need the gurney," he told the other medic.

While the medic was gone, Stephen put an I.V. into Grandma's arm.

John, the other paramedic, who knew Elizabeth from school, took her to one side, out of earshot.

"We think she may have had a heart attack. We have to get her to hospital quickly."

Elizabeth looked at him wide eyed, unable to speak.

She watched as they gently moved Grandma Rose onto the gurney and strapped her to it. They covered her with a blanket and Stephen rolled her down the hallway.

"We are going to take her to the hospital emergency room," he said, turning to her. "You can either travel with her in the ambulance, or you can follow in the car."

"If I go with Gran. Will you follow me in her car, so I can drive home, Andre?"

"You go on ahead. I'm going to call mum, let her know what's happening, then I'll drive there."

"Thanks," she said, as she stepped up into the ambulance.

Andre met up with Elizabeth in the waiting area of the emergency room at the local hospital. They sat and waited for someone to tell them what was happening.

While the two of them were talking, Andre's mother and sister arrived.

"How is she?" asked Andre's mother.

"We don't know yet," Elizabeth said. "They have been working on her for some time now."

Andre's mother took a seat next to Elizabeth. She put her arm around her, and patiently waited.

About an hour later, a tall blond man walked into the waiting room.

"Is there an Elizabeth Ghenestone here?" he asked.

Elizabeth stood. "That's me."

The doctor took a seat. "I would like to explain what's happening to your gran."

"Is she all right?" Elizabeth said, sitting beside him.

"Your grandmother has had a heart attack. She is resting peacefully at the moment, but we will have to do a surgical procedure called a bypass. Her heart has a blockage in it and we need to remove it, so that it can work properly again."

"Can I see her?" said Elizabeth.

"Yes, but only for a minute or two. Then I suggest that you all go home. We have scheduled her operation for the morning. She will need her rest now. If you go to the nurses station on your way out, they can let you know what time to be here in the morning."

The doctor took Elizabeth to the intensive care unit while the others waited. She was given a mask to wear and he led her to Grandma Rose's bed.

Elizabeth sat by her bedside and took her hand. Grandma Rose opened her eyes and looked at Elizabeth. She smiled. Elizabeth smiled back.

"You gave us quite a scare," said Elizabeth.

"Sorry," was all Grandma Rose could muster before she closed her eyes again.

A nurse came up behind Elizabeth and gently put her hand on her shoulder.

"She'll sleep now. The doctor has given her something for the pain and to keep her calm."

Elizabeth stood. "Will you phone me if I need to come back tonight?"

"Of course, now go home and try to get some rest. Your grandma is in good hands."

The nurse gave Elizabeth Grandma Rose's surgery time. She left the intensive care unit and made her way back to the waiting area.

"How is she?" said Lillian Reese.

"She's resting. Her operation is scheduled for 9:00 a.m. I'll be here at 8:30."

"I'll drive you home," said Andre.

"I'm all right, really. I can drive myself," said Elizabeth.

"You are in no condition to drive," said Andre. "I'll drive you and mum can follow us and give me a lift home."

"Andre is right, Elizabeth. Let him drive you home," said Lillian Reese.

"All right," said Elizabeth, reluctantly.

When they arrived at the cottage, Andre parked the car and followed Elizabeth round to the kitchen door. "I can come in and keep you company, if you want."

"I think I would rather be by myself for a while, but thanks for offering. I think your mum is around the front. I heard her car."

"Let me know if there is anything I can do to help, Liz."

"I will, I promise," she said.

Elizabeth and Andre walked around to the front of the cottage, where his mother and sister were waiting.

Elizabeth closed the gate behind them and made her way back around the side of the cottage to the back door. When she turned the corner, she saw Gideon sitting on the back door step.

When he saw her, he knew immediately that something was wrong. He stood, and as he changed to human size, she looked up into his eyes. Gideon remembered thinking that he had never seen such sadness in anyone's face before that night. He put his arms around her and she began to cry. He took her hand, guided her to the door and took the key from her. He opened the back door and led her inside. He sat her down and pulled up a chair in front of her.

"I came here because one of the guards at the Willow tree saw your grandma being driven away," said Gideon. "He suspected that she may have become ill, so he contacted me. What has happened?"

"Gran has had a heart attack."

"I am so sorry, Elizabeth. Mother said that your gran had not felt well for a while."

"How come she never told me?"

"You know how my mother and your gran talk. Perhaps Grandma Rose did not want to worry you."

"Well, that didn't work, did it? I'm worried to death now!"

"Not much you can do at the moment, Liz, and being angry at your gran won't help."

Without thinking, he got up and started making a cup of tea. Elizabeth watched him for a minute and then started to laugh. Gideon turned around.

"What do you find so amusing?" he asked.

"I don't mean to laugh at you, Gideon, it's just that I never envisioned in my future, watching an elf making a cup of tea in my grandmother's kitchen," she said, trying to stifle a fit of the giggles.

Gideon reached for the apron that Grandma Rose often wore when she was working in the kitchen, and put it on. She laughed even harder. Her laughter became contagious and Gideon began to laugh with her.

He sat down by Elizabeth's side and put his arm around her.

"Your grandma is going to recover Liz. I seem to feel it somehow."

She nodded, but began to cry again. They drank their tea in silence.

"I am going to stay here tonight," he said.

"You're not allowed to do that, Gideon. You know the rules."

"I am going to be a perfect gentleman."

"I'm not going to argue. It's been a long day," she said. "I'm going to go to bed early, in case I have to get up in the night."

"Me, too," said Gideon.

"Gideon, don't let Jesse know about this until we know what's going to happen to Grandma."

"I won't," he said, kissing her on the cheek. "Good night."

Elizabeth locked up the house and went to bed.

"I'll never be able to sleep," she thought, closing her eyes.

Gideon closed the curtains in the spare room. "I hope I didn't put too much sleep dust in her tea," he thought.

He waited a few minutes before he went down the hall and quietly opened Elizabeth's door. When he saw that she was asleep, he left the cottage and went to the willow tree.

"Please send word to the king that Grandma Rose has had to go to the hospital with a heart attack," he told the guard. "Tell him that I will be staying here tonight, and please ask him not to let Elizabeth's brother know what is happening just yet."

"Oh, and Ewan."

"Yes, sir?"

"Thank you for being so observant and contacting me."

Ewan saluted, "Not at all, sir."

Gideon returned to the cottage and went to bed.

Chapter Thirty Five

Elizabeth woke, bathed and dressed around 6:30 a.m., Gideon woke when she did, and they ate breakfast together.

Elizabeth had just finished washing the breakfast dishes when the phone rang.

"This is Nurse Woodbridge," said a voice on the other end. "I'm calling to let you know that your grandma is resting comfortably. When you get here, please let the nurse in reception know who you are, and she will send you to the waiting area."

"Thank you," said Elizabeth.

"After the procedure, your grandma will sleep most of the day, but you can come and sit with her for a little while if you want," replied Nurse Woodbridge.

"Thank you for calling. I'll be there in a bit."

"Don't mention it," said nurse Woodbridge.

Elizabeth hung up the phone and turned to Gideon.

"I'll go down to the Elven Realm," said Gideon. "I left a message with the guard last night. I'll go and let mother and father know your grandma is about to have…"

He was just about to say something else, when there was a knock at the back door.

"Liz?" Andre called, as he let himself in.

Gideon had just enough time to disappear before Andre entered the kitchen.

"Who were you talking to?" he asked.

Elizabeth grabbed a dishcloth, as though she was tidying the kitchen.

"Myself, of course. Don't you ever talk to yourself when you are alone?"

"Well yes, but I don't usually admit to it," he said with a sheepish grin. "I came to see how your grandma was doing. Have you heard anything?"

"I'm going to see her now. The nurse said she had a good night."

"I could drive you, if you want. I'd like to see her. Then I can report back to mum and Meg."

"I would like that," said Elizabeth. "I was planning on leaving now, if that's all right with you?"

"No time like the present," Andre said.

Elizabeth picked up her handbag and handed Andre her car keys.

"Come on then, let's go," she said, heading for the back door.

"Aren't you going to lock the door?" said Andre.

"No need. No one ever comes here."

Andre shrugged. He followed her out of the back door and around the side of the cottage to the car.

Gideon waited until he was sure they were gone, then left the cottage and made his way to the willow tree.

Grandma Rose was sitting up in bed when Elizabeth and Andre arrived.

"You look pale and tired," Elizabeth thought, looking into her grandma's face.

"How are you feeling, Gran?" she asked.

"Better," Grandma answered.

Elizabeth and Andre sat down by Grandma's bed. They had been visiting her for a few minutes when the doctor came in.

He picked up Grandma's wrist, feeling for her pulse for a second or two.

"Everything went very well. I think with a little rest, you'll make a full recovery, Rose. You can go home in a couple of days, if you continue to improve."

He turned to Elizabeth. "Don't let your grandma get too excited."

Elizabeth noticed that Grandma Rose was looking a bit tired. She stood, leaned over and kissed her on the forehead.

"You get some rest now, Gran. I'll be back to see you in the morning."

Andre stood. He touched Grandma Rose's hand. "Goodbye for now. I'll come to the cottage and see you when you get home.

"I won't come in," Andre said, when they reached the cottage, "Got things to do today, but keep me posted."

"Thanks, Andre,"

Elizabeth watched, as he sprinted along the path, jumped the closed gate, ran over the bridge and was off across the fields.

She turned the corner and entered through the back door of the cottage.

Charlie was sitting on the back step. "Is Grandma Rose all right? I saw her go away in an ambulance."

Elizabeth opened the door and let her in.

"Grandma Rose is going to be fine. I am going to pick her up from the hospital in a couple of days."

Charlie jumped up on one of the kitchen chairs and watched as Elizabeth made a pot of tea. The back door opened and Gideon came in. He gave Elizabeth a hug and a kiss, and sat down beside Charlie.

"Grandma is coming home in a couple of days, if she continues to improve."

"That's good news Liz. If it's all right with you, I would like to send Gilda up here for a few days when she gets home, just to keep an eye on her."

"I think that would be an excellent idea," said Elizabeth.

"I have a message from Thalios," said Gideon.

"What would that be?"

"He said to tell you that you must hand over the Mirronstep. The druids want it."

Elizabeth looked at him. "I won't give it to them."

Gideon was about to say something, but Elizabeth held up her hand. "I am going to take it back where it belongs. The druids don't know where the Mirronstep will be safe, but I do."

Gideon nodded, knowing it would be pointless trying to argue with her.

"Thalios is down in the Elven Realm. Perhaps we should go down and talk to him," he said.

"I'll go down to see him, Gideon, but I will be spending the night here."

They left the cottage through the back door and Elizabeth locked it. Charlie scampered down to the willow tree. It opened just as she reached it. Gideon and Elizabeth followed her inside.

Off in the distance, Andre Reese was crouched in the bushes with a pair of binoculars.

"Where are they going?" he said to himself. "I knew there was something odd going on around here, and who is that strange looking chap with her and the cat?"

He continued to watch, as they got closer to the tree. They all entered into the branches that drooped down to the ground, and disappeared.

"How strange," he said to himself.

He made his way across the field and pulled the branches of the willow tree aside, putting his hand on the tree trunk.

"It feels just like any other tree. I've climbed this tree many times as a boy."

Andre shook his head. He turned, heading back towards home, stopping once or twice to look back at the tree. "Where could they have gone? I'll talk to Liz tomorrow. I wonder where she went?"

The elven guard inside of the trunk had been watching Andre. He turned from spy hole and looked at his co-worker. "Never seen anyone do that before," he said.

"Should we tell the king?" said the other guard.

"I'll tell Lady Elizabeth when she comes back through," said the guard.

Chapter Thirty Six

Thalios was in Vandrayven's laboratory when Elizabeth entered the room.

"We will talk again later," Vandrayven told Thalios, when he saw Elizabeth.

"Of course," said Thalios, turning to her. "You and I should discuss the Mirronstep."

"Why?" she asked.

"The druids want to take it for safe keeping," said Thalios.

"That won't happen," said Elizabeth.

"If you will not give the mirror to the druids, then you must come with me and state your case to them," said Thalios.

"I'll do that. My gran is going to be in the hospital for a couple of days. So I'm going to stay up there in case anything happens."

"I will go to the druids and make arrangements for you to meet with them," said Thalios, "Please tell Rose I hope she recovers soon. I would like to visit her as soon as I can."

"Gran would like that, Thalios. It would cheer her up no end."

"You have not been for your teachings," Vandrayven said with a frown, after Thalios had gone.

"In case you haven't noticed, you grumpy old wizard. I've been a bit busy."

"You have a lot of catching up to do, young lady."

"Vandrayven, I promise I'll spend time with you as soon as this Mirronstep thing is settled. Can I ask you something?"

"Of course," Vandrayven said.

"I noticed when I found the new Grymlons, they were a little smaller than the originals."

"I went up to the tower and looked at them, too," said Vandrayven, "I think it is because they are so new. I'm quite sure that given time, they will mature and become the same size as the old ones."

"That sounds about right. I'll check them in a day or two," said Elizabeth.

"Vandrayven, I promise I'll spend time with you, as soon as this Mirronstep thing is settled."

Vandrayven turned back to what he was doing.

"I'm going to see Jesse. I'll come back and study when Gran gets home and I'm sure she is settled."

Vandrayven ignored her.

When she reached Jesse's new rooms in the west side of the castle, he was having some physio therapy with a nurse from the Human Realm.

She watched him as he struggled between two parallel bars, trying to make his legs move.

The nurse was stood back just enough to be able to catch him, if he fell.

"How is he doing?" asked Elizabeth, stepping up beside her.

"Very well," the nurse said, never taking her eyes off her patient.

Jesse lifted one of his hands, waving it at Elizabeth in an attempt to show off. He started to fall and put his hand back on the bar just in time to steady himself.

"Be careful, Jesse, don't break anything!" said Elizabeth.

"You can stop now, Jesse. You've had enough exercise for the day," said the nurse.

Elizabeth watched as the nurse helped him to his wheelchair.

"Can you wait for a bit, before you leave?" Elizabeth asked the nurse.

"I'll go down to the kitchens and get something to eat, while you two talk," said the nurse.

"I will come and find you in a few minutes, if that's all right," said Elizabeth.

"See you later, Jesse," said the nurse, as she left the room.

"To what do I owe this visit, sis?"

Elizabeth sat down. "Come here Jesse. We need to talk."

Jesse wheeled his chair over to her.

"I don't like the sound of that," he said, jokingly.

"Jesse, Grandma had a heart attack last night."

She watched as the colour drained from his face.

"She's all right," Elizabeth said, quickly. "She had to have an operation this morning, bypass surgery I think the doctor called it. I received a phone call this morning, to let me know the operation was a success, and she can come home in a couple of days."

"I want to come back up to the Human Realm with you, Liz."

"I don't think that would be a good idea, Jesse."

"Why not? There's no danger for me now. The elviron know I'm alive."

"But everyone up there thinks you are dead."

"That was years ago," said Jesse.

"Let me talk to Gran when she gets home. Perhaps we can come up with a way for you to go back up there and stay, but you're to wait until then."

"Will you come back down here as soon as you can?" asked Jesse

"I'm staying up there for now, but I'll be back tomorrow."

"I hate being stuck in this chair!" said Jesse.

"It's only temporary. I have to go, Jesse," Elizabeth said, leaning over and kissing him on the cheek. "I want to talk to your nurse about spending some time with Gran when she gets home, if that's all right with you?"

"Perhaps if I go up to the Human Realm, the nurse can look after us both until I get back on my feet."

"We'll see," said Elizabeth.

"...So that's the situation so far," Elizabeth told Jesse's nurse over a cup of tea.

"I'm agreeable to working up in the Human Realm," said the nurse. "I think I can manage your grandma and Jesse. Jesse is almost out of that wheelchair, anyway."

"I'll talk to my gran, see if she feels well enough for Jesse to be there. I actually think it may be good for Jesse to be with her. They'll be company for each other. The two of them have a lot of catching up to do."

The nurse stood to leave.

"If you need to contact me until then, Gilda will know where to find me when I'm not working with Jesse."

"Thanks," said Elizabeth.

***

Gideon stood when Elizabeth entered the Queen's apartments. Queen Paulina hugged her tightly. "I am so sorry, my dear. Rose means a great deal to us all. Is there anything we can do to help?"

"Not at the moment, your Majesty, but thank you for asking. The nurse who is looking after Jesse is going to go up to the Human Realm to work with both him and Gran. If we need any help, I promise you'll be the first to know."

"I'm going with Liz, mother. I will see you and father for dinner perhaps?"

"I will look forward to it," the queen replied.

"Goodbye, your Majesty," Elizabeth said with a slight curtsy.

The Queen nodded and smiled as she turned away from them both and left the room.

"Where are you going?" asked Gideon, following Elizabeth out into the hallway.

"I'm going back up to the cottage."

"I will come with you," said Gideon.

"I think I should go up there alone for now," said Elizabeth.

"Why?" asked Gideon.

Elizabeth took his hand in hers. "I'm not sure, but I think we're being watched when we go into the willow tree. I want to find out who it is. I can't keep a secret if the secret is standing beside me."

Gideon frowned. "We have never been discovered up until now, but point taken. Send for me if you need me."

When they reached the main hall, he let go of Elizabeth's hand and called for a carriage to take her to Humadria.

As Elizabeth entered the inside of the Willow tree, Ellis, the guard on duty stopped her.

"Sorry to trouble you, miss, but not long after you and Prince Gideon came in here from the cottage, that young man who visits you, came up to the tree trunk. He tapped on it and walked around it, as though he was trying to find a way in."

"Has anyone ever done that before?" she asked.

"Not that I am aware, miss. Should we do anything about it?"

"No, I'll handle it, but thank you for bringing it to my attention," she said.

Elizabeth came out of the willow tree, cautiously, walked over the bridge and opened the gate.

Just as she was about to walk along the pathway, movement caught her eye. Elizabeth turned to see Andre standing at the other side of the river by the bridge.

"Why are you just standing there?" she shouted to him.   Andre came over the bridge. Elizabeth stood, holding the gate open for him.

"Where did you come from Liz?" he asked.

"You know where I came from," she thought, as she smiled at him. "Come on into the house and I'll make us some tea."

He followed her along the path, and Elizabeth unlocked the back door.

"I thought you told me that there was no need to lock your door?"

Elizabeth ignored him. She entered the house, and Andre followed her in.

"Sit down and I will make us a pot of tea, then I'll explain a few things."

Andre sat at the kitchen table, and watched as she made the tea.

She turned to him. "Would you like some biscuits?"

"Yes please, Liz."

She took the biscuit tin out of the cupboard above the tea kettle, put it on the table, and removed the lid. Andre picked up a biscuit, broke it in half and dunked it into his cup.

Elizabeth sat opposite him and took a sip of her tea.

"The reason I left the door unlocked when we left to visit Grandma, was because there was an elf in here. He didn't leave until he knew that you and I had gone."

Andre grinned. "You don't have to be sarcastic. I was only asking."

"No really, I'm absolutely serious. He made himself invisible when you walked in the back door. That's why you heard me talking. I was talking to him."

Andre sipped his tea, and put his hand into the biscuit tin again. He pulled out a chocolate biscuit, broke it in half and dunked it.

"I saw you go into the branches of the willow tree with a blond chap, but I didn't see you come out again. I suppose this elf lives in the willow tree." Andre said, grinning.

"Under it, actually," Elizabeth replied.

Andre choked on the bite of soggy biscuit he had just popped into his mouth.

Elizabeth jumped up and patted him on the back. He picked up his cup and gulped down some tea. She sat back down when his coughing subsided.

"The reason I am telling you this, is because I'm going to be married soon, to the elf that was in this house yesterday," she continued. "I think it would be nice if you and Meghan could be there to see me wed. The problem is; you and your sister would have to keep the secret. No one must know of the elves. Can you keep a secret Andre?"

Andre stared at her. "Is this some sort of elaborate joke?" he asked, as he stood and poured himself another cup of tea.

"No!" Elizabeth replied.

Charlie had been listening outside, through the slightly open back door. She entered the kitchen, brushing up against Elizabeth's legs.

She bent down and stroked the back of Charlie's head.

"How are you today?" she asked the little cat.

As Elizabeth spoke to Charlie, she winked.

Charlie looked up at her, then at Andre.

"I am well, thank you," the little cat replied.

Andre's eyes became wide as he stared down at Charlie. He looked at Elizabeth. "She just spoke."

Charlie looked up at him.

"And now she looks as though she's smiling."

He put the teacup down and promptly slumped to the floor.

Elizabeth slid out of her chair and turned him on his side, in case he threw up.

"What is wrong with him?" Charlie asked.

"He's fainted," said Elizabeth.

"Is he going to die?" Charlie said.

"No, Charlie. People don't usually die when they faint."

Andre slowly came to, minute or so later. When he was able to sit up, Elizabeth managed to get him up into a chair.

"I feel as though I'm going to be sick," he said.

Elizabeth put her hand on the back of his head and pushed it down between his knees. Andre stayed there until he felt better. Charlie sat by Elizabeth waiting for the drama to be over.

Andre looked at Charlie. "You know I could have sworn the cat spoke."

"I did," said Charlie.

Andre rolled his eyes.

"Don't you dare faint again!" said Elizabeth.

"I'm fine," said Andre.

Elizabeth sat back in her chair. Andre stared at her. "Now do you believe me?"

"Yes," he said, turning slightly pale again.

"I'm going to stay here at the house tonight. Why don't you and Meghan come back tomorrow and I will tell you more. Remember, you mustn't say a word to anyone, not even your mother."

"All right," said Andre.

"Are you going to be okay to walk home?" she asked.

"Yes," Andre replied, scratching his head.

He walked out of the back door and along the pathway.

"Call me when you get home," Elizabeth shouted after him.

He waved without turning around.

"He was a bit shocked, wasn't he," said Charlie.

"Cats don't usually talk," said Elizabeth.

"I don't speak around humans," Charlie said.

"That's very wise. If you do, something horrible might happen to you. Don't worry about Andre, he'll be all right. It'll give him something to think about though."

"Can I stay here with you?" asked Charlie.

"I would like that. I don't really feel like being alone at the moment."

Elizabeth got ready for bed. When she came out of her bathroom, Charlie was at the bottom of her bed. She pulled back the covers and slid between them. She had just put her head on the pillow, when Merlyn appeared beside Charlie.

"If you want to stay in here, you both have to go to sleep," she told them.

They looked at her, nodded and settled down.

She woke to the morning sun shining through the bedroom window, Merlyn and Charlie had left. She went to the kitchen and made herself a cup of coffee.

She stood at the kitchen sink, looking out onto the garden, and her heart felt heavy.

"Feels odd, Gran not being here," she thought. "She's usually already up by now, making breakfast or cleaning around the cottage, or something."

Elizabeth drank her coffee and got dressed. She cleaned up the cottage. She was getting ready to leave for the hospital when Gideon came in through the back door.

"Good morning," he said, kissing her on the cheek.

"Good morning. I'm going to visit Gran."

"Do you need Gilda?" he asked.

"I talked with Jesse's nurse. I'm thinking I might bring Jesse up here and she can look after both of them."

"That is a good idea," said Gideon. "I will go and bring my father up to date with the situation."

Chapter Thirty Seven

Three days later, Elizabeth picked up Grandma Rose from the hospital.

"The district nurse will be phoning you to set up an appointment," the nurse told her, handing her a bag with medicine and dressings for Grandma's wounds. "She will come in and check on your grandma, to make sure she has no infection and her wound is healing properly."

Elizabeth wheeled Grandma Rose to the car, put her in it and took the chair back. An orderly took it from her at the entrance.

On the way home Elizabeth glanced at her grandma once or twice. "She looks so pale and tired."

When they reached the cottage, Elizabeth helped Grandma Rose into bed.

"Can I get you anything, Gran?"

"I would love a decent cup of tea, dear," Grandma said.

Elizabeth kissed her on the forehead. "It's good to have you home."

Grandma Rose smiled. "It's good to be home."

"I'll get right on that tea," Elizabeth said.

When she returned with the tea, Grandma opened her eyes and sat up a little. Elizabeth put the tray on her grandma's lap.

"Thank you," Grandma said, sipping the tea. "It's really good to be home."

"I have some chores to do," said Elizabeth. "I'll look in on you in a few minutes."

She closed her grandma's bedroom door behind her, went back into the kitchen and poured herself a cup of tea.

"Thank goodness for the quiet," she thought.

The back door opened and Gideon came in with Jesse's nurse.

"Why don't you have a cup of tea, Gideon, while I introduce Nurse Houseman to Gran."

The nurse followed Elizabeth down the hall and into Grandma Rose's bedroom.

"Gran, this is Nurse Houseman. She's going to look after you for a while."

"Aren't you Jesse's nurse?" asked Grandma.

"Yes, I am."

"Shouldn't you be looking after him?"

"I thought it might be nice if Jesse came up here," said Elizabeth. "That way, she can look after both of you. I'm sure you would enjoy the company."

"How will we explain him to everyone? They think he's dead," said Grandma.

"Jesse the boy died," said Elizabeth. "The person down in the Elven Realm is now Jesse the man. We could pass him off as my cousin from Uncle Stephen's side of the family."

"What a splendid idea," said Grandma. "I would love to have Jesse up here with me."

Elizabeth left the two of them together, so they could get acquainted. When she got back to the kitchen, Gideon, who was now human size, was putting spoonful after spoonful of sugar into his teacup. Elizabeth sat down opposite him and took a sip of her tea.

She was just about to say something to him when the back door opened again. This time it was Andre.

Gideon stood quickly and was about to disappear, but Elizabeth put her hand on his arm. "Don't. Stay where you are."

Andre looked up as he entered the kitchen.

When he saw Gideon, he stopped, looking him up and down.

Gideon, who by now was standing beside Elizabeth's chair, returned the stare. Elizabeth stepped between them.

"Andre, this is Gideon, the elf I was telling you about. Gideon, this is Andre. He and his sister have been friends of this family since we were all young children."

Andre looked down at Elizabeth. "All I see is a strange looking male dressed in funny looking clothes. He doesn't look like an elf to me."

Elizabeth turned away from him. "Gideon, please show Andre what a real elf looks like."

Gideon closed his eyes, bowed his head and shrank down to about a foot tall, then looked up at Andre, waved at him and vanished.

With that… Andre promptly fainted.

Gideon re-appeared, grew to human size and looked down at him. "Is he all right? Does he do that often?"

"Just lately he does," Elizabeth said, kneeling down and turning Andre on his side.

They waited patiently for him become conscious.

Andre finally sat up and looked at Elizabeth. "I did it again, didn't I?"

Elizabeth nodded.

Andre gave Gideon a sheepish look as he began to get up off the floor. Gideon stepped forward and extended his hand. Andre took it and Gideon helped him up.

"I'm sorry," said Andre, "I must seem awfully ill mannered."

"Not at all," said Gideon. "It must feel very strange for you to meet someone like me, for the first time."

The two of them took a seat at the kitchen table and Elizabeth made more tea.

"Well, what now?" said Andre, "Of course I have questions," he continued, looking at Gideon, "but where do we go from here?"

"I know," said Gideon. "Let's take him down to Kimadrian."

Elizabeth laughed. "I'm not sure he could stay on his feet for long if we took him down there. Perhaps we should save that for another time."

"Take me where?" said Andre, gulping down his tea.

"To the Elven Realm, where Gideon comes from," Elizabeth said, pouring him another cup.

"I would love to go down there!"

"Not today," said Elizabeth. "I have to look after Gran today, but if you bring Meghan here tomorrow afternoon, I'll take both of you down there. You must promise me though, Andre, not to say anything to Meghan. Let me tell her."

"All right," said Andre, drinking the rest of his tea.

"I look forward to seeing where you live," he said, shaking Gideon's hand. "Talk to you later, Liz."

Andre left by the back door.

"Why did you let him see me?" said Gideon.

"Because he saw all of us go into the willow tree. Sooner or later, he would have become curious enough to find out for himself. This way, we can keep the situation under control."

"I think you are a very smart human, my beautiful Liz, but I have to go now too. I'll see you in the Elven Realm."

He kissed her goodbye.

Elizabeth went to her grandma's room. The nurse was sitting in the corner, knitting. When Elizabeth saw her grandma was asleep, she beckoned for her to come to the kitchen.

Nurse Houseman followed her down the hallway and took a seat at the kitchen table.

"I'll tidy up a bit, then I'll go and get Jesse, but first I need to go shopping for Gran. Could you give me a list of the things Jesse likes to eat, so I can shop for him, too?"

"I'll go back to Rose's room and write a list while you clean up."

Elizabeth tidied up the kitchen and the living room. She took the list from Nurse Houseman and drove into Oaklade to shop.

After she returned home, she put the shopping away, and began putting some lunch together for her grandma and nurse Houseman.

She had just left Grandma Rose's room, when the front doorbell rang.

Elizabeth turned around, went down the hall way and opened the door. Standing in front of her was George Westbury.

"Mr. Westbury. What a nice surprise! Well don't stand on the door step. Come in," she said, stepping aside.

George Westbury entered the house, and Elizabeth stepped forward and gave him a hug.

"To what do we owe the pleasure? Would you like a cup of tea?" she asked him, as he followed her down the hall to the kitchen.

"I never turn down a cuppa," said George.

He followed Elizabeth into the kitchen, where she made tea for them both.

"How is Carrie?" Elizabeth asked, pouring tea into a cup and handing it to him.

"She's doin' well, and thanks for askin'. I hear from Thalios, that your grandma is ill."

Elizabeth sat at the table. "She gave us a bit of a scare, but she's home now and recovering nicely."

"Glad to 'ear it," said George. "Thalios has asked me to come here and get you."

"What for?" asked Elizabeth.

"The Judicial Druidic Council wants to meet with you," said George.

"It's about the Mirronstep, isn't it," said Elizabeth.

"They won't let it go easily," George said, with a grin.

"Well, there's no time like the present. I'll go and tell Gran I'll be gone for a while."

"Thalios said to tell you that you will need to bring the Mirronstep with you," said George.

Elizabeth had stood and was about to walk down the hall to her grandma's bedroom, calmly turned and faced George.

"I will not."

"So be it," said George.

She turned back towards Grandma Rose's room, knocked and entered.

"Who was that at the door?" Grandma asked.

"It was George Westbury. Would you like to see him, Gran? He's come to take me to go in front of the Druidic Council."

"Oh, goodness me, no! I don't want anyone to see me like this. I look awful, but you go ahead and go with him. Let me know when you get home and tell me all about it."

Grandma turned to the nurse. "I'll be in good hands with Susan," she said with a smile.

"I'm terribly sorry. Where are my manners? I didn't ask your name and you are going to be looking after my brother and gran. Susan is it?"

"Yes," said Nurse Houseman. Please call me Susan. Nurse Houseman sounds so formal."

"Well, Susan, I'll try to be back as soon as I can."

"You go on, dear. We'll be fine here."

Elizabeth returned to the kitchen and took the car keys from the hook by the door.

"Come on, George. The car is around the side of the house."

George followed Elizabeth along the path and around the corner.

"How did you get here, George?" she asked, noticing no other cars.

"I got a lift from a friend."

The two of them got into Elizabeth's car.

"Where to?" she asked.

"Do you know where the Folly is in Faringdon?"

"Yes, we used to play around it when we were kids. They cleaned it up, didn't they. Don't they charge you to go up to the top now?"

George Westbury nodded. "Some people will pay to see anything. Yes, that's where we need to go."

Elizabeth drove through Oaklade, then turned right and headed towards the village of Buscot. They continued to Faringdon and then headed to Faringdon Hill.

At the top of Faringdon Hill was the Folly.

The two of them got out of the car and began to make their way upward.

"I remember when we were at school, we learned about Follies," Elizabeth said, as they walked. "As I remember, most of them are tall, narrow brick buildings that rise high into the air, much like this one. We kids were told that there are many Follies in England. I also recall that they are called Follies because they were built for absolutely no reason, but they're fun to climb. If you could get inside one and climb to the top, they had breath-taking views."

"Ay," said George, ambling along beside her, smoking his pipe.

"I don't believe it!" Elizabeth said, when they reached the top of the hill, noticing the newly washed and refurbished Folly. "This place was so broken down! The door was barricaded to stop us kids from getting in. Now look at it."

"They charge a few bob to go up to the top now," said George.

"Well, that's not too bad," said Elizabeth. "We used to squeeze under the broken part of the door and climb up the ladder inside, to see the view back then. A pound or two is a small price to pay to stop it from being demolished. Do many people come up here?"

"Sometimes," said George, turning away from the tower. "This way, we have to go into the woods."

They entered the trees, and George looked around, just to be sure they were alone. Then he led her to a fallen log, rotting on the ground. George sat on the log and put his hand down between his legs. He pressed on an unseen button and stood quickly. The log moved sideways, revealing a stairway that led under the ground. He started down the steps with Elizabeth close on his heels. When they reached the tenth step, George stopped, pressing a spot on the wall. The ground above them moved onto itself and for a moment it went totally dark.

George lit a match and looked around him. To his right there was a wooden torch, lighting it with the match he was holding, he pulled it out of its holder.

They can't afford electricity?" she thought, following him.

The two of them continued downward. The steps seemed to go on forever. At last they came to a bottom step. George put the torch into an empty holder on the wall.

George and Elizabeth walked along the dimly lit passageway, until it took a sharp turn to the left. They continued until they came to a large round room, with a low roof with corridors branching off in all directions.

George stood in the middle of the room and waited. A few seconds later, Thalios appeared from one of the passage ways.

"You do not have the Mirronstep?" he asked.

She returned his gaze. "No, I don't."

Thalios sighed. "I was afraid of that. Please come with me."

The two of them followed Thalios down one of the passages until they came to a door. Thalios knocked politely before opening it. George and Elizabeth followed him into the room.

Thalios closed the door behind them.

Five druids were seated in high back chairs, behind a long wooden bench high above them.

George Westbury bowed to them and backed away until he reached a chair by the door. He took a seat as Thalios stepped forward. Elizabeth stayed beside George.

"If it pleases your lords," Thalios said, "This is Elizabeth Ghenestone. She is here at your request to discuss the matter of the Mirronstep."

The druid, who was seated in the middle of the five, stood.

He looked older than the others and wore a golden girdle, resembling the one Thalios had around his waist.

"Please step forward," he said to Elizabeth.

"You don't scare me you old codger!" she thought, as she approached the bench.

"We are the High Druidic Council. My name is Mordan. We are here today to ask you what you intend to do with the Mirronstep."

Elizabeth looked from right to left, taking in the five faces above her.

"Well?" he said.

"I am going to take it back to where it belongs," she said.

"And where might that be?" asked Mordan.

Elizabeth looked up at him. "I'm not going to tell you."

"We looked after the Mirronstep for many years, before you came along. The Mirronstep is our responsibility," said Mordan.

"And you lost it," said Elizabeth.

"But you found it," said Mordan, "and we thank you for that. Now we want it back."

"I won't give you the Mirronstep, But I will give you the small mirror you had hidden," Elizabeth said.

"Ah… yes," said Mordan.

"Just what was the purpose of the small mirror?" asked the druid on the left.

"You had it here all this time and you didn't know what it was for?" said Elizabeth.

"We used to," said Mordan.

"That was hundreds of years ago," said the druid on the left.

"When the Mirronstep became lost, we kept the mirror and the book, but we didn't know what they were for," said Mordan.

The Mirronstep

"The small mirror is the way back when the Mirronstep is used," Elizabeth explained. "Without it, a journey through the Mirronstep is only one way. The Mirronstep itself will be taken and put into the care of someone who will keep it safe. The book is a journal of what happens when the Mirronstep is used. I'm going to keep it."

Let me make this clear," she continued, never taking her eyes off the council. "This is not open for negotiation. I assure you that the Mirronstep will be in good hands. But I won't under any circumstances tell you where it is."

There was an awkward silence for a few moments.

"Please wait here," Mordan said.

The five of them filed out of the room, exiting through a door to the left.

Elizabeth began to pace back and forth.

Five minutes later, the druids re-entered the room and took their places at the bench.

Mordan stood once more. "We agree."

Thalios stepped up beside Elizabeth and took her arm. She turned and looked at him.

"It is done. We must leave now," he said.

Elizabeth looked up at the five druids and bowed. To her surprise, they all stood and bowed to her.

With Thalios guiding her by the elbow, they left the room. George Westbury stood, bowed to the panel, and followed Thalios and Elizabeth.

Thalios escorted them to the steps that would take them back up to the Folly.

"Are you coming Thalios?" asked Elizabeth.

"I cannot," he replied. "I am to be punished for taking the small mirror and the book from here."

"What sort of punishment?" she asked.

"Because of the good that came from the Mirronstep, my punishment is light," said Thalios. "I have to remain here and wash the floors of the druid's chambers. I will have to perform this duty for one month, as a penance for my deception."

"I'm sorry, Thalios," Elizabeth said.

"Not at all," said Thalios. "My punishment could have been a lot worse."

"When will we see you again?" she asked.

"If my old knees hold up to all the floor washing, I will come and visit you and Rose as soon as I can," he replied.

George Westbury shook his hand. "Don't you be a stranger to me and the wife."

"I'll be knocking on your door and asking for some of your famous bread and honey before you know it," said Thalios.

George pulled the torch off the wall and lit it. He and Elizabeth walked along the hallway and up the steps. He pressed against the wall and the darkness above their heads opened up. George extinguished the torch and placed it back in its holder for the next user.

"Let's get you home, George," said Elizabeth.

The two of them made their way back to the car and Elizabeth drove George to Avebury.

It was early evening by the time Elizabeth arrived back at the cottage.

When she entered by the back door, she found Grandma Rose in her robe, drinking tea at the kitchen table.

"How did it go?" she asked.

"It went well. The druids agreed to let me take the Mirronstep back where it belongs. You must be feeling better."

"Susan said I had to get up and move around," said Grandma. "She said my wound will heal more quickly, if I get my circulation going."

"Where is Susan?" asked Elizabeth.

"She is making the bed in the spare rooms. One for her and one for Jesse," said Grandma.

"I'm going down to the Elven Realm, Gran. I'll talk to Susan before I go."

Elizabeth was walking down the hall, when Susan came out of one of the rooms. "How did it go?" she asked.

"The Mirronstep will not be going back to the druids," said Elizabeth.

"Good," said Susan.

"I'm going to the Elven Realm, Susan. I have some things to do. When I'm finished, I'm going to see if I can get Jesse up here."

***

"I want you to wait for me," she told the carriage driver, when they reached the castle.

She went to her rooms where she cast a spell to make the Mirronstep visible. Over by the window, the air shimmered slightly and the Mirronstep appeared.

She opened a cupboard by the bed and said some words in elvish. Both the small mirror and the book appeared. She put the mirror in her pocket, and made the book disappear again. She covered the Mirronstep with a blanket, and put it under her arm, before going back to the carriage.

"Please take me to Humadria," she told the driver. When they reached the gates to the town, Elizabeth jumped out with the Mirronstep under her arm.

"Should I wait, My Lady?" the carriage driver asked.

"Do you have any business here?" asked Elizabeth.

"I have a daughter who works in the linen shop," the driver said. "If you're going to be a while, I would like to spend some time with her."

"You mean Phyllis's Linens?" asked Elizabeth.

"Yes, My Lady, Shelagh, my daughter, works there during the day. She rents some rooms on the floor above."

"I might be gone for a while," Elizabeth said.

"I can stay there. She won't mind," said the driver. "I've done it many times when I've had to wait for a passenger."

"I'll go to the shop when I return and ask for you," said Elizabeth.

"Right, My Lady. See you then."

When Elizabeth had walked a little way and there was no one around, she said, "baladion gallagry," as she moved her hand along the length of the Mirronstep. Both the mirror and the blanket disappeared from sight.

Elizabeth made her way through the streets of the Upper Realm of Kimadrian, looking as though she had something imaginary under her right arm. She stepped out of the willow tree and headed straight to her car.

It began to rain, on the way to West Kennet, but that couldn't dampen Elizabeth's good mood.

"I hope I can help young Sir Gareth," she thought, as she parked by Silbury hill.

Elizabeth got out of her car, pulled on her rain coat and picked up the Mirronstep.

She crossed the road. Wind and rain whipped at her coat as she manoeuvred her way through the turnstile. She made her way up the side of the field, turning right and into the Long Barrow.

When Elizabeth reached the room at the end of the man-made burial mound, she rested the Mirronstep against the wall.

"Sir Gareth," she called. "It's Elizabeth."

He appeared with his little ball of light.

"I have come to keep my promise," she told him.

He looked at her and around her, frowning. "Where is the mirror?"

"Just trust me, Sir Gareth. Do you remember where you died?"

"It was such a long time ago," he said, shaking his head.

"Didn't you say that you were somewhere around here?" asked Elizabeth.

"But I cannot leave here," said Sir Gareth.

"Just tell me a general area," said Elizabeth. "I'll cast a spell to find your bones. Without your body, I can't take you back."

Sir Gareth thought for a moment. "I think it was about a quarter of a mile or so in the direction of Silbury Hill."

"I'll be back," Elizabeth said, heading back out of the long barrow.

She turned left and headed back down the slope until she came to the road. Elizabeth crossed the road and stopped. As she closed her eyes, she could feel the rain dripping from her scalp and through her hair.

"A knight of Arthur lies around.

His bones now hidden in the ground.

Reveal him now. He cannot stay.

He no longer wants to lay this way."

The Mirronstep

Elizabeth opened her eyes, slowly looking around. A few feet away, a light shimmered a couple of feet off the ground. When she reached the light, Elizabeth looked down. There was a sword laying on the grass. She knelt down and put her hands flat on the ground either side of the sword. The ground opened up and the bones of a human, long dead, appeared in the dirt.

Elizabeth ran to her car, opened the boot and found a large black plastic bag. She ran back to the grave and put the bones in the bag together with the sword. She returned to the barrow where Sir Gareth was waiting. Elizabeth noticed the look on his face and pulled only the sword out of the bag, handing it to him. He turned it over, then looked at Elizabeth and grinned.

"It has been a very long time since I held this sword."

"Glanflisemy Refleclo," Elizabeth said.

Sir Gareth jumped with surprise, as the Mirronstep appeared by the wall.

"Do you trust me?" she said.

"To do what?" asked Sir Gareth.

Elizabeth held out her hand. "Come on, I'll take you through the mirror."

He took her hand and together they stepped into the Mirronstep.

They popped out of the other side, falling to the floor.

Sir Gareth looked around him. "This is the room where the Mirronstep was."

Elizabeth was in a large room with stone walls.

"Not unlike the walls of the castle at Kimadrian," she thought.

She looked out of the window. Down below there were dozens of people dressed in the same style of clothes as Sir Gareth. Elizabeth turned when she heard muffled sobs from behind her. Sir Gareth was sat cross legged on the floor, crying.

"What's the matter?" she asked.

"I never thought that I would ever get home," he said, between sobs. "I know I am dead, but I thought that I was going to have to stay in that dark room for ever."

"Let's get you buried and see what happens," said Elizabeth.

Sir Gareth stood. It was beginning to get dark, as the two of them slipped out of the castle and Sir Gareth led Elizabeth to a nearby burial ground.

She found a shovel and dug a hole deep enough to hold the bones and the sword. Elizabeth poured Sir Gareth's remains out of the bag and into the hole. He bent over and put his sword over the top of them.

Elizabeth shovelled the displaced dirt, until there was only a small mound.

"Now what?" he said.

"Now we wait and see what happens," Elizabeth answered.

The words were hardly out of her mouth when a light appeared above them. A woman dressed in a long white robe appeared in the light, and slowly moved downwards towards them.

Sir Gareth looked up at the woman.

"Mother!"

The woman in white smiled and held out her hand to him. He took it, looking back at Elizabeth.

"It's all right, you can go now," she said. "I was waiting for something like this to happen. Go, you can be at peace now."

The woman turned to Elizabeth. "Thank you."

Elizabeth nodded to her. Sir Gareth and his beloved mother moved upwards as though being transported by an invisible lift. As they did so, the light they were in, faded into darkness until they were gone. Elizabeth found her way back to the place where they had arrived. She took the small mirror out of her pocket and pushed her hand against it. In a split second, she popped out of the Mirronstep, landing back in the barrow. She picked up the Mirror and headed back to her car.

"One more stop to make, before I give the druids the small mirror," she said to herself, as she drove out of the car park.

It was dark by the time Elizabeth reached the church at Highwell. This time she parked on the street, in front of the alcove that led to the iron gate; which in turn led directly to the side door. Elizabeth took the Mirronstep out of the boot of her car and stepped through the iron gates to the alcove.

She tried the side door, but it was bolted from the inside. She stood back and waved her right hand from right to left. The ringed handle moved slowly in a clockwise direction. She stepped forward pushing the door open.

A cold breeze blew by her face as she stepped into the darkness and closed the door behind her.

"It feels so spooky in here without the light of day," she thought.

She turned towards the Warnefield chapel, propped the Mirronstep against a pew and pulled the door in the floor open.

"It's even darker down there!" she thought, as she peered down the steps.

She stepped down two steps and felt for the light switch. The lights came on.

"Well that didn't make much of a difference," she said, into the darkness.

She sprinted back up and grabbed the Mirronstep, turned and stepped down into the crypt.

She stood for a moment, letting her eyes get used to the dimness.

"Monk, are you here?" she said, quietly.

Elizabeth heard a noise behind her and turned. One of the gargoyles standing against the wall, snorted and caught her eye, but didn't move.

Elizabeth stood still returning its gaze. The gargoyle, seeming to take offence at her stare, dropped down as if to pounce and let out a snarling sound.

Elizabeth smiled, "Not this time, you overgrown gryphon," she said.

The gargoyle spread its wings and rushed at her. She held up her hand and pushed against the air. The gargoyle was shoved back by an unseen force. It hit the wall hard and landed on the stone floor. It stood and was about to rush at her again.

"I don't want to hurt you, but I will, if you come at me again," she said, holding out her hand, ready to push him away again. "Go about your business. You have no need to protect this church from me."

The gargoyle backed away, returning to its place.

She turned to see the monk standing behind her. His head, which was still under his arm, had a pleasant smile.

Elizabeth picked up the Mirronstep. When the monk saw it he dropped his head onto the floor. It hit the concrete slab, bounced a couple of times before landing at Elizabeth's feet.

She rested the Mirronstep against the wall and picked up the head. She placed it gently back under the Monk's arm.

"Thank you," he said. "Might I trouble you to wipe the dust from under my nose," he added, moving his nose around, trying not to sneeze.

Elizabeth pulled a tissue from her pocket and wiped the monk's nose.

"Thank you, again" he said. "Is that what I think it is?"

"Yes. I told you I would bring it back to you if I found it. I will leave it with you under one condition. You must not give it to anyone else."

"I won't," said the monk.

"Where do you want me to put it?" Elizabeth asked.

"There are two gargoyles at the end of the crypt. Please put it between them and I will instruct them to guard it," said the monk.

Elizabeth carried the Mirronstep over to the end wall of the crypt, where the gargoyle that had attacked her was standing. As she approached, the one who had not attacked her stepped aside to make a space for the mirror. Elizabeth gingerly approached, placing the Mirronstep in between them. The one that had tried to attack her a few minutes earlier, snarled at her from the corner of his mouth.

"Oh shut up," she said.

The gargoyle closed his mouth.

Elizabeth backed away, not trusting her back to them. When she felt she was a safe distance, she turned and almost bumped into the monk. She looked down at his face.

"Now I have a reason to be in this dark, lonely place," he said.

"I have to get going now," Elizabeth said, "would you like me to cast a spell, so that the Mirronstep is visible only to you?"

"I would appreciate that," said the monk.

Elizabeth said a few words in elvish. The Mirronstep shimmered, but did not disappear.

"Only you, the gargoyles and I can see it now," she told him.

The Mirronstep

"How delightful, I will come with you to the steps," said the monk.

They walked along the aisle way, until they came to the bottom step of the crypt.

"If ever you need the Mirronstep, just come and see me," said the monk.

"I'll do that," said Elizabeth.

She turned off the light, and climbed up the steps. She closed the door to the crypt, and left by the side door of the church.

Elizabeth waved her hand, re-locking the door, returned to her car and drove back to Oaklade.

She tried to be quiet when she entered the cottage, not wanting to wake her grandma.

"I had intended to go back down to the Elven Realm," she thought, but it's getting late. So I'll stay here with gran for the night."

Elizabeth bathed and crawled into bed.

As she slept, she dreamed, she saw two little girls, one blond haired and one dark haired. They were playing together. As they played, the dark haired one turned to Elizabeth and said, "Don't get in my way!"

Elizabeth woke with a start, sweat covering her brow. Somehow, the dream filled her with dread. She looked at the clock. It was 6:00 a.m.

"I think I'll get up and make breakfast," she thought, getting out of bed.

When she reached the kitchen, Susan was already making breakfast for Grandma Rose.

"I'll take it to her," Elizabeth said, picking up the tray.

She made her way down the hallway, knocked on the door and entered.

Grandma Rose was already sitting up in bed.

"Good morning," said Grandma.

"Good morning, Gran," Elizabeth replied, putting the tray on her lap.

"How did it go yesterday?" Grandma asked.

"I am going to give the small mirror back to the druids," said Elizabeth. "I've put the Mirronstep in a safe place."

"Where?" asked Grandma.

"I'm not going to tell you, Gran. If you don't know where it is, then you won't have to lie, if you're asked."

"I'm agreeable to that," said Grandma.

"I'm going to start working on a design for my wedding gown when I get back."

"I'll talk to an elven designer for my outfit," said Grandma.

"I hope you'll be well enough to help me with mine, gran."

"I'm sure I will," said Grandma.

There was a knock at the door. Nurse Susan came in. "It's time to get you up and around, Rose. We don't want you to have another heart attack, now do we?"

Elizabeth looked at her grandma and smiled. "I have to go back down to the Elven Realm," she said, getting up to leave. "I'll see you later."

Elizabeth left the cottage and went into the Willow tree. She ordered a carriage to the castle.

"I'm so excited for the future!" she thought as the carriage sped across the elven countryside.

Epilogue

Elizabeth Ghenestone was about to be married, but things were changing and life would become dangerous and complicated. But that is another story…

The End.

Author's Bio

Jacqueline Nydam was born in the United Kingdom. She now lives in Oregon. Jacqueline loves to spend her spare time riding horses with her husband, and taking long walks with their dogs.

She occasionally returns home to the U.K. to visit her family and friends.

Cover Artist

Victoria Knight is an Oregon artist whose talents range from murals to book covers. www.victoriaknightpaintings.com.

THE MAGIC BEGINS HERE...

Elizabeth Ghenestone was born in Oaklade. Her ordinary life is ripped apart when her parents and brother are killed in a mysterious head-on car crash.

She discovers her true identity when she moves in with her grandmother, and is thrown into a fantastic world of magic, danger, and mystery.

Available from Amazon